D0340247

PENGUIN BOOKS

UNDUE INFLUENCE

Anita Brookner was born in London in 1928, spent some postgraduate years in Paris, and taught at the Courtauld Institute of Art until 1988. Of her novels Penguin publish *Lewis Percy, A Start in Life, Brief Lives, Hotel du Lac, A Closed Eye, Providence, Family and Friends, Look At Me, Fraud, A Family Romance, A Private View, Incidents in the Rue Laugier, Altered States, Visitors* and *Falling Slowly*.

'The Brookner world mesmerises. There is much to be learned from those who inhabit its corridors of desolation'
Susan Hill, *Mail on Sunday*

'Brookner is a true original and, in her own way, a true poet of the modern city'
Adam Lively, *Sunday Times*

ANITA BROOKNER

Undue Influence

PENGUIN BOOKS

PENGUIN BOOKS

Published by the Penguin Group
Penguin Books Ltd, 27 Wrights Lane, London W8 5TZ, England
Penguin Putnam Inc., 375 Hudson Street, New York, New York 10014, USA
Penguin Books Australia Ltd, Ringwood, Victoria, Australia
Penguin Books Canada Ltd, 10 Alcorn Avenue, Toronto, Ontario, Canada M4V 3B2
Penguin Books (NZ) Ltd, Private Bag 102902, NSMC, Auckland, New Zealand

Penguin Books Ltd, Registered Offices: Harmondsworth, Middlesex, England

First published in Viking 1999
Published in Penguin Books 2000
3 5 7 9 10 8 6 4 2

Set in Monotype Bembo
Printed in England by Clays Ltd, St Ives plc

[1]

It is my conviction that everyone is profoundly eccentric. Those people I pass on my way to work every morning almost certainly harbour unimaginable fantasies. Nor are my neighbours entirely to be trusted. Once my mother and I were disturbed by the sounds of a ferocious altercation coming from the flat above ours in Montagu Mansions, yet the following day we were able to address our usual greeting to the stately widow who lived there and who was visited, as far as we knew, only by her son, an economist at the Department of Trade and Industry. Shortly afterwards she informed my mother that she was going to live with her son in Maida Vale. This was somehow understood to be a sensible arrangement, arrived at in a mature manner, although to judge from that epochal argument it seemed less than reasonable. She was in the habit of looking in on my mother, who rarely left the flat. 'Poor boy, his marriage did not work out,' she said, with a lovely show of tolerance, but my mother reported the gleam of victory in her fine eyes. She had promised to keep in touch after she moved, but my mother died and the widow failed to put in an appearance. I dismissed this as normal behaviour, and was able to do so because by that time I had come to realize that most people are entirely inconsistent and that one is advised to treat them gently, keeping one's scepticism to one's self. Not to let it show is a desideratum of civilized behaviour.

My other conviction is that everything is connected. That widow in the upstairs flat, whom I knew only slightly, I immediately identified as the mother of the man I observed drinking his coffee in the café in Marylebone Lane where I occasionally stop on my way to the shop, for no better reason than that he had a cowed and submissive look which could have been caused by nagging from more than one quarter. A scenario immediately suggested itself: the wife and the mother at odds, the mother waging ceaseless and not very subtle war against the wife and finally bearing her son away in triumph, like the warrior she was. To the victor the spoils. This man in the café, with his fair bent head, his meek neck, looked like one of those Christians bound to be thrown to the lions. And his mother would have been accustomed to thinking of herself as her son's accredited girlfriend, her companion on holidays, her escort on social occasions. This sort of mother never forgives this sort of son for indulging in sexual activity, and should he marry, which in many cases he does in order to get away from his mother, will act as if she has received a mortal blow from which she may not recover. Her performance, which will be carefully calibrated, will necessitate anxious telephone calls from the son; she in her turn will have no hesitation in calling him at his place of work, sometimes in tears over an implied snub from the wife, by whom she purports to be baffled. 'But I'm his mother!' she might say, in the face of certain objections to her frequent visits, so that relations would be broken off and the son would have to visit his mother surreptitiously on his way home. Finally there would be a demonstration of the wife's unworthiness, like the one my mother and I had overheard, and the die would be cast: mother and son would live together as if no marriage had taken place. The man drinking his coffee in Marylebone Lane wore a clean shirt every day and had neatly combed hair, like a schoolboy. I imagined his mother inspecting him before he left home. A wife would be too busy.

Naturally it is likely that none of this was true. This man in the café might be unattached, and our widow in the flat above entirely innocent. Except that she gave out an aura of unfulfilled sexuality that led one to reflect on the penalties of widowhood, and the troubled legacy to children – although as far as I know she only had the one son. Apart from this there was nothing in her demeanour that was unseemly, or rather there was nothing else in her demeanour that was unseemly. But she seemed unusually combative, as if a campaign were in progress. My mother was the only woman she did not view as an antagonist, largely because my mother was so polite. She knew that the widow – Mrs Hildreth – felt sorry for her, was mildly amused by this, but was good-hearted enough to play her part. Playing her part involved venturing no opinions. And I think she admired the woman's gusto, imperfectly concealed by a worldliness that was acquired rather than innate. Her eyes would roam round our plain living-room, with its oak furniture – even a settle! – its large blurred green carpet on the hardwood floor, its densely patterned curtains, the volumes of Ruskin in the bookcase, as if William Morris were still alive, and she would condemn it out of hand, reflecting complacently on her own swagged and cushioned apartment, on which my mother had reported with perhaps justified satisfaction.

We never saw the son, which enabled me to identify him with the stranger in the café. But the curious fact is that I saw Mrs Hildreth again long after these imaginary events had taken place. I saw her from the back, lingering outside Selfridges, and I noticed how much older she seemed, her neck bent in that characteristic elderly stoop, although her hair was as carefully burnished as it had always been, and her ankles were still slim above the obstinately high heels. She had not given in. On the other hand she looked idle, absent, and she was in the original neighbourhood.

'Mrs Hildreth?' I said. 'Do you remember me?'

Her eyes, when they focused on me, seemed slightly strained, as if her sight were failing.

'It's Claire, isn't it?' she said finally.

'Yes, it's me. How are you?'

'Oh, still out and about, you know.' She gave a poor smile.

'Still in Maida Vale?'

'Yes, although the flat is too big for me now. My son married again, you know. I'm on my own now.'

Come to think of it I had not seen the man in the café for some time. Married again! Then the story was over. Except that it never is, is it? Mrs Hildreth's alteration was now explained, as was her withdrawn expression. She stood as if expecting me to tell her what to do next. Clearly she was now without occupation, one more old lady submitting to the inevitable shipwreck.

'You must miss your son,' I said, not quite innocently.

'David? Oh, I usually see them at the weekends. They live in Burgess Hill now. David collects me in the car. But I'm quite glad to get home again – I don't believe in outstaying my welcome.'

There was no rancour in her tone, no wistfulness either. This was what convinced me that her life was nearly over. Her eyes looked out bleakly, in an effort to see beyond me. She did not ask me how I was, although she seemed content to stand and talk. Seeing her there, still smartly dressed but somehow quite lost, I was forced to abandon the story I had told myself about her. Sometimes connections are misleading. Her son was probably short and dark and complacent, not at all like the worried man in the café. But I was correct, I thought, in supposing that he had finally got the better of his mother, for in doing so he had somehow killed her. The luxuriant widow I remembered had nothing in common with this obedient relic. I felt I should do something for her, ask her to lunch, at the very least call her a cab. She must have sensed my hesitation, for she gave me a smile that was all comprehension. I wondered if she remembered that my mother had died. If so she had not mentioned the fact, nor had she inquired after her.

'Give me a ring some time,' she said, laying a hand on my arm. 'Don't be shy.'

In that moment I realized that she was probably quite blameless, always had been, that that long-extinct argument – so powerful, so brutal – was probably quite misleading, that she was simpler than I had supposed, simpler than I was, and that the connections I had made were sometimes skewed, the result of a life spent watching rather than in taking part.

People are mysterious, I know that. And they do reveal mysterious connections. But sometimes one is merely anxious to alter the script. It was not the first time I had been guilty of a misapprehension.

[2]

I was at home in the flat when my mother died, having just returned from the hospital to pick up the nightdresses I had washed and ironed for her. She had seemed very tired when I left her, but no more so than usual. The telephone rang just as I was making myself a cup of coffee. 'At least you had time to say goodbye,' I was assured by the ward sister, but I rejected this. The idea of saying goodbye to my mother seemed outrageous, barbaric. Yet I knew that I should never see her again.

My friend Wiggy came and spent the evening with me, introducing an element of normality into a day which had been given over to making arrangements, though truth to tell there were few enough of these. We had no relatives, so there was no Book of Numbers genealogy to work through. My mother had wanted to be cremated, as if this were somehow a fitting conclusion – or perhaps an unexpected one – to a life entirely lacking in drama. I had kept my face impassive when she discussed this, and had assured her that everything would be taken care of. By me: this went without saying. She faltered a little when she realized this, which was why it was only mentioned once. Neither of us had any thoughts on the afterlife. There would be no resurrection. This, if anything, cheered me: I had no desire to spend eternity praising other people's God. Nor did I very much want to see my father again, clumsy as he had been after his first stroke, his useless right eye covered by a patch. I had spent some years working as his secretary, and had thus missed out on the career of which my mother spoke so hopefully. In any event I had thought him an unworthy partner for my mother, and he had the peculiar faculty of blunting my imagination. I longed for my mother to have had worthy suitors, regretted on her behalf his thick tweed-suited body, the stick he used, even in the flat. We were both dutiful, of course, my mother because she was a dutiful woman: I myself felt less humble but knew that life was simple only when one concurred with the wishes of others. In itself this is a dangerous weakness, but it seemed obligatory at the time. I was glad when he died. My mother spent a dazed week huddled in her chair, as if he might reappear at any minute. After that I think she knew a measure of contentment. She had always struck me as a contented woman. She belonged to the era before women complained.

My mother had been an art student when girls at the Slade wore long belted smocks and had waved and curled hair. I know this – about the hair, that is – because there is a portrait of her by Sir Gerald Kelly in our dining-room. He seemed to have caught her essence, although she was very young at the time: she is seated in three-quarter profile, with her hands in her lap, the hair caught with particular precision. She has that absent-minded dreaming look that women had in those days, and which must have been *de rigueur* for girls of a certain class. She married my father, a civil engineer much older than herself, as soon as she had finished her studies. I never saw what must have attracted her, apart from a certain stolidity, a certain reassurance. I imagine that they enjoyed furnishing the flat with its curiously uncomfortable furniture; at least nothing was ever changed after he died. I suppose that I shall keep everything as she left it, since I have nowhere else to go. And anyway I am fond of Montagu

Mansions, and I can walk to work in Gower Street and back again in the evening. Come to think of it my life is as divorced from the world as my mother's had been. Yet I find it impossible to imagine her as ever having entertained the thoughts that have kept me so busy over the years.

I wanted her to have had a romantic life before the days when my father's stick heralded his passage from one room to another and his heavy body subsided into a chair, the stick propped up by his side. I objected to him on aesthetic grounds, although the lost look in his remaining good eye stirred me to uneasy feelings of compunction. I wanted my mother to have had lovers, although I could see that this was impossible. She was simply too transparent to entertain disloyal thoughts, although she had been very good-looking as a girl. Her looks faded somewhat after her marriage. Sir Gerald Kelly has caught something of her true nature in that passive seemly three-quarter profile. It behoved me to play my part, in deference to her innocence. To all intents and purposes I was the good daughter, and I believe that was how others saw me, as if I had inherited my mother's blamelessness. At moments I even believe this may be true, although it is not entirely true. Those holidays I take, with her blessing, are not spent exclusively in French provincial towns looking at cathedrals, although such towns are as amenable to adventures as any other place. It is enough for me to entertain my mother on my return from Chartres or Amiens or Bourges or Strasbourg with an account of the byways of the town visited, and with the photographs and postcards to prove that I was there, to make me feel straightforward, reconnected with her worthiness in a way that has been studiously mislaid from time to time. Besides, I like French cathedrals, although not perhaps the flashier ones. Vienne and Autun are more to my taste than Troyes, although Troyes has a lot going for it. Le Mans was the only dead end: Dijon came close. Coutances was pleasant. Mostly I walked, speculating on the people I passed, on the conversations I overheard. These are the consolations of the solitary walker, and the habit has stayed with me. Misconceptions are inevitable, but as I am never put to the test they somehow fail to signify. In any investigation I should be a most unreliable witness.

I believe that my mother's life was one of almost pious simplicity. I believe that she thought that I would marry as she had married, obediently, and that this would come about naturally, or rather supernaturally, given that we knew hardly anyone. My mother's life was a straight line from her cradle to what was now her grave, or rather her ashes. Once I got my job with the Misses Collier I was out all day, so could hardly envisage how she spent her time. I knew she did what women, or rather ladies, did when she was a girl: shopped in the morning, went to town in the afternoon, although 'town' in her imagination consisted of the Royal Academy, the Tate, and the National Gallery. I was introduced to these places at an early age and for some years kept up the habit, although gazing in silence is a somewhat lonely occupation. It was during a visit to the National Gallery that I met my friend Wiggy, Caroline Wilson. We were both standing in front of *The Execution of Lady Jane Grey* when this small person remarked, 'Silly of her to have worn her best dress.'

'Maybe not,' I responded. 'There is nothing like making a lasting impression. Besides, she owed it to the painter. She probably knew he had all those highlights in reserve.'

'Do you like it?' she asked. 'I can't quite decide.'

'I don't object to it,' I answered. 'I just think the size is a mistake. But I suppose he wanted to get in all those wisps of straw in the foreground.'

I took her home with me for tea. My mother was enchanted by her, and not only because Wiggy is an artist of a sort. She paints portrait miniatures of babies and small children from photographs, so that doting grandmothers can have them framed and keep them on their bedside tables. She lives above a café in Museum Street, and is the quietest and most tactful person I have ever met. Naturally I never told my mother that Wiggy had been the mistress of a married man for the past six years; there was no point in worrying my mother with that sort of information. Sometimes I wondered if she knew what an illicit affair involved. I would not have put it past her to doubt the validity of such attachments, although Wiggy and I were of an age to have chalked up a certain amount of experience, most of it uncertain. But even so, the rueful quality of the experience notwithstanding, I always felt I knew more than my mother ever had.

On *her* bedside table my mother kept the first present my father had ever given her, a copy of *The Golden Treasury* inscribed 'To Madeleine, the epitome of womanhood'. This had always struck me as noble but inadequate, as if he had to trust the poems to do his courting for him. And yet there was something decent about that gift: it could foretell nothing but marriage. They all got married in what I think of as the old days. My generation hardly goes in for it in the same way, too enlightened, I suppose, too progressive, too career-orientated. I admit that my notions of marriage are archaic, as I suspect is the case with most women. In my case there is a particular reason for this, or perhaps one I have simply adopted from my reading of the bundles of defunct women's magazines stored in the basement of the shop where I work. Most date from the early 1950s, an age when men wore hats and went to the office and women stayed at home and wore aprons and mysterious underclothes. These articles are immensely reassuring, as if marriage were a seamless garment with no snags in the fabric.

The magazines abound in fascinating disclosures. The letters to the dignified women who are supposed to know about these things all evince the same perplexity, albeit in different guises. 'Should I let my boyfriend go all the way?' The answer is always the same: if he respected you he would not demand it, even suggest it. This prospect of shamefaced young people – for the young men must have been in a state of disarray – is amazing to me. These days intimacy takes place at the beginning of the affair rather than at the end, and the women giving the advice are only too eager to reveal their own histories of alcoholism and anorexia. In the letters to 'Worried. Ealing', tolerance is urged on the less than happily married. Also humorousness. This might have made for an easier life but it seems unnecessarily fatalistic.

It is the illustrations to the stories that capture my attention, one in particular: a woman is shutting the garden gate of her house behind her as she prepares to do her morning shopping. She wears gloves and a small hat shaped like a pancake; she has a wicker basket over her left arm. The gate behind her has the sort of sunray pattern that probably still exists somewhere, for people do not change their garden gates in obedience to the dictates of fashion. Needless to say we do not have that sort of gate in the environs of Montagu Mansions. I do not know what this woman does when she gets home again. She manages to be elegant in an old-fashioned way. It would not occur to her to worry about her weight.

From three o'clock onwards, or so it seems to me, she anticipates her husband's return on the evening train. What does he think as he strides manfully in at the sunray gate? Not a lot, I would say. They are both bound to be very well-mannered. On what happens when they retire to the bedroom, having spent the evening darning socks and listening to the wireless, the magazines are silent. A virginal discretion is maintained throughout, as if married couples need no instruction, are privy only to their own secrets. Sex is underdeveloped, and yet it seems so peaceful. Naturally someone of my generation could not envisage such a union, which seems faintly dreadful. And yet the image of that woman in the pancake hat, on her way to the sort of shops where customers are served by a man in a brown overall, has stayed in my mind for some time. It holds a definite attraction, as if one might, if one were very lucky, attain to a similar plateau of satisfaction. The woman in the pancake hat wears an elusive smile. Maybe her husband is not such a bore after all.

I do not wish this consummation for myself. Rather, I wish it retroactively for my mother, of whose life it is so natural for me to think. My mother was taken straight from her parents' house to this slightly forbidding flat where her husband had pitched his tent some years previously. The kitchen cupboards were still filled with his first wife's glass and china. There had been no children of that earlier marriage, although my mother would have welcomed them – she was still young enough to crave companions. And the stout authoritative man to whom she was married was no companion. I knew this at once, from a very young age. It was not given to my mother to wear the elusive smile of the woman in the magazine. Her smile was always a little puzzled, as she made her dutiful way round the galleries. I dare say my birth was the ultimate proof of her married life. For that reason she loved me too much, as I loved her. We were both discreet about this, tacitly acknowledging the absence of a man who would have made possible an easier relationship, one less charged with the mournful consciousness of lost alternatives. I never heard her complain, yet as my father grew more handicapped and more selfish her smile became more diplomatic, as if aware at last that this was not a normal life for a woman with a simple loving nature. As a widow she remained virginal. I would have liked her to marry again; instead she kept up an unalterable wifely routine, shopping in the morning, looking at pictures in the afternoon. I was a sort of company, I suppose. Not for a moment did I seriously think of leaving her alone, and yet it now occurs to me that this was what she was waiting for, her final release into freedom.

On the evening of the day on which she had died, and died in the company of strangers, I said something of this to Wiggy, who merely remarked, 'It's you who are free now. Will you make any changes, do you think?' She views our lives as anomalous, as I do. She loves her married man, but knows that he has arrested her development: no garden gate and shopping basket for her, and yet I know that with her country background she would accede almost gratefully to such a condition. As for me, my days have settled into not very interesting compartments: our life, now my life, at home, and the excursions into what I think of as cathedral territory, where minor adventures may or may not take place. None of this is entirely satisfactory, which is why I have become something of a mental stalker. In my observations, as I go about my days, I feel as if all my activity has been forced upwards, into my head. I know remarkably few people in what I am tempted to call real life, and yet I seem to get closer to them when I construct their lives for myself. Wiggy says I should write a novel, but in fact I read very little. Working in a bookshop makes one acquainted with titles rather than texts, and in the evenings I long to get out and about. I walk a lot. That is how most evenings are spent.

'When will you go back to work?' Wiggy asked me.

'In a day or so, I suppose. Well, no, after the funeral, in fact. They won't want to see me before then.'

All at once I was filled with a painful longing for my working life, now denied to me for a decent interval of observance. (But it seemed to me that my mother had died long ago, and more recently in those mute days at the hospital, when she was almost pulseless.) I love my work, which takes place at the top of Gower Street, in a second-hand bookshop called Ex Libris. It belongs to two aged sisters, the Misses Collier, Muriel and Hester, although only Muriel sits behind a desk, usually reading. Hester, who is the elder of the two, and that means in her mid-eighties, turns up every afternoon with a cake for our tea, which is my signal to emerge from the basement and put on the kettle. Hester is pretty deaf, but very spirited; Muriel is more austere. They were both Land Girls during the war, which may explain their durability, despite Muriel's knotted legs and Hester's hearing aid. They seem to be in the best of health, although both are frighteningly thin. It is difficult to imagine their existence away from the shop, which they inherited from their father, St John Collier, on whom they have bestowed the status of a man of letters, although I dare say he had already claimed this for himself. It is their intention that his various writings should be gathered into publishable form, be privately printed, and be available in the shop. They are, and always have been, unmarried. Father looms large in their conversation. Mother rarely gets a look in.

My job is to extract St John Collier's articles from piles of rotting newspapers and magazines, to transcribe them on Muriel's huge upright Royal, and to arrange them in some sort of order. 'Naturally you will feature in the Acknowledgements,' I am assured. The late man of letters operated on several fronts, as a minor belletrist, as a contributor of nature articles to *Reynolds News*, and, on the strength of his having been a lay preacher in his youth, as the author of homilies in those women's magazines that I find so beguiling. These homilies are not half bad, if you care for that sort of thing. Reassurance seems to be the keynote, as if God had cheerful plans for us all. To tell the truth I prefer these messages to the ones about the spotted wagtail and the willow warbler, which occupy another sizeable section of his output, but I plough on conscientiously, amid the smells of defunct newsprint and the occasional floating fragment of disintegrating paper. I do all this in the basement, where the foreign language books are kept. I am rarely disturbed by customers. In fact most people do not realize that the shop is open for business, since the door sticks so badly that it is almost impossible to gain admittance.

'You must do something about the door, Muriel,' shouts Hester.

Muriel looks up briefly from whatever she is reading. 'We need a man for that,' she says, and the subject is dismissed.

I have no fantasies regarding Muriel and Hester, who have always struck me as creatures of the utmost rectitude, and therefore somehow not interesting. I prefer those who go about their business with an obvious burden of feeling. 'The Man of Feeling' was the title of an (unpublished) essay by St John Collier, which will be the lead in our book. It is incredibly complacent, like his interpretation of God's purpose. But I prefer those unconscious gestures, those suddenly lowered eyes that give away inner conflict. I can read them like a book. This I prefer to all those books I have not read and whose titles I know so well. I could sell you anything in the shop, since I am so familiar with the stock. But I prefer the living flesh and its ambiguity. I am in my element there, a hunger artist whose hunger is rarely satisfied.

During the few days I spent alone after my mother's death I was able to observe a slight alteration in my behaviour. These days were worse than I had anticipated. The floorboards echoed as I moved from my bedroom to the sitting-room, and I was reminded of my father's lumbering progress, and also of the slight feeling of fear I had always experienced at his approach. This fear had always been baseless; my father was not a threatening figure, merely an inconvenient one, but it now occurred to me that he must have been unhappy. He was in a position to register his deterioration; his one good eye was sharp, and he knew that he was now a clumsy elderly man, whose wife's relative youth disturbed him, as if he had not sought it in the first place.

Their marriage had always struck me as a cynical arrangement. My mother, impractical as she was, had little hope of an independent life, particularly as she had a slight fear of the outside world and was only able to function if she kept to a rigid routine. It probably reassured her to be taken over by a will stronger than her own. She must have felt a certain relief as this substantial stranger translated her from one life to another. As for my father, his predominant emotion must have been gratification. My mother, at the time of her marriage, was young, certainly unspoilt. I doubt if he were very experienced himself, in spite of that brief first marriage that had ended when his wife died of cancer. 'To Madeleine, the epitome of womanhood.' As he seemed to descend gratefully into uxorious habits, and as I was alerted to these at a young age, I sensed that what he appreciated was a certain continuity, with my mother drafted in to make sure that the pattern was not disturbed.

This she did impeccably, and perhaps for this reason was secretly relieved when he died, after a second stroke, gracelessly, in hospital, his hand fumbling under the sheet. She too had observed her period of mourning, in the flat, as I did now, before resuming her regular way of life. But it seemed to me, as she went out in the afternoons, to some gallery or other, that she was still fearful, or perhaps more fearful than she had been when my father was alive. For this reason she sometimes spent whole days at home, reading, in the silence of the long summer afternoons. This made me uneasy, but she showed no signs of depression, discontent. My return home in the evenings, from whatever I had been doing, occasioned a joyful smile. The book was laid aside; she was ready for my news. I offered it, with suitable omissions.

I once, rashly, asked her if she were lonely. She frowned in concentration, duty bound to be accurate, to render an account, to herself as much as to me.

'Not lonely, exactly,' she said. 'But an odd thing happens. I think back to the people I knew when I was young, and realize how good they were to me. My friendships seemed to me then, and seem to me now, so secure! As an only child – like you, my poor darling – I relied on my friends a great deal. We lived a little way out of London, and everything seemed safe. In the evenings I could go over to a friend's house and we would go out for walks. Can you imagine such simplicity?'

'I go out for walks too,' I reminded her.

'But, darling, your walks are dangerous! London is hardly the place for an evening walk. I am anxious when you are out. Not that I should ever try to stop you.'

'Nothing has happened to me.'

'Of course not, you are a sensible girl. But I remember those evening walks I took with my girlfriends, one in particular, Cathy; we were inseparable. I would walk to her house, and then she would walk me back to mine, and so on. It sounds silly, I know, but there seemed to be a golden haze about the evenings then. Very few cars. And we discussed secrets, although of course we had none to speak of.'

'What happened to her? Cathy, I mean.'

'Well, she married very young. She was eighteen. She had been to a cousin's wedding and met a man not much older than herself, and in due course he very properly proposed to her, and they were married. In her wedding dress she looked different, older, and for the first time in my life I became aware of separation. It affected me deeply. Cathy and her husband moved away, and the evenings were never the same again. It struck me at the time that in any event I would be excluded. That's what makes me so unhappy when I hear about children being excluded from school. It is a brutal business: one never quite forgets it.'

'So you were lonely, then. Even then.'

'Well, of course. But I had already met your father. He was at the same wedding, a friend of Cathy's parents. And it seemed to me that Cathy conspired to encourage us: she probably wanted me to feel, what? Not left out. Because our conversations were no longer transparent. Her husband-to-be was rather jealous of an intimacy in which he had no part. And your father was courteous, respectful.' She paused. 'He restored my pride,' she said finally.

'That doesn't seem to me a very good reason for marrying the first man who asks you.'

'Oh, but it is, Claire. Not that I hope you'll ever understand this.'

'And now?'

'Well, I have no friends now. Cathy and I still send Christmas cards, but that is all. These days I only have acquaintances, neighbours, people I pass in the supermarket. We inquire pleasantly after each other's health. And at my age I can hardly expect to make new friends. But I can't honestly say I'm disappointed about this; it seems part of a natural process. I appreciate my quiet life. Of course, I miss your father.' My expression must have been sceptical, because she shook her head and smiled. 'The early days of our marriage were lovely,' she said. 'We had holidays – Venice, the South of France – and it was delightful to have a companion. And we had weekends in the country, looking for things for the flat. I knew he was a good man. But then he had that little accident (she meant his stroke) and I had to get used to looking after him. He loved me, you know. And he was so proud when you were born.'

Reading between the lines I could see that my father's stroke had put an end to her physical life, but I was careful not to raise this matter. In any event she would not have enlightened me.

We had lived affectionately, but also carefully, together, each anxious to protect the other's privacy. It comforted her to know that I was respectably employed, while in my basement I was able to chart her tentative afternoon progress down Bond Street to the Royal Academy, or on the bus to the National Gallery, or in a taxi to the Tate. I could have done that last journey on foot, but my mother had become frail, and in the weeks before her death had not gone out at all. Her death was like her life, modest, self-effacing. I was unprepared for it. Perhaps I wanted to be. A superstitious, even terror-stricken part of me was glad that she had left no trace. Yet I knew that I should miss her for the rest of my life.

I was also in a quandary about what was expected of me. The flat was mine, but I hated to be alone in it, and besides, there was no food. Was it in order for me to go out for a meal? I felt ridiculously self-conscious, as if the whole world must be aware of my plight. I concluded that the sensible thing to do was to stock the bare cupboards and the fridge. There was an all-night supermarket at the top of Baker Street, and I was surprised that it was so empty, until I realized that it was nearly ten o'clock at night. I had spent the whole day in a swoon of memory and reflection. The evening air reassured me; I was not in a hurry to return home. I took a walk: George Street, Marylebone High Street, New Cavendish Street, into the unpopulated regions of Wimpole and Harley Streets. It was finally the absence of people, of familiars, in this minatory district, that caused me to turn back, but the experience was salutory. I vowed to resume those evening walks that I had previously kept short in deference to my mother's anxiety. I was less lonely in the street than I was at home.

As I let myself into the flat I reflected that it would be pleasant to know that there was someone already there, albeit in another room. I saw the point of a marriage even as discreet as my mother's. Yet what I felt was a wistfulness all my own, a dangerous longing for company. And not any company. I thought with pity of my mother's girlhood, her evening walks with her friends, the wedding at which she had been eagerly and awkwardly introduced to my father, their long, long engagement . . . I thought of her as a virgin, sacrificed, and then I thought of the days of their companionship, in Venice, in the south of France. And I almost envied them. I thought of my friend Wiggy, waiting in for a visit from her lover, and grew angry on her behalf. Better a marriage, however brief and unsatisfactory, than an arrangement such as hers. I thought I ought to get married; I thought that Wiggy should. It seemed to me that neither of us had the least idea how to go about this. If anything Wiggy's case seemed even more extreme than mine. Yet when she rang, as she had taken to doing every evening, I detected no unhappiness in her voice. She is dear to me, but we share no secrets. I visit her for a cup of coffee in her flat in Museum Street; she is always taciturn and even-tempered. She says I cheer her up, by which she means that I entertain her. She loves my stories, my fantasies (everything is connected), and settles back to listen. After which I usually go on my way quite light-heartedly, feeling in control, colourful. Except that my mother's absence has made me too aware of my mental processes, aware too that I have tried to supply myself with a form of company that now appears ghostly, too obviously invented. Somehow I feel uneasy about my behaviour, in a way I could not quite define. I looked forward to going back to work. What I needed was the soothing company of St John Collier. Surely no one could devise a better ally in difficult times.

The food which I had bought, and which I should have to

buy, again and again, seemed insubstantial, the plastic carrier bag pathetic. I placed the contents on the kitchen table: a grapefruit, butter, a tin of coffee. This was not a meal. In the last days of her life my mother had subsisted on tea and biscuits: I now did the same, shamefully. I seemed to have lost my amused perspective on the world. The only respite was to get out of the flat; buying the food seemed to me nothing more than a pretext. In those dark streets I recovered slightly, as if it were my destiny to go about, a wanderer on the face of the earth, unclaimed. This was how I spent those not quite innocent holidays in cathedral cities, making opportunities for myself which now seemed to me equally shameful. And I was hungry. The prospect of a meal, served in decent surroundings, now seemed enticing, and I resolved to eat out in future. I would take Wiggy with me, although I knew that she might prove recalcitrant. She was a home-loving creature, and seemed to have resigned herself to a life of waiting, as if her lover might look in at any minute, although as far as I knew his visits were infrequent. I had often wondered how she put up with this. I could not conceive of such passivity, at least for a woman at the end of the twentieth century, although I had the example of my mother constantly before me. But my mother was *hors catégorie*; no one could elect to live that way now. And in any event, with her death, a new order was established, one in which I had only myself to rely on, in which the future would be of my own making.

Somehow I must arrange affairs so that these dreadful days and evenings were not to be repeated. I was uncertain how this was to be achieved, but I thought, or rather hoped, that serendipity would play a part. It had not so far let me down. The job at the shop had come about almost without any effort on my part. I had answered a mysterious advertisement in the *Spectator* which merely stated that help was needed on a private literary project. I had telephoned the number given, had been summoned for an interview, and once I had got past the recalcitrant door had met both Colliers whom I had immediately classed as unworldly, much more unworldly than I was. They had engaged me at once, which seemed to me suspicious, until they showed me the basement. This was gloomy, not quite clean, and smelled of gas.

'You will not be disturbed,' Muriel assured me. 'We get very little call for foreign language books, though why that should be I can't quite understand. A certain number of academics visit us in the summer. Those who know where to find us, that is. They tend to come back. Pleasant people.'

The peaceful silence of the shop had surprised me. It was not out of the way, far from it, but it had a provincial air, as if it were in a side street in Ludlow, or Barnstaple. And then Muriel, behind her desk, did not look like a shopkeeper. She had a distant aristocratic appearance which she had no doubt cultivated as being suitable for the daughter of a man of letters. What had surprised me was her superiority, which was genuine. Yet here was a woman who had devoted her life to this dusty enterprise, as though it were a genuine calling. I did not then know about her days in the Land Army, which would have seemed to me as remote as the Peasants' Revolt. Rather I imagined suitors battling their way in vain through the obstinate door, and being held at arms' length by Muriel Collier's distant but well-mannered smile. She seemed to accept me without question, or maybe she was simply anxious to get back to her reading.

'Have you had many applications for the post?' I inquired cannily. I had already removed my coat.

'One or two,' she replied. 'They seemed disappointed when I explained the work to them. I think they saw themselves putting together something more contemporary. And they were unsuitable in ways I could not quite understand. So modern, you know. Young men with their shirts hanging out. And one older man smelling of drink who evidently thought I should have heard of him. He had a beard, and a collection of mannerisms. I could see that he despised me. Called me "Dear lady", detected spinsterishness. Well, I am a spinster; I make no apology for that. How soon do you think you could start?'

I was startled, had not expected to come so far so quickly. I said that I could start at once, if that was what she wanted. She gave me a smile that lit up her pale austere features.

'You had better familiarize yourself with the material,' she said. 'And there is a café round the corner if you require lunch.' She spoke as if lunch were a reckless indulgence. 'And my sister comes round at about four o'clock with something for our tea. I'm sure you will be happy here. But,' she held up an admonitory hand, 'I must be sure that you will take the work seriously. My sister and I revered our father. These days, I dare say, he would appear unsophisticated. But he wrote in happier times, before all this satire.' I did not point out that satire was mainly the product of the long dead Sixties. I was anxious to get down to work. When she mentioned the minuscule salary, also characteristic of the Sixties, I understood why all those young men with their shirts hanging out had turned the job down. This was a time warp. St John Collier, whose *œuvre* I was about to disinter, was no less a figure of the past than was his daughter. When Hester arrived that same afternoon, her presence announced by an eager shout from outside the door, which her sister was then obliged to open, I felt immensely at ease.

I might also say at home. St John Collier's writings struck me as entirely worthy, although the added attraction was the piles of obsolete women's magazines in which most of them were entombed. The nature articles I could deal with more or less summarily. But in the basement, on my own, except for a very occasional customer, I could indulge my curiosity, not in the great man himself, but in all those horoscopes, those letters of advice – so prudent, so circumspect – written, I suspected, and replied to by the august woman whose photograph was featured at the top of the page, those constipating recipes, and above all the illustrations to the stories, with their winsome lady role models (except that nobody had them then) and their air of gentility which even I, a spoiled product of a later age, felt bound to admire.

Nostalgia for the shop struck me painfully, but I still had this peculiar interval to observe. Truth to tell it rather frightened me, while the poor array of comestibles which I had dumped on the kitchen table and still not put away made me heartsick. I felt as if someone should be looking after me, but had the sense to see that this attitude was dangerously unhealthy, even archaic. I still had the weekend to get through, and this I knew would be difficult. Weekends were supposed to be festive; they were to be anticipated joyfully. I had always found them somewhat problematic. I seemed to sleep badly on a Friday night, and of course towards the end of my mother's life I hardly slept at all. She had died on a Sunday, which I knew would forever colour the day which even happy people find burdensome, at least towards the evening. I could do what everybody else did, go to a six o'clock film, if that was what I wanted. That left the matter of food. I was by now quite hungry, and it was still only Friday. I resolved to telephone Wiggy and invite her, quite casually, out for a meal. In Wiggy's company I should feel less awkward, less conspicuous; my bereaved state would be less obvious. And if necessary I should eat out every evening, early, on my way home from work. But I still longed to get back to the shop, and the Greek café round the corner, and Hester's cakes. An extraordinary shift seemed to have taken place in my habits and customs. I suppose that this is the inevitable result of a death in the family.

On the Saturday morning Muriel Collier telephoned to ask how I was. I thought that was good of her, and gratefully assured her that I was fine. My voice seemed strange to me, and evidently to Muriel as well, for I was told that I need not come back to work until I felt like it. I promised her that I would be in on Monday, trying not to sound too eager. Then I rang Wiggy, and suggested a meal, which I thought might inaugurate various other meals. I thought the timing was right: her lover never appeared at the weekend but devoted himself to familial pursuits in the Home Counties.

'All right,' she said cautiously. 'Where would you suggest?'

'Oh, we'll find something,' I promised her. 'I'll pick you up around seven.'

So I did, but our dinner was not a success. Two women on their own amid the Saturday night revellers did not make a good impression. There is a stigma, even now. I said as much to Wiggy, who did not particularly want to be reminded of this. Not that her lover ever takes her out for a meal. It is rather that his presence in her life gives her a feeling of being accompanied, and this, however illusory, confers a certain composure. For one dreadful minute in the course of the evening I saw that she felt sorry for me. That was no doubt why she said, 'This is fun. Let's do it again.' But the pasta (which, come to think of it, I could have cooked at home) seemed hard to digest, and the noisy restaurant was beginning to give me a headache. I longed to be out in the homegoing streets, alone, though I knew that I was condemned to such occasions for the foreseeable future. Wiggy knew this too, but we were honour bound to observe the proprieties.

'I'll ring you tomorrow,' she said, with a tentative squeeze of my arm. And we parted, I think, gratefully, which merely added to my sadness.

I walked the usual route home, slipping from shadow to light to shadow again. The flat was warm when I let myself in; although it was early May the weather was still chilly. I thought I might spend the following day, Sunday, tidying my mother's room, throwing away all the childproof pill bottles which at the end had remained unopened. I went to bed discouraged, but I slept deeply and woke with a slightly lighter heart. I spent the morning and a good part of the afternoon tidying and cleaning: this was no doubt how I should spend all my remaining Sundays. This thought made me sad all over again, and I went to bed far too early. That is why, perversely, I overslept on the Monday morning, and was late arriving at the shop. Muriel raised her eyebrows slightly and pointed downwards. I thought she was consigning me repressively to my duties in the basement, but in fact all she meant was that I should not make too much noise. We had a customer.

[3]

At first the man in the basement looked to me like an older and more careworn version of the man with bowed head in the café in Marylebone Lane who was not Mrs Hildreth's son and for whom I had imagined a whole illusory history. (I am not infallible.) This man had the same air of lassitude, which I detected in spite of his polished appearance. He was formally dressed for his visit to a dusty bookshop, although he could not have known that it would be quite so dusty. He wore a finely tailored grey suit with a faint chalk stripe, a very white shirt, and highly polished shoes. I think it was the brilliantly laundered shirt that led me to make the comparison with Mrs Hildreth's putative son, as if this man too had emerged from the hands of a watchful woman, and had set out, fully caparisoned, to encounter the hazards of the ordinary working day.

Except that this man obviously had no connection with the world of work: he was too careful, too immaculate. And besides what sort of man do you find in a bookshop at ten o'clock on a Monday morning, unless he is some sort of don, about his own affairs? This man, however, was too presentable to be one of the academics we get in from time to time. He turned briefly when I said 'Good morning' before turning back to the shelves. I had an impression of a fine blond head and a fair-skinned face prematurely worn into furrows of anxiety which gave him an elderly look, although his figure was tall and upright and rather graceful.

In his hasty return to his earlier perusal of the shelves I sensed a reserve. This man would not waste time on a strange woman, with whom in any case he was not on terms of familiarity or friendship. I found him attractive, more attractive than the prospect of a day with St John Collier, who had begun to acquire a patina of benign tediousness. I pitied those two girls having to listen to him throughout their childhood, although the experience seemed to have done them no harm. Their respect for their father had remained intact, a fact at which I could only marvel. My own father had never emitted a single philosophical or semi-philosophical dictum, so that I had learned at an early age not to look to him for enlightenment, or even very much in the way of affection. He found me as tiresome as I found him, but I had never quite resolved the factors that made us so antagonistic.

I took the cover off my typewriter and pretended to be studying my papers. It would be impolite to start work with this man at my back, although he was paying me no attention. From what I could judge he was reading his way steadily through whatever came to hand, as if he had found sanctuary in our basement and was in no hurry to leave. I also detected an almost unnatural stillness, almost a watchfulness about him, as if he were sensitive to my own inactivity, or as if he knew that I was not normally an inactive person whom he had no wish to constrain by his presence. For this reason he was conscious of me, as I was of him. I shuffled the typewritten pages on my desk; clearly I could not start on the women's magazines while he appeared to be reading Heine's collected poems. I corrected a few typing errors, resolving to work properly, in a resolute fashion, when he had gone. But he showed no signs of going, and in the end I merely sat still, with a pen in my hand, as if to give an impression of profound thought.

He did not much worry me. I am at ease with men, to whom I am inclined to forgive much. This, I thought, was the direct legacy of my unfortunate father, to whom I forgave little. I was fifteen years old when he had his first stroke, and I became used to his clumsy presence, but also to his irascibility, as if not enough deference were being paid to his condition. He was inclined to sulk when he considered himself to be neglected. In fact he was not neglected, but he was quick to sense when my mother was tired, or when I warily brought him a cup of tea and was forced to watch while it ran down his chin . . . And that awful last sight of him as he lay comatose in the hospital, his hand still about its business under the sheet. 'It's the catheter that's bothering him,' said the nurse, but she was young, and as embarrassed as I was.

For that reason I appreciated wholeness in men, whatever their moral character. The partners I have chosen have all been well set up, viable, as if I need to know that they carry no trace of mortal illness, that I am not threatened with their decrepitude. My worst nightmare is to be shackled to a sick man, for I have seen what physical sickness can do to the mind. I dare say my father was aware of his lamentable appearance. I am sure he was aware of my lack of love for him. But with a young person's primitive instincts I was frightened of ugliness, wanted to have nothing to do with it. To have him in the flat all day was bad enough. And to be fair I was not entirely to blame. He did not care for me, although he pretended to do so. He cared only for my mother, who tended him faithfully. He found my childhood noises distasteful, which was why I soon learned to be quiet, so as not to remind him of my presence. I was anxious not to have to encounter him, although this was impossible, as he installed himself in the living-room and stayed there, in his chair, unavoidably present. For this reason, when I came home from school, I made straight for my bedroom. I read a lot in those days. I have a picture of myself furiously reading, my fingers in my ears to drown out the sound of his harsh altered voice, which came out as a groan, as if he were angry all the time.

No doubt he was angry, yet he was determined to live, whereas I, again with the ruthlessness of a young person, thought it would be more appropriate if he would simply disappear. I was nineteen when he had the second stroke, the one that killed him. Until then all I knew of men was impairment, inadequacy. After that I wanted only a certificate of durability, unaltered features, easy unthinking movements. Presumably daughters are more easily influenced by their father's habits and appearance than by their worth. The idea that my father could have provided me with worldly instruction was simply laughable. Who could learn from a man so gracelessly concerned with what remained of his damaged life? Or so I thought, in my ignorance. In mitigation I can state that he was inclined to dismiss me as unimportant. It was not until he was dead that I began to relax. It was shortly after his death that I took, at my mother's urging, my first tentative holiday. I like to think she remained in ignorance of what was to become something of a habit. In any event my holidays were never discussed in detail. We pored over the photographs and postcards together – rood screens and tympanums, choirstalls, misericords, clerestories and elevations – as if these had had exclusive claims on my attention. I faltered when I found that she had compiled several albums of the postcards, which she kept in her bedroom. She was so innocent herself that I am sure she managed to think me innocent as well.

I am alert now to signs of damage in a man. If this is combined with physical excellence I feel a perverse desire to take him over, as if his weakness excited me. When the two conditions are combined – attractiveness and hesitation – the conjunction is often spectacular. I sometimes think that my childish ruthlessness has survived undiminished, but in fact I am careful to cause no harm. Indeed I disappear discreetly, leaving several questions unanswered. I wish that this particular pattern did not impose itself, that I could happily offer affection without that slight feeling of vengeful satisfaction. On the whole I have managed quite well. It is just that my mother's death, and the sight of those photograph albums, which kept company by her bed together with Palgrave's *Golden Treasury*, had weakened me. And perhaps I was undergoing the influence of St John Collier's sweet-natured assertions, as if to believe in a happier world were within the capacity of even fallen creatures like myself. For I knew myself to be at fault. The intolerance I had manifested towards my father had left a stain, which was why I was such a solitary person. A solitary person with a longing for wholeness, an experience which would cancel all the others. A baptism, if you like.

The man in the basement, of whose presence I had become uncomfortably aware, as he had of mine, smelled discreetly of some subtle scent which was far removed from the blasts of aftershave one was likely to encounter in the early morning. He gave an impression of almost futile luxury, which was implemented when he drew a snowy handkerchief from his sleeve and flicked a small speck of dust from his fingers. He implied an army of servants, either that or a lonely and obsessive drive towards perfection, probably the latter. He was obviously rich, certainly idle. I imagined his empty day, every gesture aiming at sublimity. He had an iconic presence, and yet I was able to observe the occasional involuntary grimace which creased his fair thin-skinned face. He was a man torn between achievement and frustration, the balance tilted towards the latter. When I sneezed he gave a violent start, as if recalled to familiarity with greater upheavals.

I offered to make him a cup of coffee but he refused effusively. I was beginning to find his continued presence rather tiresome. At the same time he impressed me as attractive. I wanted to know his story, which I was quite capable of inventing for myself. Perhaps because I had been thinking of my father I thought I detected an unhappy home background, an invalid sister to whom he was deeply attached. This selfless sister – for she would be all virtue, as in one of St John Collier's scenarios – would urge him to go out and enjoy himself. But the poor fellow would be half-hearted in this pursuit, would seek refuges, indeed basements, where his presence would impress but would remain unchallenged. This same sister would oversee his appearance, which would always be faultless, this being a subject on which they would naturally concur. I had no way of knowing how accurate or inaccurate this picture was, but I did not doubt that I was intrigued. I looked at my watch and realized that he had been silently reading for thirty-five minutes. By this time he could have had one or two of Heine's poems off by heart. Either that or he was translating them. Perhaps he too was a man of letters. But he looked too ineffable, and also too unhappy, for that. I altered my estimate of him. He was a dilettante, a caste I had always admired.

'Can I help you?' I said finally, slightly irritated by the lack of effect my presence was having on him. Besides, I wanted to get on with my work. I was aware that before my enforced absence I had come across an article boldly entitled, 'Emphasize your good points!' (nowadays it would be called 'Maximize your assets!', in deference to the market economy) which suggested that St John Collier's favoured publications were emerging from their post-war obedience, and were exchanging austerity for a certain tentative assertiveness. This in turn, but the thought must have been lying dormant, alerted me to the unpleasant fact that St John Collier was running out of time and myself with him. The pile of magazines had shrunk dramatically: my task was almost completed. I had no doubt that Muriel would keep me on for a bit, but she did not really need a full-time assistant. My task had been to devote my attention to St John Collier, and this I had done; editorial work simply amounted to putting the articles in chronological order. Changes of an unwelcome kind seemed to be inevitable. I resolved to ask Muriel whether it might be interesting to write some sort of Foreword, an account of St John's early life, perhaps. She could tell me the facts and I could string them out into some sort of narrative. The idea appealed to me. I had got used to him; he was safe in my hands. Besides, his philosophy was so user-friendly, the best of all possible worlds, as someone or other had said. Trust and hope would never let you down, he seemed to imply. I should have liked to believe that he was right.

'Are you looking for anything in particular?' I asked, rather more sharply than I intended.

'*Jenny Treibel*,' he replied. 'You don't seem to have a copy.'

'We have *Effi Briest*,' I said. 'Are you particularly interested in Fontane?'

'Oh, I have several copies of *Effi Briest*,' he replied. 'It was some of the other stories I was after. They are rather hard to come by, you know. You are my last hope.' He gave a heart-breaking smile. 'I have tried almost everywhere I can think of.'

'The London Library?'

'Oh, but you see I must have my own copy.'

He looked worried, distressed, more distressed than one should look in the face of a slight contretemps.

'Most people come in for the French,' I remarked chattily, anxious for some reason to put him at his ease.

'I prefer the German writers,' he said, with the same heart-breaking smile, as of one confessing to a weakness. A man who was not quite a man, I reflected. The idea had a perverse appeal.

In my mind's eye I had an image of a book with a red and white cover brought in, with a job-lot of texts, by a university student after graduating. (We get plenty of these.) This book was entitled *The German Library* and was in good condition. Muriel had put it on one side, on one of the tables, with the intention of reading it herself. As far as I knew it was still there. The name Fontane, which was certainly there, came to me distantly but with a sense of certainty. I have an excellent photographic memory. I remembered something like 'Shorter Fiction', also on the cover.

'I think I can find you a copy,' I said. 'But not straight away. If you'd like to give me your name and address I'll let you know.'

He looked even more worried, as if this were classified information, but divulged both his name and an address in Weymouth Street. I knew it well, of course, for it was on the route of my evening walks. I promised to be in touch and accompanied him back up the stairs. By now he seemed anxious to leave. With a pleasant expression, or so I hoped, I watched as he wrestled with the door.

'Give it a good tug,' said Muriel, raising her eyes from her book. 'It needs seeing to, but we haven't the right instruments. We need a man.'

At this he looked alarmed, as if she had expected him to take off his coat and get down to it straight away. (She probably had.) We both watched as he extricated himself. Then Muriel went back to her book, and I lingered for a few minutes in the shop. I found the red and white volume under a pile of others on the table, waiting to be shelved. I took it downstairs with me, as if I were going to put it away.

At six o'clock that evening I telephoned the number he had

given me. 'Mr Gibson?' I inquired. 'It's Claire Pitt, from the bookshop. I've found a copy of *Jenny Treibel* for you, but it's in English. Would you like me to keep it for you?'

'Could you perhaps send it?' he said.

'Oh, I'll drop it in,' I assured him. I was anxious to verify my theory about the invalid sister. 'I'm often in the area.' This at least was true.

'Claire!' came Muriel's voice. 'I'm locking up.'

He was quite likely to have forgotten my name already. 'Claire Pitt,' I repeated, then suddenly wondered what on earth I was doing. His voice had sounded thin and melodious, as if he were on his best behaviour, anxious to reassure. Definitely the invalid sister, I thought.

I picked up the book, said goodnight to Muriel, and went home. In the course of the evening I glanced through it, beguiled by some of the names ('Victoire', 'Lisette'). I would ask him to lend it to me, I decided. Just for a few days. That way I could deliver it to him all over again.

I have no interest in the German Romantics, or indeed in any other kind of romantic, with or without literary status, but the stories seemed limpid, accessible, but somehow remote in time, rather like the man who had been looking for them. I did not go so far as to read *Jenny Treibel* so as to seem more knowledgeable than I really was; such stratagems were not in my nature. I really do not know what I had in mind at that stage. Sometimes an attractive appearance is enough, so that one is inclined to endow the person who possesses such an appearance with other gifts, grace, intelligence, some sort of accomplishment. And this tall fair stranger had seemed so incongruous in our dusty basement, as if he were visiting from another world where everyone was well dressed. The wincing nervousness seemed out of character but it was easy for me to excuse it. It was the reason for this that I was determined to examine. The man had either suffered some sort of psychic injury that had left him otherwise intact or he was under great strain. There may have been, probably was, illness somewhere in the background, and with this I could sympathize all too readily, as my experience had taught me to. I had frequently felt shame at my own resistance to my father's tragedy, but I believe my instinct was correct. It is sometimes necessary to keep one's distance from misfortune, however harsh this may seem to others.

The man in the shop seemed more affected by this dilemma (if it existed) than I had ever been; he was far gone, if not in suffering, then no doubt in awareness. I should have liked to discuss this matter with someone, or even to have put the man on his guard. Your sympathy is quite adequate, I should have said; do not allow it to become excessive. Vulnerability is commendable; masochism is not. There was no possibility of my ever saying this. But I believe that my desire to say it was present even on that first day. I felt both pity and impatience, as if enormous efforts would be needed to impose the realities of life once more before it proved too late. In this I may have been prescient. Spotless heroes (I did not doubt that he would be spotless) often owe their survival to agencies more worldly than themselves. It was something to think about, something to remind me of the fairy stories I had read so obsessively as a child. I put it no higher than that.

[4]

It was not his sister who was the invalid. It was his wife. This I learned the following evening when I delivered the book. 'Martin? Who is it, darling?' came a voice from another part of the flat.

'Would you excuse me a minute,' he said. 'My wife . . .'

I was left standing in the middle of a room which was the complete antithesis of our plain-living high-thinking rooms at home. This room was an unironic tribute to the nineteenth century. Looped curtains of dark blue chenille obscured most of the light from the two tall windows that looked out over Weymouth Street. The floor was covered by a large red and blue carpet which someone other than myself could no doubt have identified and dated. On a marble chimneypiece stood a gilt clock under a glass dome and two glass candlesticks dripping with lustres. In the middle of the room stood a round walnut table on a single pedestal; a smaller version of this was placed between the windows. Two enormous wing chairs, covered in blue and green damask, further obscured the light. These chairs, it seemed to me, were not designed to be occupied. My parents' chairs at home were upholstered in a vague orange and brown tapestry; they had high backs and wooden arms and were functional and austere. Surrounded by this opulence, which I was left alone to admire, I felt a vague residual distaste. I did not know how long I was supposed to stand there (for it seemed to me impossible to sit down) and the muted conversation which I could hear coming from another room activated some primitive memory of earlier overheard intimacies.

The light was dim. A couple of opaline lamps supplied what there was; there was no ceiling rose. At home we had been lit by a plain chandelier, for which the word was if anything complimentary: three unadorned wooden arms supported bulbs in parchment shades. This too had given a bad light; my mother's and father's reading lamps had supplied the rest. Here I was conscious of light being deliberately excluded. Everything had a high finish. It was warm and silent. I searched for the source of this warmth but could see no radiators. The marble fireplace held a steel grate filled with dyed blue hydrangeas. This struck me as the only artificial element in this nightmare interior in which everything was designed in relation to everything else.

I began to wish that I were out in the street, enjoying, if that is the word, one of my solitary walks. I reckoned that Martin Gibson had no business to leave me standing there while he pursued some conversation in another room. From what I could overhear this conversation was muted but enthusiastic, the sort of tone adopted in a sickroom. So I was not wrong about the illness, I thought. There was a sense of a conspiracy that left me attending vaguely on the sidelines, a mere spectator, or rather auditor. And yet I had no other role. The role that was assigned to me I had devised for myself. Martin Gibson, whom I had admired in the shop, seemed now to be reduced to a sort of servant, emptied of substance by a wife who was somehow impotent, laid up; his manhood, such as it was, would be subsumed by her needs. I felt sorry for him, but my pity was edged with irritation; this was the kind of call I was bound to answer. I saw myself as Potiphar's wife, embracing a reluctant

Joseph, and felt the sort of reprehensible excitement to which I was prone. I knew my character was poor, that I could lay claim to few moral qualities. In these moments I thought of my mother, her artlessness, her careful days in the belted smock, copying from the model, and the sadness that her friend's wedding had occasioned. I knew that such simplicity was beyond my reach, let alone my grasp. That was why, at the age of twenty-nine, I stood in a stranger's room calculating my chances.

When Martin Gibson returned his face showed a certain animation. 'Cynthia, my wife, would like to meet you,' he said. 'If you are not in a hurry do come and say hello.' He lowered his voice. 'She sees so few people these days. She says her illness has driven all her friends away. So when she hears a strange voice . . .'

'I'm sorry your wife is ill,' I said. 'What is the matter with her?'

When I looked back on this remark I found it intolerably crude. Though plain it was evidently unanswerable, for Martin Gibson, who was, I noted, still wearing his chalk-striped suit, looked as if this were the one question that no one in their right mind would have thought appropriate.

'Her heart,' he said. 'And her nerves, of course. Poor darling.'

I wanted to hear more, but little more was to be vouchsafed. I thought of one of the books my mother had insisted I read, about a man with an ailing wife. My mother had thought it a masterpiece; I had not. This had disappointed her. 'It's not the saddest story ever told,' I protested. 'Why was he so helpless?' She had smiled. 'It is circumstances that make us helpless,' she replied, and I saw that she was looking back to her own past years of incarceration. I said nothing after that, but my dislike for the story increased, and has remained.

I followed Martin Gibson along a corridor and into a bedroom lit by more opaline lamps, but more brightly. I hardly had time to register more than the fact that the wife lay in a large bed, or rather lay back against a multitude of pillows, with manicure implements on a small tray on her knees. I had an impression of blondeness, of a round face, of anxious eyes. She was immaculately made up, and did not look in the least ill, yet when she spoke her voice was hoarse, and the hand she held out to me, and which I took, was hot and moist. She was wearing some sort of peignoir, coral pink, with a certain amount of lace, and she smelt of the kind of scent which should be reserved for decisive women executives looking forward to a career in the boardroom. I imagined, though I could hardly turn round and look, a whole armoury of such scents, indulgences brought to the sickroom by the devoted husband who would naturally be at a loss in such a situation and who would seek the advice of the sales assistants behind the beauty counters. My mother had never used more than a simple cologne. But this was no time to think of my mother.

'How do you do?' I said. 'Claire Pitt. I brought your husband's book. I didn't mean to disturb you.'

'My dear,' said the hoarse voice. 'If you only knew how eager I am to see new faces. My life, as you can see,' she gestured around the room, upsetting the tray with the manicure instruments which her husband bent eagerly to retrieve, 'is confined to this one room now.'

'I'm so sorry,' I said.

'Of course Martin could have collected the book,' she said sharply. 'He is quite free in the daytime. In fact I make him go out; I know he likes to walk. I insist that he does so, though I suspect he doesn't always enjoy it.' She flashed him a smile which revealed another, earlier woman, mischievous, not entirely kind. She would have been lovely, I reckoned. She was still good-looking in a ruined way, although I was touched to see that her cheeks had taken on a little colour since I had entered the room. Her hand still held mine, as if to prevent me from leaving.

'Who looks after you in the daytime?' I asked, since it was clear to me that she had no interest in myself.

'Oh, Sue is here in the daytime,' was the reply.

'Your daughter?'

She laughed. 'Did you hear that, Martin?' she said. Her tone was not quite friendly.

'The nurse,' said Martin Gibson, not registering the implied insult. At least I thought it was an insult. If these people did not sleep together that was hardly the husband's fault. Nor was it entirely hers. She did seem ill; the heat of her hand was disagreeable. Yet it would have been rude to have disengaged my own. My eyes strayed to the bedside table, on which stood a flowered china candlestick, and a photograph, in an Art Nouveau silver frame, of a white Scotch terrier sitting in a basket. Her eyes followed mine, and she smiled slightly, as if she had discerned my curiosity but was not disposed to satisfy it. 'Yes, my poor dog had to go,' she said. 'Along with all the rest.'

'I'm so sorry,' I said again, since this seemed to be expected of me. 'If there's anything I can do . . .' I still do not know why I said this.

'Of course, it broke my heart when Martin had to give up his teaching,' she went on.

'Oh?' I looked at him inquiringly, but he seemed resigned to being a mere attendant.

'European literature, at London University.'

'But that must have been terrible for you,' I said, turning to him.

'It was,' said his wife. 'And for me too. His students used to love to come and talk to me. If they had a little problem it helped them to confide, you know.'

I reflected that she might enjoy other people's problems,

particularly those of young people who are still tender enough to trust. No doubt she had designs on whatever problems I might have. As if in answer to this the hot hand grasped mine even more tightly. I felt a slight desire to escape.

'Yes, the secrets I've heard. Of course it was the girls who wanted to talk. Their love affairs. They were all in love. Most of them with Martin.' She smiled. I watched as the smile faded. 'The weekends are the worst,' she said to my surprise. 'Nobody comes. And there's not a sound from the street. I hate it here.'

'Darling,' her husband pleaded.

She ignored him. 'What do you do at weekends, Claire?'

'Well, I don't like them much either,' I said, startled into honesty. 'On Saturday evenings I have a meal with my friend Wiggy . . .'

'Your boyfriend?'

'No. Wiggy is a girl.'

'Why is she called Wiggy? Is there something wrong with her hair?'

'Her hair is fine,' I ploughed on. 'And on Sunday . . .'

'Oh, Sunday!' The hands were now clasped reminiscently, for which I was grateful. 'When I was well we always went out on Sundays. The Compleat Angler for lunch, and then a drive. The car had to go, of course. No point in keeping it in the centre of town. And Saturdays too. We used to go looking for things for the flat. I see you are admiring the lamps.' I realized that her eyes had never left my face.

'My parents used to do that,' I told her. 'Before my father got ill. He . . .'

Her hands flew to her face. 'Oh, don't tell me about illness. It's life I want to hear about. Life!'

'Darling,' interjected the husband. 'You're getting tired.'

'Yes, I'm tired,' she said gratingly. 'But I haven't heard anything about this young person.' Not surprising, I thought, since she had expressed no interest. 'You can tell me anything, you know,' she said, clasping my hand again. 'Come again. Come on Saturday. Bring that friend of yours with the funny name.'

I disengaged my hand with difficulty. Martin – I was now disposed to think of him as Martin – moved forward and rearranged her pillows.

'I'll get your infusion,' he said. 'And then you must sleep.'

'Yes,' she said, exhausted. 'I must sleep. Goodbye. Until Saturday. Don't forget.'

'Did she mean that?' I asked Martin, as he shut the door quietly behind him.

'Well, yes, she did. She sees so few people. It would be a kindness . . . Of course you are under no obligation . . .'

'I don't mind,' I said. 'I'll come on Saturday. I'll bring Wiggy. If that's all right with you.'

'Most kind. And now I'm afraid you'll have to excuse me. Cynthia will want her drink. And then I'll have to get her settled for the night . . .'

'Of course. I understand.'

'Until Saturday, then.'

'Goodnight,' I said.

At that stage I had no intention of returning on the Saturday. Let them find some other form of entertainment. I felt particularly bad about introducing Wiggy's name into the conversation, if conversation was what it had been. She had enough trouble dealing with me. I knew she would rather have stayed at home than sat through those artificial evenings out which looked likely to become a ritual. She would keep these up as long as I did. There was no way she would welcome the idea of sitting by a solipsistic stranger's bed. Unlike me she had a companion.

Out in Weymouth Street, the evening only slightly darkening at nine o'clock, I felt lonely, ejected from the intimacy of countless bedrooms. Not that this particular bedroom had impressed me. What had impressed me was the fact that the woman had felt confident enough to be slightly rude to her husband. That was the sort of confidence I could never acquire, since I should never marry. I knew this suddenly, out on the pavement in Weymouth Street. I raised my eyes to the Gibsons' windows, but they were now dark. I decided that Cynthia Gibson was both sentimental and malicious: sentimental because of her hot hands clinging to mine, malicious on account of her husband on whom she was dependent but who insisted on treating her like a child, or like the invalid she was. It had been the frustrations of a healthy woman that had come through to me.

And the stifling comfort of those paradoxically comfortless rooms! The careful lamps everywhere, the cluster of milk-glass vases on the console in the hall! He would have been the collector in those days when they motored round waterside towns and villages, she the signer of cheques. That they were wealthy was in no doubt, but I sensed that the money must be hers. They were not old, but they were elderly; he might be forty to her fifty, or even fifty-three. That would account for her acerbity, as if the poor fellow could be credited with a capacity for infidelity. She was probably the only woman he had ever known. As a young man he would have been excited by her, by her hot little hands, her air of authority. And by her money, which had entitled her to put a high price on herself. She had no doubt discerned the erotic potential in a shy young man, had teased and flattered him into a state of excitement, under the watchful eye of an experienced mother. I was making this up, of course, but it struck me as entirely feasible. She would have been thirty-five to his twenty-five when they met, and it would have been a white wedding, never mind the flattering expertise with which it had been anticipated. 'Life!' she had said, in tones of ardour and despair. Something harsh had broken through, the first sign of authenticity in that whole strange scenario. I felt as if I had spent an evening at the theatre, but had not much appreciated the play, perhaps had not understood it. For once I was conscious of my own lack of experience.

I knew only simple transactions, in which there was no room for connivance or complicity, certainly not subjection, submission. Maybe the time had come for me to learn these higher or lower arts. Martin Gibson's appeal to me was in this category. His wife had shown me that. The strange visit had taught me this particular lesson. There are no accidents. Everything is connected.

The light had gone, the evening was under way. In Wigmore Street I found a café, went in, and ordered a toasted sandwich and a cappuccino. What did those people eat? Something refined, no doubt, in the best possible taste. I licked a crumb from the corner of my mouth, paid the bill, and left. My meal had taken twenty minutes. When I reached home the flat seemed to me a haven of plain dealing, the hardwood floor a guarantee of straightforward behaviour. For a moment I wished I was the sort of girl my mother had been. Then I went to bed, determined to put the evening out of my mind. In this I partly succeeded.

On the following day I was hardly surprised when Martin Gibson came down the stairs into my basement. The cautious steps could surely announce no other.

'Good morning,' I said, with possibly a slight edge to my voice. 'What can I do for you today?'

'Oh, nothing, nothing. I came to thank you for your visit.'

'Not at all.'

'It made such a difference to Cynthia,' he went on. 'She sees so few people.'

'So she said.'

'She's talked about it, you know. She was quite thrilled . . .'

'How long has she been ill?'

'Two years, slightly more.'

'And she doesn't go out at all?'

'No, not any more.'

The slight animation faded from his face; he looked haggard and handsome. 'So if you could come on Saturday? With your friend? Just for half an hour or so.'

That morning, as I walked to work, I had been aware of the first truly fine day in a spring of predominantly grey skies. I wondered how I might fare if I were condemned to view it through the shrouded windows of that awful flat.

'I'll come,' I said.

His expression lightened at once. I think he was quite unaware that I might have other plans. Besides, I had no other plans. And it was so long since I had seen gratification on another's face that my decision seemed to be quite rational. At the same time I knew that I had left simple rationality quite a long way behind.

[5]

Wiggy was not best pleased with the evening I had in store for her, but had evidently decided that I needed consoling, indulging. In fact we were both in need of diversion, or perhaps development in the direction of something more serious. Her life was no more satisfactory than mine was, although she never complained. As for myself, I was no doubt in search of significance – not that I knew what that should be. One thing was certain: I was not destined for the happiness of a settled life, whether or not I longed for it: I was not one of the elect. 'Oh, for a closer walk with God,' the radio had moaned at me on the previous Sunday, when I was about the business of clearing my mother's effects out of the flat. Indeed, I had thought. One would venture a few criticisms, of course, if admitted to the Presence, a few reminders of broken promises. The lion does not lie down with the lamb, one would observe; swords have manifestly not been beaten into ploughshares. And what was my Father's business, exactly? To judge from the Old Testament it was about being angry. In which case how had such an angry Father had such a charming Son?

This was not for me. I was resigned to the laws of this rough world. I would take my chance, and with it the penalties, for there are always penalties. I had spent that morbid Sunday wondering if simple happiness were available to all and had come to the conclusion that it was not. One had to make a determined bid for it, and I did not quite know how this was done. Friends of mine who had married young had revealed that they were no strangers to triumphal calculations and this had puzzled me. I was no romantic, but part of me wanted the process to be effortless. Instead of which I had taken the only options I thought I had, and had considered myself secure against disappointment. The disagreeable element in all this was that I knew that nothing would come of such manoeuvres, invigorating though they were. I returned every time to the *status quo ante*, whereas those same friends seemed to move quite easily into further stages of maturity, leaving me on the outer margin, waiting for my life to begin. Needless to say, this awareness was concealed, though not always from myself. In my former circle I was the entertainer, a role which I had adopted, and which was, I knew, appreciated. Yet it was surely no accident that I rarely saw those friends now. My role was becoming harder to sustain. If my way of looking at the world was hazardous, it was, by this date, largely unalterable.

As always my mother's life was the standard by which I measured my own, although I had learned disaffection from my father. I had concluded that happy families belonged in some mythic category, together with promises that had not been kept. Even in the fairytales which I had read greedily as a child I had been disturbed by the absence of pity, by the slyness and guile that was regarded as quickwittedness. Many years later I realized that I had taken this creed as my own, yet my innocent mother had thought it suitable for a child. Presumably the more subversive message had passed her by when, a child herself, she had read the same stories. One speaks of unawakened women as virtuous, though this may not have been their intention. In my mother's case both were true. She never wavered in her purpose of making our lives as agreeable as possible, even after my father had changed from a courteous companion to an intractable and self-absorbed invalid, not seeing that it was owing to her excellent care that he had lasted so long.

The only uncensored feeling I ever discerned in her was unconscious relief when he died. Even this she failed fully to register, and therefore experienced no guilt. She resigned herself gratefully to her pastimes, pictures and books, and to myself. It was I who was guilty when conscious of the disparity between her life and my own, though I think – I hope – that she remained in ignorance of this. In truth my black heart had had few occasions on which to manifest itself. But I had only to picture my mother and her girlhood friend, their heads together, wandering through the summer evenings, to feel unworthy. Yet even they had been subject to change. Marriage had transformed my mother into a woman, although she remained a girl at heart. Marriage had put an end to the blamelessness of those evenings, which she was never to know again. The same may even have been true of her friend. I no longer thought it odd that they had not kept in touch. Both would now have been conscious of concealment, of secrets no longer to be shared. I thought my own methods were healthier. For me concealment meant distance. Perhaps it was time I took another holiday.

I had suggested to Wiggy that if we looked in on the Gibsons at about six o'clock we could escape after at most half an hour on the pretext of dinner. This seemed to me more satisfactory than a later hour, when Cynthia Gibson would no doubt be tired. I had noted her sudden slump into exhaustion from my previous visit. Had I stayed longer, I knew, she would have become febrile, querulous. I remembered her husband's assiduity in marshalling me out of the room. Looking back to say goodbye I had been shocked by the sudden deterioration in her appearance, her colour faded, her mouth bitter, set in a grimace which may have been habitual. Therefore I was relieved, for my own sake, as well as Wiggy's, when the door was opened by a robust-looking girl in a white coat, the nurse, presumably. 'Hi,' she said. 'Good timing. I was just about to leave. Your visitors are here, Cynthia,' she called. 'I'll just see if she wants anything, then I'll make myself scarce.' She laughed pleasantly, revealing dazzling teeth. Had I been ill I should have found her presence reassuring. Nothing could conceivably go wrong in the presence of those teeth.

But I was not ill, and I wondered if it were entirely in order that she should be wearing earrings and that the white coat should be open over a blouse and a pair of pin-striped navy blue trousers. I wondered this again when she returned to the hall, took out a comb, and stationed herself in front of a small and no doubt venerable mirror. She was good-looking in an uninteresting sort of way, with large blue eyes and regular features. The white coat came off and was hung in a cupboard.

'Sue, darling,' came a cry. 'Don't leave me without saying goodbye. After all I shan't see you until Monday.'

The nurse, Sue, presumably, gave us a conspiratorial wink, and said, not much lowering her voice, 'She's been like that all day. Restless. Fortunately you'll be a bit of a distraction. Only don't stay too long, will you? And remind Martin to give her her pills. I'm coming,' she carolled. 'Ready or not.' It was evidently her job to coax and tease, to provide affectionate banter, even to flirt. She would, throughout the day, be the unfortunate woman's sole companion. I felt equally sorry for them both.

At first sight all I could see of Cynthia Gibson were those greedy little hands clasped round the nurse's neck, disturbing her recently combed hair. Therefore it was not really surprising to see the nurse stroll over to a dressing-table confected out of some antique table and a nineteenth-century looking-glass in order to put herself to rights all over again.

'Good evening, Mrs Gibson,' I said. 'It's Claire Pitt; do you remember me? And this is my friend, Caroline Wilson.'

'Of course I remember you. You bad girl,' she added. 'You told me you were bringing another friend.'

'No, no. Caroline is called Wiggy. That's probably what you remember me saying . . .'

She took no notice of this. 'Martin,' she called out. 'Bring the champagne. I want Sue to have a glass before she goes.'

'You shouldn't,' I protested, for form's sake.

'I'll let you into a secret,' she said, leaning towards me and releasing a wave of scent. 'Tomorrow is our wedding anniversary, Martin's and mine. That's why we're celebrating. We always do.'

'Show them the photographs,' said Sue, favouring me with another wink.

'I will, I will. Now give me a kiss and go. Which boyfriend is it tonight?'

'The ironing, in fact. See you Monday. Don't do anything I wouldn't do.' At this point a spectral Martin appeared in the doorway with a bottle of champagne and several glasses held between the fingers of his left hand, like a bouquet.

'Give Sue a glass quickly, Martin. She's in a hurry. Where on earth had you got to? I was beginning to think you'd gone out.'

This was to be the pattern of our entire visit. We sat on either side of the bed, ignored, while various items of what actors call business were performed for our benefit. After Sue had left, it was, 'Come round to this side where I can see you both,' but in fact either the sight of us did nothing to stimulate her interest or she had forgotten who we were and why we were there. It was difficult to maintain the fiction that my previous visit had so thrilled her that she could not wait to see me again. If anything she was more interested in Wiggy, who wore her usual polite pleasant expression. I was proud of her; I always knew she would not let me down. Cynthia Gibson sensed this and asked Wiggy what she did. Without waiting for an answer she reached out and felt, indeed fingered, the stuff of Wiggy's skirt. 'Pretty material,' she said. 'I had something like it once. Martin! Where are you?'

By dint of valiant effort and a good deal of social expertise I managed to tell her that Wiggy and I were best friends, that we always met for dinner on a Saturday, that we were delighted to have looked in, in my case to renew acquaintance, in Wiggy's case to meet someone whom I had described as fascinating (this was true though not quite in the sense she might have expected), that we were sorry to make this such a short visit but that restaurants always got so crowded on a Saturday that we must be on our way . . . I could see that she was not much interested in this but I felt I had to furnish the silence, or what would have been a silence. Her husband, as before, had retired to a dusky corner of the room. I need not have bothered. I realized that he was there as audience, while Cynthia's role was to divulge information, about herself, mostly. It was clear that she was used to doing this, had behaved in this manner all her life. If Martin were audience we were little more than props, brought in to express appreciation. It was true that she was unfortunate; what was interesting was the fact that her will was intact. She was entitled to ignore what did not please her, which included anyone whose interest in her was less than her own. The mute husband, unnecessary now that the champagne had been poured, was witness to what she no doubt thought of as her enormous popularity.

He was, if anything, out of place, a man among women, for the atmosphere surrounding Cynthia Gibson was feminine, conspiratorial. I saw that it was the function of the nurse to provide the repartee that he was too sombre to deliver. Yet how he must have loved her! Even now his eyes never left her face.

What must one do to inspire such love? Clearly it had nothing to do with superior qualities. Maybe it was the fascination exerted by sheer selfishness. I had never come across this before. All the people I knew, including the Colliers, father and daughters, were good and I had accepted this as the right true order of things. Now, as Cynthia Gibson held out her glass for more champagne, I began to see that there was a quicker easier way to secure a man's attention. Clearly it only worked in the case of a man. Wiggy and I were hardly eligible. 'Darling,' he warned. 'You won't sleep tonight.'

'And don't be such an old fusspot,' she said. 'I don't know why I don't just finish the bottle, since these two girls aren't interested. Where did you say you were going for dinner?'

'Charlotte Street,' I said firmly. In fact we were going to an Italian restaurant in Tottenham Court Road.

'I used to eat out a great deal before I was married,' she said. 'In those days I was terribly in demand. The Caprice, it used to be. That was my favourite. Now, of course, I don't go out at all.'

'I'm so sorry,' said Wiggy. I knew she was entirely sincere.

Cynthia gave a brief bitter smile. 'Off you go, then. Leave me to Martin's tender mercies.' As if on cue he approached the bed noiselessly, removed her champagne glass, and smoothed her brow. The look she gave us was not entirely innocent. Even a trophy husband is better than none, she seemed to imply. There are always errands to be run, services to be performed. And there are gratifications even now that you may not suspect.

We stood up awkwardly. 'It's been so nice,' she said. 'You'll come again, won't you? And next time I'll show you those photographs. The wedding photographs,' she reminded us. 'It was such a pretty day.'

I did not like this but there was nothing I could do about it.

And besides I had seen her head fall back in the gesture which was now curiously familiar. I knew that gesture, the sudden vulnerability of the exposed throat. My mother, who had so recently left me, had fallen back in exactly the same way, during her last days in the hospital. And my mother had no devoted husband to monitor her every movement, only my poor self. I felt pity for Cynthia Gibson, but also a measure of contempt. I felt she could manage better if she tried. These feelings I now extended to Martin who was ready to usher us out of the door. I realized that apart from making welcoming noises he had not uttered a reasonable sentence all the time we had been there. Wiggy and I had wasted our sweetness on the desert air. And yet there was no doubt that in some fashion we had been necessary.

The dear street! How good it was to breathe a saner air. Even in this adamantine part of town, with all the doctors and the dentists present in spirit if not in the flesh, the evening smelled sweet. Only the shop selling surgical appliances was there to remind one, or rather to remind others, of decrepitude, mortality. We walked along in silence, aware of the fine weather. It was the first real summer evening, an evening for sitting in gardens or outside some café, as I had so frequently done in France. We were still imprinted with the scene we had so recently witnessed. Another's illness does that to one, makes one aware of one's own strengths, intact, ready to be used. I loved life, even my life, even Wiggy's. By the flower stall in Tottenham Court Road men were thinking that it might be in order to buy a peace offering before going out again to the pub. Overnight, it seemed, tulips had given way to peonies, their tight flower-balls an un-English shade of fuchsia. Only that morning I had seen a pouter pigeon strutting across Baker Street, thinner nimbler relations scattering tactfully ahead.

'Poor thing,' said Wiggy finally.

'Terrible,' I agreed. 'Yet not a very nice woman,' I added.

'Oh, Claire, how can you say that? Just think of her days trapped in that room, with only the nurse for company.'

'And the husband,' I reminded her.

'Yes. He was rather attractive, I thought.'

We both pictured the undoubtedly handsome but rather lifeless figure sitting silently in attendance on a fragile chair in a symbolically dusky corner of the room, as if his place were destined to be in the shadows, lit only by his wife's exigencies. How he had darted to his feet when she showed signs that tiredness was beginning to overtake her! Yet he had hardly said a word to us when we left.

'I'm not quite sure why we were there,' Wiggy went on.

'Neither am I. I told you how it came about. But I think we were a bit of a disappointment. I think she felt let down.'

'But she was excited, you could see that. She had made up her face, done her hair. And that white thing she was wearing looked expensive. The sort of thing you wear when you want to make a good impression. She was like a child, wasn't she?'

Yet I had been aware of a complicated woman.

'He'll want us to go again,' I warned.

She looked at me. 'You seem to know him quite well.'

I let this pass. 'And we'll probably go, although we shall feel quite inadequate. She was ungracious – even you can see that – and yet I feel we failed her somehow.'

'I could sketch her,' said Wiggy thoughtfully. 'She'd probably like that. She wouldn't have to talk, or anything.'

'I doubt if she ever stops.'

'Oh, Claire.'

'She wants to show us her wedding photographs.'

'Well, that's not so terrible. I don't mind looking at photographs. And her wedding was no doubt the happiest day of her life.'

I did not particularly want to be involved in a parade of

sentimentality. In any event I am allergic to weddings, having attended too many. But Wiggy is a nicer person, more generous, less judgmental. 'I think the sketch is a better idea,' I said. 'Then perhaps we could back out. After all we don't know her. And she doesn't know us.'

'I found her rather touching,' said Wiggy. 'And we must disappear tactfully. Perhaps we should leave our telephone numbers. That way they can contact us if anything happens.'

By 'anything' she meant death. In which case it would be Martin who kept in touch. Why he should do such a thing was not immediately apparent. But it was true that they were both avid for company. They were friendless: that was what struck one about them. Presumably they had abandoned their former friends (for they must have had some) when illness struck. Or perhaps it was one of those rather terrible relationships in which each fed off the other. Certainly Wiggy and I had been reduced to bit parts. Neither of us had been asked a single question. It was enough that we were there, mute witnesses to Cynthia's drama. And yet she had accepted our presence as if she had known us for many years. I have observed this phenomenon before: it is a manifestation of overriding self-love. And even so there is something innocent about it. 'I knew you'd be interested in my views,' seems to be the assumption. One's own views are thought to be completely subordinate.

'One more visit, then, with your sketch pad,' I said. 'I don't want to get too involved.'

But I did. There was a certain excitement to be derived from this situation, and it was dangerous. I could not quite define the danger, but it had something to do with Cynthia's strength and Martin's weakness. I wanted him to rebel against the role she had chosen for him, to reveal some impatience, some manliness. I felt she had deprived him of that. In an odd way I admired her for it.

We had a pleasant evening. The strange visit, into which we had been almost conscripted, gave us something to talk about. The time when Wiggy felt she had to be tactful with me seemed to be over. Our friendship was renewed. We both appreciated this, and parted once again the easiest of friends.

[6]

By Monday I had put the Gibsons out of my mind. I had a more immediate concern: I had all but finished with St John Collier, and I had to convey this to Muriel, while expressing my eagerness, which was entirely genuine, to do justice to the rest of his life. There was no point in delaying this: I had no desire to spend days in the basement doing nothing. And the lifestyle of the Fifties was beginning to pall. I envisaged something a little more discursive, a little more challenging.

'There's his book,' said Muriel. 'Or rather the notes for his book. He never finished it. I don't think he even started it, but he made notes, in proper notebooks. They're still at the house. If you come home with me this evening you could take them back with you. Keep them here, of course. There might be some extracts that could be used . . .'

'His book?' I asked.

'It was to be his life's work,' she said sadly. 'But he waited too long. Maybe that is the way with all long-term projects. They keep one company in a reassuring kind of way. And then one day it's too late. But he talked about it as if it were a going concern. My poor father had few diversions in his life, the shop every day, his two girls at home. My mother had died when Hester was still young. She devoted herself to me and to Father. And as you see we carry on his way of life.'

'You never thought of doing something different?'

'Well, there was the shop, you see. We knew he was going to leave it to us.' She sighed. 'And in the end we did what he wanted us to do. Girls did in those days. It's only when you're old, Claire, that you see how unjust this was. He didn't want us to marry, though Hester was a beauty. You may not think so now . . .'

'Oh, but one can see that,' I protested, for Hester, and indeed Muriel, still impressed, despite the hearing-aid and the stick. What was appealing about Hester was her smiling eagerness, without thought of reward or reciprocity. She would appear every day with freshly-made rock cakes in a greaseproof bag and appreciate our comments, as if they were not regularly offered. Muriel was more circumspect; she was the breadwinner, after all; she was obliged to be businesslike. Though she appeared to pay it only minimal attention she kept the shop going. I had no idea what her overheads were. In any event the house in Marchmont Street was theirs. St John Collier had done that much for them. But I thought it sad that they had never moved out.

I was also surprised that they lived, and always had lived, in Bloomsbury. To judge from St John Collier's philosophy I had imagined them to be denizens of some leafy suburb or garden city. But I suppose that what was once an accident of geography had hardened over the years to a conviction that he was part of a 'set', an authentic Bloomsburian. That there was room for such people I did not doubt; not everyone had Virginia Woolf's capacity, though whether she ever noticed him when they passed in the street, as they must have done on occasions, would have been highly unlikely. He, of course, would have raised his hat, lifted his stick, given a pleasant smile of recognition. I thought even more kindly of him, ploughing his simple furrow with unshaken belief in his own observations. He would have taken it badly when she died.

But by that time, in the blessed aftermath of war, he would have felt a timid hope that he too would be acknowledged as a venerable local character. Whether or not this was ever the case would not now be known. But I am sure that he had a very wide constituency of like-minded people, simple people satisfied with a reassuring message of goodness and hope. All over the country women (and they would have been predominantly women) would open their magazines and read his page with obedient smiles. The nature articles, though more rigorous in style, might have appealed to men. They did not much appeal to me. But I too had been avid for his advice, which seemed to belong to a lost age of contentment. We were more divisive now, more fragmented. To begin with we all worked. St John Collier's readers were largely passive. There was another illustration which I treasured, that of a woman sitting in an elephantine armchair, her ankles neatly crossed. She is reading by the light of a standard lamp with a fringed shade. Perhaps she is reading St John Collier's page. In any event she looks at peace with the world.

'His book?' I prompted, for Muriel had gone off into a reverie. It took her a second or two to focus on me. She is old, I thought with a tremor, but it was impossible to feel pity. Pity is for the weak, the incompetent, the unsuccessful: Muriel was none of these things. She had been in her way a pioneer, a liberated woman. If she had regrets they did not show. She rarely smiled, but that was all of a piece with her austerity of manner. I think she was fond of me. I think they both were. I fitted in. I did not work ungraciously; I did not have a Walkman clamped to my ears; I did not make excuses to leave early. Hester was gratified by my appetite for her cakes. Muriel was gratified by my enthusiasm for her sister's contribution. Neither Muriel, Hester, nor of course myself thought to entertain each other at home. This would have raised unwelcome questions of status, of familiarity. And I think we all sensed that home was a private affair, not open to the scrutiny of strangers.

'It was to be called *Walks with Myself*,' she answered me. 'Like all men of his generation he was a great walker. Not like today, Claire, although I'm glad to know that you walk to and from work. Every Sunday – and it had to be Sunday, the only day the shop was shut – he would take his stick and go out after an early lunch, or sometimes a late breakfast.'

'Where did he go?'

'Nowhere very spectacular. He would explore different areas of London, Putney, Kennington, Southwark. Bloomsbury, of course, he knew by heart. And then he'd come home after four or five hours and we'd have tea. High tea, it was called in those days. Ham and salad and fruit cake. And he'd sit back quite tired and absolutely satisfied, although I doubt if he'd spoken to anyone the entire time he was out.'

'So he was going to describe all these various places? It sounds a marvellous idea.'

'I think there was going to be a great deal of description, certainly. He never told us much. But one Sunday I remember there was a heavy frost and we didn't want him to go out. But he did and saw some skaters on a pond somewhere. Dulwich, I think it was. He told us about that. I think what he wanted to do was to offer reflections. His book was to be a companion for the solitary walker.'

'I wish he'd written it.'

'Yes, poor Father. But those walks were his freedom, his only freedom. His life was very limited without my mother. That was why we never left him.' She smiled sadly.

I imagined the two girls, upright then as now, whiling away their Sunday afternoons, preparing the high tea, waiting for the wanderer to return. They too must have been lonely. But I should never know that, for their code forbade confidences.

Muriel had never spoken so much as she had on this particular occasion.

'I'll give you his notebooks,' she went on. 'Though I doubt if they're very coherent. Perhaps a few descriptive fragments . . .'

'I think that would be lovely,' I said.

'I'll bring the notebooks in with me tomorrow. Unless you'd like to come home with me,' she said doubtfully, clearly regretting her earlier invitation. It seemed to me that she wanted no one, not even myself, as witness to their way of life. I thought of Sunday preparations in that narrow kitchen (for it would be narrow, like the rest of the house), water dripping from an ancient tap into an enamel bowl, massive brass burners lit under an equally massive kettle.

'If you're sure you don't want any help,' I said.

'No, no. Ah, there's Hester. Open the door, would you, Claire. She never could manage it.'

There was nothing for me to do, but she did not suggest that I go home. I had no desire to go home. Our flat, now my flat, depressed me, though, like the Collier girls, I should stay there because that's what my father would have wanted. He had made a great show of telling me that my home would always be secure. I had not been grateful at the time, though I suppose I was grateful now. I had never seen myself as a householder, rather a solitary walker in the manner of St John Collier. I felt entirely sympathetic towards his book. *Walks with Myself* was an admirable title. I took the project to my heart, reflecting once again how goodness clings to some lives and not to others. Those girls, Muriel and Hester, handsome in their youth, as their ruined looks testified even today, would have been dutiful, uncomplaining. They would have felt a closeness on those Sunday afternoons, which would seem tame, risible, to any daughter today. And that would have been the climax of their week, that their abiding impression of intimacy. I did not quite feel sorry for them. Nor, of course, did I envy them. My own life seemed irregular by comparison. There was a freedom there that was not always comfortable. Boundaries keep people out; mine served only to keep me in. I shrugged. My life was my own affair. I needed no instruction.

It was their contentment that baffled me. Either that or their containment. My mind kept returning all that evening to the Colliers and their world. I was unenthusiastic about a further walk. I supposed I should start walking properly when I had reached St John Collier's instructions on the matter. This occasioned a certain reluctance: I was not yet ready to be drafted into the Collier camp. I was not like the girls, as I was beginning to think of them. I was free, certainly, but that freedom was ironic, not quite the real thing. I was free because nothing was required of me. I was therefore superfluous. This I knew to be true, but the truth was so unwelcome that I seized my purse and my keys and went out to the all-night supermarket. In the late evening this always seems to be populated by solitaries, people who look drained by the strip lighting. This is one more instance of deregulation: shopping at night. The shoppers would avoid each other's eyes, though I read that such places are settings for romance. We are embarrassed in case anyone should think that this is our reason for picking up half a dozen eggs and a small granary loaf. This is what most people seem to buy, and our purchases look puny. This is one further reason for embarrassment, proof of the exiguous nature of our domestic arrangements. On my way home I saw something even more shameful: a pair of men's shoes abandoned in the gutter. They were not even particularly worn, evidence of exasperation rather than poverty. Their owner must have gone home defiantly in stockinged feet. One sees such sights in the city, particularly in the growing dusk, yet one never learns the story behind them. Even my capacity for invention balked at the shoes, which were so clearly not connected to anything. Or anyone. Strange how one received intimations of solitude at this time of day.

I was a little piqued that Martin Gibson had not presented himself to tell me how rapturously our visit had been received. In fact, I now realized, it had been a failure. I had been mistaken: the onus was not on the Gibsons to express appreciation. It was on myself. His continued silence implied that some sort of offence had been taken. Cynthia was the sort of woman to take offence, displaying hurt feelings, but not deigning to explain them. So one-sided were her preoccupations that explanations were deemed to be unnecessary. She would consider herself to be tragically let down, by everyone, including her husband. Indeed I wondered whether he were not the source of her discontent. His tacit assumption of responsibility for her condition would be held against him, the diversions he planned for her perceived as the makeshift arrangements they truly were.

But it went deeper than that. Did she expect him to make love to her? She was still a good-looking woman; in her own eyes she would be ravishing. She would have been demanding as a wife, scornful of his weakness, though it served her well enough now. Any other man in the same position would have found a discreet alternative; she may even have despised him for not doing so. There would have been taunts . . . Yet that mixture of exceptional good looks and exceptional hesitation, which I myself had found so challenging, must have concentrated her attention in the first place. I did not know her background, but I had no difficulty in inventing it: money, comfort, ostentation, philistinism. She would have had an uncertain temper, which others would rush to anticipate and to turn aside. The parents would have been in some superior branch of commerce, manufacturers of something useful, aristocrats of the middle class. She would have been Daddy's girl, although it would have been Mummy who would have seen to her appearance. I was sure that she would refer to her parents as Mummy and Daddy even now. Presumably they featured in those wedding photographs she was so anxious for us to see. 'Such a pretty day,' she had said, as though it were an episode in fairyland. The honeymoon would have revealed a different woman. Presumably Martin had never got over the shock.

I was anxious to know if I were right, but clearly our acquaintance was too slight for me to make any overtures. There was no earthly reason why such an acquaintance should be prolonged. But just as irrational people do involve one in their concerns I found myself thinking about them quite a lot. They were somehow a better subject of study than the virtuous Colliers. My feelings modulated between distaste and excitement, which should have been a warning to me. When I realized that I had some stake in their relationship I repudiated the notion. It had nothing to do with me nor I with it. I would hold on to my status as an acceptable person. Not a good one, but at least not underhand, not so far.

Therefore, when he did appear, on the Thursday, I was rather annoyed. Ten large black notebooks sat next to my typewriter; I was looking forward to my day's work.

'I'm sorry to have left you without news,' he said, by way of a greeting. 'I'm afraid Cynthia has had a slight setback.'

'Was our visit too much for her?' I inquired.

He looked startled. 'Oh, no, not that. It was just that Sue announced that she wanted to take a fortnight's holiday.'

'Oh dear.'

'Yes, well, I managed to persuade her not to.'

'You would have had to be at home all day,' I observed. 'Of course the agency could have sent someone else.'

'But Cynthia might not have taken to her.'

'But you managed to persuade Sue . . .'

'Yes. She saw the state Cynthia was in.'

'She's all right now?'

'Yes, but it left her awfully tired, you know.'

It had clearly left him exhausted. 'Would you like a cup of coffee?' I asked.

'Well, yes, if it's not too much trouble. It's very kind of you.'

He blushed slightly, as if he were not used to accepting even a token kindness from a stranger. What demons did he exorcize by constant service to others? What self-denial, what self-abnegation did he consider to be required of him? I handed him a mug. He looked round vaguely. 'There is no saucer,' I said. I suspected that he had had no breakfast. Beware of men who come to you hungry for nothing more than sustenance. After a moment I opened the drawer of my desk and extracted one of Hester's rock cakes which I offered to him on a sheet of A4 typing paper. He ate it meekly.

'Is there no one else who could give you a break?' I asked. 'Family?'

'Not really. Cynthia was an only child. Her parents are both dead.'

'And on your side?'

'Only my mother. She lives rather far away. In Norfolk.'

'Whereabouts in Norfolk?'

'Blakeney.'

'I know it.' Our last family holiday had been in Blakeney, shortly before my father had got ill. It was perhaps the only memory of unity, of normal family life, that had stayed with me. I remembered the sea, barely sea at all, just an illusory expanse at the far rim of the marshes, the birds, and my mother's contentment.

'Perhaps your mother . . .'

He grimaced. 'My mother and Cynthia don't get on. They are both strong-willed women. In fact my mother doesn't get on with me, particularly.'

'Oh, that's very sad.'

'She married again, you see. I didn't care for my stepfather. He took me out in his boat once, to make friends, you know, and I was frightfully sick. My mother was furious. She thought I had let her down.'

'And it didn't get any better?'

'No, it didn't. I moved to London after Cambridge. We didn't keep in touch. They came to our wedding, of course, but they didn't take to Cynthia's parents. My mother, I'm afraid, is a snob.'

'You must have been relieved to be married,' I said. 'I'm sure it was the happiest day of Cynthia's life. She implied as much. And of yours?'

'No,' he said. I looked at him, surprised.

'I would have been a good bachelor,' he said apologetically. 'I loved my work, got on well with my students. I knew Cynthia was used to a more opulent way of life than I was. She wanted all these *things*, tables, curtains and so on. My bachelor flat had suited me well enough. And then there was the question of the students whom she insisted on advising. I knew that was wrong.'

'Not necessarily, surely?'

'Oh, yes,' he sighed.

'But you love her?'

'She is my life,' he said. That was manifestly true.

'You gave up your job?'

'It probably took up too much of my time. And when Cynthia got ill . . .'

This illness appeared to me to be complicated. Oh, I did not doubt that there was an underlying weakness. But that the will was involved somewhere along the line I did not doubt either. Cynthia was used to being unique, the family princess, destined to live happily ever after. Since that was her fate she had embraced it in the only way available to her. She disliked women, that much was clear. Wiggy and I had simply proved to her that we were no competition. That was why she had insisted on seeing us.

'So if you could bear to come again?' he said. 'It breaks up the day for her. And she does talk about your visits, you know. It would be a great kindness . . .'

I made a decision. 'Wiggy said she'd like to sketch her,' I said. 'She's a professional artist, you know.'

His face lit up. 'She'd love that. She still cares for her appearance. Well, you saw that.'

'She's lovely,' I said, quite sincerely. That air of a full-blown rose just going to seed was one I could appreciate. It went with ample forms, still visible beneath the elaborate negligées, anxious eyes, and a mouth that implied that no quarter would be given. She looked like what she was: a hardened coquette.

'Not this Saturday, perhaps,' he was saying. After a brief and no doubt regretted burst of candour he had reverted to his worried state. 'Perhaps in a week's time?'

'Saturday is a good day for us,' I reminded him. 'It's when we go out to dinner.'

'That would be so kind . . .'

'Why don't you give me a ring? We left our telephone numbers.'

'Yes, yes, that would be best. I'll get her over this business of Sue first. She took it rather badly.'

'I'll wait to hear from you,' I said. 'Or if you'd prefer to drop in to the shop . . .'

'No, I mustn't take up any more of your time.' He gave me the first direct look of our acquaintance. I looked back, pleasantly. This was evidently too much for him. Within seconds, it seemed, he was gone.

[7]

I thought a lot about Martin Gibson in the days that followed. The potent irritation that he inspired in me, and no doubt in others, faded into a sort of reluctant sympathy. He now appeared as a man who had always been subject to coercion, and who had not known how to deal with it. I thought about that scene on his stepfather's boat and of its aftermath, the mother's anger. I could even see her point of view. The awkwardness of introducing her son to her future husband had been compounded by her son's lamentable performance, which she would have felt bound to laugh off, to dismiss, while all the time the boy, shivering and miserable, had a higher claim on her sympathy. She would have been in the full flush of excitement at the prospect of a new marriage, while the man would have been exasperated at the puniness of his future stepson. I saw this man as the sort who habitually arouses feelings of fear in those less opaque than himself. I saw him as red-faced and athletic, well set up, hearty, the sort of man to appeal to a widow still of an age to marry again. I saw the boy's infinite distress at the prospect of having to share his mother with this man. He had said that they did not get on, which implied that some sort of showdown had taken place after this incident. I reconstructed his life carefully: Cambridge, he had said, then a bachelor flat in London, where he had been perfectly content. He would have been mildly popular with colleagues, immensely popular with students, who would have been beguiled by his handsome looks into seeking opportunities for further interviews, with in fact further intimacy in mind.

I doubt that this had even taken place. He would have been careful, scrupulous, and beyond that genuinely wary. He would have seen his work as a safe haven, but one which could be ambushed. In order to gain total possession of such a man it would be necessary to remove him from his work, from those loyalties to dead writers which few could share. A woman like Cynthia, all instinct, would have known this. The daily presence of young people, all so much younger than herself, would have been a preoccupation. She had retaliated by annexing them. Those afternoons when she had probed for their confidences seemed to me another form of coercion. She would have claimed that she was helping him, when in fact she was undermining his authority. Besides, it is extremely underhand to extract a confidence. The intimacy that the students sought from Martin was in fact imposed by his wife. This would have seemed dubious to anyone who had the interests of the young people at heart. He would have known this, as would certain of his colleagues. A mild difficulty with the work prescribed would have been turned into a drama of divided loyalty. Confession is addictive: in addition, some of these young people would have been far from home. A sympathetic ear was not to be forgone, particularly a sympathetic ear into which it was possible to own up to a mild crush on the husband of the woman who professed complete understanding of the predicament.

Cynthia's suspicions would have been justified by such artless outpourings. Her antennae were so finely adjusted that she could see how the land lay. She could see temptation where none existed. She would have known by then that her husband was afraid of women, and would therefore have been extremely circumspect. She would have told him repeatedly that he was working too hard, would have interrupted his reading with all manner of winsome requests, would have made much of tiredness, retiring to bed, but hailing him from the bedroom. By a process of erosion she would have divested him of many pleasant evening duties . . . Had her famous illness dated from here? And since her splendid body harboured a genuine weakness had it not seemed more urgent to take care of Cynthia rather than of those healthy young people, and all those dead authors?

But why had he married her in the first place? I could see that he must have been woefully inexperienced, easily impressed, and fatally subject to wills other than his own. How had they met? Here my imagination supplied the details. Cynthia's father, in his capacity as benefactor of the college, would have attended an official dinner, one of those dinners which are a form of flattery, in the pious hope of receiving further donations. Financial difficulties would have been invoked in the President's speech. Everything would have been made perfectly clear. In America, I believe, such donations are sometimes rewarded with an honorary doctorate. But Cynthia's father – what was his name? – would not have been after a doctorate but after a husband for his daughter, whose volatile temperament was beginning to generate tiresome fusses at home. The young lecturer would have seemed to him to fit the bill. It would have been easy enough to strike up an acquaintance, to seek his advice on what was needed for the Romance Languages department, child's play to invite him home (one of those flats in Orchard Street, I decided). From that point his wife could take over. And his daughter, of course.

That was my construction, and it pleased me. But what if he had genuinely fallen in love? Cynthia was a capricious woman, her caprices visited on women as well as men. What if *she* had genuinely fallen in love? I had observed the remnants of a certain passion there, the imperiousness on her side, his sombre commitment to her well-being. Was there an incompatibility which still tormented them? What I thought I had picked up from her signals was a heartfelt disappointment that had turned to rancour, and on his side an awareness of his own incapacity. He would have felt impotent, as he had under his mother's scolding, unable to rectify a fault which stretched back into childhood. He would have persuaded himself that he must strive mightily in order to be readmitted into favour.

Normally I sympathize with women. I know from my admirable mother how lowering it is to tolerate – and to have to tolerate – an inadequate man. Yet Cynthia did not appear to me to be entirely exonerated from blame herself. I disliked what I thought of as her frivolity, which seems a strange charge when she was confined to bed with an illness about which I was sceptical. I felt that she should have made more of an effort, rather than display herself to her own advantage in a pathetic situation. I felt indignant that her husband had lost his freedom. I suspected that he still worked, surreptitiously, that he spent his days in some library, wondering if he could confide to paper those ideas he had once had, when he had thought that his life would be a life of study. A book, perhaps, which would vindicate his ruined present. He would know that it had been ruined. Yet that knowledge would goad him into further zealousness, so that the path that had been chosen for him, or rather that he had chosen to follow, for better or worse, now had the force of a duty, or rather a commandment. And whatever disappointment he now felt would be as nothing to the disappointment of his wife, that disappointment he was now bound to palliate by his devotion, even by his love. It would be an affair of honour. And I could see that he was an honourable man.

All the same I felt a distaste for the situation which was entirely on my own account. Why had I been tricked into a show of niceness which was not in my nature? What business did I have with these people who, I reminded myself, knew nothing about my circumstances, and worse, showed no desire to know? I had been privy to Cynthia's allusions and to Martin's guarded confession, yet at no point had any information been sought in return. This bewildered me; it seemed a kind of wilful obtuseness, the kind that should be disclaimed. Either that or a genuine indifference. But I did not think it was indifference. What it was, I decided, was a terrible kind of urgency, as if the Gibsons' case was so strong that it must be put at all times. This was their secret, I decided: they had both decreed, with some justification, that they were tragic figures, whose pleas must be heard at a higher court. They were not simply solipsists, they were soliloquists, drawn together in a fateful bond which demanded witnesses. There was no room, there was no *place*, for outsiders, for third parties. My role was to register their predicament, in which they were so far gone that nobody but themselves could understand it. They had attained to a higher collusion than that which I imagined existed between married couples. This was truly a remarkable union.

I said some of this to Wiggy, who merely remarked, 'You find him attractive, don't you?' This irritated me. Of course I found him attractive; his attractiveness was not in doubt. But in an awful way neither was Cynthia's. I could not see her, as Wiggy saw her, as a simple unfortunate, whom we were bound to visit in the spirit of nineteenth-century ladies visiting stricken cottagers. To begin with the Gibsons were too rich, or rather Cynthia was. It was for them, for people in their position, to extend patronage. It was their determined refusal to perform this task that I found both rebarbative and exciting. I was determined to extract some sign of reciprocity before I was done with them. It would be hard, I knew; their monumental selfishness, which I saw as a tragic selfishness, like King Lear's, would be difficult to crack. Lear, of course, was fully persuaded of his rectitude; he absolved himself throughout. I loathed the play, had done so ever since I had seen it on a cultural outing from school. But I had to admit that it made for good stagecraft.

I was waiting for Martin to materialize in my basement, as he had done before. I did not really expect him to telephone: the telephone was far too direct, too confrontational an instrument for him to use. I had given him my home number, but for several days there was no message on my machine. This meant that I passed my days in a state of semi-alertness, listening for his steps on the stairs. This also meant that I could not quite give full attention to my work. In this I was aided by St John Collier, whose notebooks were proving a bit of a let-down. I could detect no real enthusiasm for the passing scene in his wanderings; he probably just wanted to get out of the house. Yet having decided that he would walk on Sunday afternoons he found himself bound to do so. He would have been aware of the girls at home, waiting for the wanderer to return and perhaps to reward them with a choice of anecdote. In fact he had nothing to say, and the notebooks merely recycled his earlier material. Thus he would note: 'Parsons Green. Dead squirrel by side of road; closed eyes, thin downturned mouth.' And then, with an effort, 'How often do we reflect on those who have gone before, and to whom we feel indebted!' This seemed to me to be a failure of nerve; St John was the victim of his own mellifluous method. That *Walks with Myself* would never amount to anything must have been obvious to him. It certainly was to me.

And yet the project had my full backing. This seemed to me the sort of book anyone could write, and therefore should write. But at the end of his life, and these fragments struck a valedictory note, St John Collier must have registered the melancholy fact that he had amounted to very little, that his daughters were his most fervent admirers, and – who knows? – that he was a little tired of their reverence and might have preferred something more robust in the way of appreciation. He would have been tired in every sense, tired of his loneliness and his life of duty, tired even of his Sunday walks, tired especially of the obligation to maintain a professional persona, when he had nothing, or very little more to deliver. There was one note of enthusiasm: he had seen a rainbow when he was walking on Primrose Hill. Naturally he had taken this as a sign of benevolence, that same benevolence that he now ascribed to Nature rather than to God, unless, as was likely, he saw the two of them in collusion. Only a very sweet disposition can square that particular circle.

I therefore vowed to do my best for St John Collier, although this might involve creative editing on my part. In all conscience I thought of myself as his humble biographer. I would ask Muriel more about her father's life and interpolate some details between the passages of his own writing. I had been impressed by Muriel's still verdant devotion, by her account of those solemn Sundays, the fruit cake, the tap dripping into the enamel bowl (although this last was my own invention). I thought of them as a family of saintly celibates, the flesh subdued by the spirit. Yet there must have been moments of regret, perhaps of curiosity, which would have been instantly repressed. That was why I detected a heavy-heartedness somewhere in the notebooks. I felt disturbed that such a good man should have known unhappiness, or perhaps only stirrings of unhappiness, at the end of his life. 'Hampstead Pond,' he wrote. 'Skein of geese. Winter coming.'

The temptation to take a walk on my own account was very great. It was now high summer, and the basement, of which I was fond, had come to seem intolerably confining. I took to going out at lunchtime, not to eat – a sandwich would do – so much as to stroll and satisfy my hunger for faces. The city was now filling up with tourists, who reminded me that I could soon be a tourist myself, if I chose to. But there seemed to be no future in this idea, at least not one that I could see. It was on my return from one of these lunchtime excursions that I found a note propped up on my typewriter. 'We should be very happy to see you both on Saturday, if convenient. Kind regards. M. G. Please forgive note.'

I informed Wiggy of this. Her enthusiasm seemed to have diminished, as had her sympathy. My own sympathy had never been very active in the first place. I therefore decided to be as pleasant as possible in these strange circumstances. This proved to be a wise decision. 'It's my birthday!' was Cynthia's greeting to us as we were admitted to the bedroom. This was all but shouted, as a champagne glass was waved in our direction. 'And my silly husband says I shouldn't be drinking. I *always* have champagne on my birthday. What have you brought me?' she said, as Wiggy withdrew her sketchpad from its plastic bag.

'I thought I'd do a drawing of you.'

'Wiggy is a professional artist,' I supplied.

'Oh, not now. This is a celebration! Martin, give the girls a glass of champagne. Did he tell you that that silly girl wanted to go off on holiday? The idea! As if either of us could take a holiday! Still, we talked her out of it, didn't we, darling? Now, what have you two been up to?'

As usual she did not wait for an answer. Our lame recitals seemed to die on the scented air. They were interrupted from time to time by a repeated, 'It's my birthday!' These threatened to dwindle in conviction but were quickly resuscitated. All we could do was smile and congratulate her all over again. But then that was what she wanted us to do.

I have always felt slightly embarrassed by birthday celebrations, because the onus is always on the bringer of gifts. We had brought nothing, not even flowers. But even flowers can go wrong, arrive on the wrong day, or find no one in to receive them. I remember my mother telling me of her confusion on going into a shop to order some birthday flowers to be sent to an acquaintance, to be told that her credit card had expired. Although she had her chequebook in her bag she had felt rebuffed. 'And Janet would have been so disappointed,' she told me, as if the shop had refused to serve her. The incident had seemed so redolent of failure that she was quite surprised when her friend telephoned on the following day to thank her. The uncertainty seemed stronger than the relief. Of course we had not known that Cynthia was celebrating her birthday. What am I saying? We hardly knew Cynthia, who was now reminiscing about birthdays gone by. There had always been parties, she observed. She was the sort of woman who marked all rites of passage in an exceedingly public manner. Two spots of colour burned in her cheeks, yet the atmosphere in the room was glum.

All at once she stopped in mid-sentence and her face froze in a woeful expression. Her eyes widened. 'Martin?' she said. He bounded from his corner. 'I think perhaps . . .' he said.

'Yes, of course. We must have tired you, Cynthia. You must rest now. And many more happy returns,' we wished heartily, as if to cover the uneasiness of the moment with the fervour of our goodbyes. 'We'll see ourselves out,' we told Martin, anxious now only to leave. 'Thank you so much,' he said. He looked up from the bed, his eyes haggard. 'So nice to have seen you. We enjoyed your visit, didn't we, darling?' But Cynthia, looking bewildered, did not reply.

'What did you make of that?' asked Wiggy, when we were safely out in the street.

'It's obvious, isn't it?'

'You mean . . .'

'Quite.'

'Poor old thing,' said Wiggy. 'I don't think I feel like dinner, do you?'

We were both shaken by the impropriety of the episode, myself more than Wiggy. Until then I had not really considered Cynthia to be ill, ill that is as my father, my mother had been ill. Her illness had seemed essentially decorative, tricked out as it was by her soft pillows and her immaculate appearance. Now I saw these accessories as a last resort, a form of dandyish wilfulness, of defiance. She was no stoic, but she had perfected a stoic's defences. This again was evidence of the power of her instincts. Had she used her mind to perfect the same strategy she would have been admirable. As it was she was profoundly pathetic.

By unspoken common consent we walked in silence, up Harley Street to the edge of the park, before turning back again in the direction of Cavendish Square. But this area was irritatingly devoid of passers-by. Life was what we wanted. More life! 'We should have some coffee, at least,' said Wiggy, and we walked the length of Wigmore Street in search of it. In the café where I remembered eating a toasted sandwich we sat down gratefully at the back, away from the door, Wiggy with her unopened sketchpad, still in its plastic bag, on her knees. 'How awful if I'd forgotten it,' she said. 'We could never have gone back.'

'No,' I agreed. 'We can't go back.'

That this had now been decided by what seemed like an outside force was something of a relief. We relaxed, ordered more coffee, eventually a Danish pastry. All round us the evening was merely beginning. Two girls at the next table seemed to be discussing a colleague. 'She tried to talk her way out of it,' said one. 'She didn't know I'd caught on.' 'I never liked her,' said her friend. 'Still, you have to make allowances, don't you?' 'Not me,' said the first one virtuously. 'I never make allowances.' She lit a kingsize cigarette, and sat back, challenging anyone who might conceivably suggest that she should. I was impressed. Wiggy, aware of my growing interest in their conversation, brought me back to the matter in hand with a discreet warning look.

'We might send her some flowers,' she said.

'Good idea. I'll get on to it.'

'Roses, I think, don't you?'

'Yes, she'd like that.'

We were both disturbed by the evening's events. Even the girl at the next table seemed threatening. Embarrassment, I knew, would come later. We should not have intruded into the Gibsons' private drama, and yet we had been invited to do so. Their need for an audience – or perhaps for help – had made itself felt throughout. It occurred to me that for all their uninviting, even forbidding manners they wanted some sort of encouragement that neither of them was equipped to provide. Perhaps anyone would have done. But in the end we had let them down. It was probable that at this stage no one could have helped. I thought with some irritation of Martin's mother in orfolk. Surely she might have put in an appearance? But she 'didn't get on' with Cynthia, and this I translated as a total breach. And tomorrow was Sunday, when the nurse would not be there. I longed to eliminate Sunday, thinking of the two of them, polite and terrified, in their dark flat.

Suddenly the noise of the café seemed unbearable. I wanted to be out in the beautiful air, savouring the last of the evening. The following day would be Sunday for me as well, a day on which nothing happened, or could be expected to happen. There was another complication: when would Martin get in touch? He had left his telephone number on the note posted on my typewriter, but given his temperament, his agonized sensibility, I knew that he would not welcome an inquiry. We had indeed been witnesses, but to something we could not talk about. This would prevent him from appearing in the basement again, and no doubt from telling me more about himself. The emphasis had shifted once more back to Cynthia. The weak exert a tyranny denied to the more robust. At least that was how I now saw it. Irritation, so ready to surface, was curiously absent. My imagination failed me, put to flight by a more insistent reality.

'Are you all right?' asked Wiggy.

I collected myself. 'I'm fine.'

Wigmore Street was blue with the last of the evening. We both breathed in deeply.

'I'll ring you tomorrow,' said Wiggy. But in fact we were both anxious to be alone.

As it turned out Sunday was not so bad. It was enough just to be intact. I took a long walk round Hyde Park and Kensington Gardens in the afternoon, and, like the Colliers, ate a substantial meal when I returned home. I felt guiltily safe. I went to bed early and slept deeply. On the Monday morning I went to Selfridges and ordered some pink roses. On the card I wrote, 'With love from Claire and Wiggy'. This seemed adequate until I remembered that if Cynthia were somehow restored to relative health, as I hoped, she would have already forgotten who we were.

[8]

I waited uneasily for something to happen. Was it in order for me to telephone and inquire? Or was the situation so embarrassing that it was better to revert to my status as occasional, even random visitor? I thought that there might have been some acknowledgement of the flowers, until, like my mother, I reflected that flowers often fail to arrive, or arrive on the wrong day, at the wrong address. Indeed, given these potential mishaps, I wondered whether the flowers had not been a mistake, or that they had not in fact been delivered. In which case no acknowledgement could be expected. In retrospect it seemed to me that the flowers had struck a false note, that it would have been better for all of us, Martin and Cynthia included, that that particular visit had not taken place. Nevertheless the onus seemed to be on the Gibsons, or at least on Martin, to get in touch. If he did not it was because there was no reason for him to do so. We were, after all, completely marginal. I concluded that the Gibsons had retreated into their peculiarly watertight relationship. Either that or the flowers (which may not after all have arrived) had been registered as some sort of error, both formal and over-eager. In any event there was no indication that either Wiggy or I were needed, even remembered. This was both a relief and a puzzle. Yet try as I might – and I did try quite hard – I did not see that there was any further role for me to play.

One evening I got home from the shop to find a message on my machine. 'Hi! This is Sue? Mrs Gibson's nurse? I'm sorry to have to tell you that Mrs Gibson passed away last Wednesday. Mr Gibson asked me to let you know. He can't come to the phone right now. Bye.'

I was enormously, even disproportionately shocked. That a woman whom I had suspected of the direst stratagems had actually died seemed to me an outrage. In fact any death is an outrage. The death even of a stranger connects one with one's own losses. My hands were shaking as I dialled Wiggy's number. Interestingly, she was as shocked as I was, though she had less stake in the matter.

'What should we do?' she asked, genuinely at a loss.

'We ought to offer sympathy. Pay our respects, or whatever people do say in these circumstances.'

'Yes, but they'll have had the funeral, won't they?'

'I certainly hope so. And anyway it would have been private. After all they didn't seem to know anyone.'

'Strange, that. She never mentioned anyone else.'

'We may have answered a passing need.'

'No more than that, surely. I don't see any reason why we should get in touch any more. We'll have to write, of course.'

'I think we should go round. Show our faces.'

'Claire . . .'

'A brief visit, of course. I thought Saturday. Just to be tactful.'

And to see that everything is in order, I thought. Or not.

We agreed that we would go to Weymouth Street on the following Saturday afternoon, when Martin would presumably have composed himself. What would it signify for him, this death, annihilation or freedom? I imagined him emerging from the gloom of that flat like Lazarus from the tomb, a free man, but a man with no experience of freedom. How would he use it? Or would it simply take him the rest of his life to get used to the idea? What did one do with freedom anyway, when it was unacceptable, as it undoubtedly was in this instance? Freedom requires courage, and he had none. Without courage freedom declines into existential anxiety, the panic that had briefly afflicted me when I had stood alone in the flat on hearing of my mother's death. I had recovered, or so I thought. But Martin, I suspected, would not manage so easily. His propensity for guilt, and his obvious loneliness, would stand in the way. Particularly the loneliness. That was why my instinct for turning up in person seemed to me to be the right one. I did not speculate further on my motives. Indeed in that moment of awe at the malign workings of fate I did not speculate at all.

On the Saturday afternoon the door was opened to us by the nurse, still in her white coat. Apart from the coat she looked vaguely dishevelled, or rather less composed. Her face was paler than I remembered it, and the earrings had gone. It occurred to me that she might be genuinely upset by Cynthia's death. In essence they were the same sort of woman, flirtatious, frivolous, flippant. Their camaraderie may have been authentic, although the tone of their exchanges would have driven a serious person mad. But perhaps it is essential to keep up a pretence of recovery just around the corner when someone is ill. This necessitates falsity, all manner of lies, draws patient and nurse together in a terrible complicity, or rather one that seems terrible to outsiders. Apart from the necessary subterfuge this girl struck me as innocent. She would simply have followed the rules that Cynthia had laid down. These would have involved above all monstrous flattery, which would have been quite in order, given the circumstances. That the nurse could manage this gave some indication, I thought, of her own character. Both she and her patient were in some sense female and more female than I was.

They were female in a rather old-fashioned way, arch, teasing, happy to be deploying those obsolete instinctive skills even when there was no man around on whom to practise them.

I could never manage that, which explained why I had failed to come up to Cynthia's standards. Wiggy too is entirely unpretentious. And yet our faces had ached with the effort of supplying some of the hysterical appreciation on which the sick woman had come to rely. Quite simply, we were not part of the conspiracy. She must have considered us intolerably slow-witted. No wonder she had expressed disappointment, justifiably so in her own estimation. And the flowers would have been another awkward touch, funereal. I felt ashamed, slightly disgraced, felt wrong in being present on this Saturday afternoon, when ordinary people were at leisure, when Wiggy and I would soon be at leisure ourselves. In the dark hallway, where we stood uncertainly, there was no indication of how we were to proceed. I even thought it better if we simply left a message and made our thankful way home. But this thought was ridiculous. And besides it looked furtive. Already our whispered conversation seemed out of place, like the gossip of servants. Apart from ourselves there was no sign of anyone else being present.

'You're still here, then?' I asked the nurse.

She made a face. 'Looks like it,' she said. There was no further explanation.

'Who is it?' came a voice from the bedroom. A woman's voice. We were still standing in the hall.

The nurse sighed, more at the sound of the voice than at the necessity of explaining our presence. 'You'd better come in,' she said.

In the drawing-room the opaline lamps were lit, although it was broad daylight outside. But these rooms had always seemed intolerably dark, which may have accounted for Martin's low spirits. It occurred to me that he must have loathed the flat, which had no doubt been a wedding present from Cynthia's parents, whom I remembered locating in Orchard Street. The dog had had to go, she said. No wonder: there was no room for an animal in the midst of all these appointments. And maybe even Martin had rebelled at walking a small dog up and down Harley Street. He was hardly a man for a run in the park. No doubt Cynthia had been much affected. She was the sort of woman who would have whispered confidences into the dog's ear. I thought of both Martin and the dog, imprisoned. And yet Martin had the freedom of the streets, at least in the daytime; she had allowed him that. No doubt I was wrong in imputing lack of feeling to Cynthia. It was not feeling she lacked but sympathy, or rather empathy. She simply could not see what it was like to be another person.

'Who is it?' said the voice again, rudely, I thought.

A woman who bore a ghostly resemblance to Martin himself entered the room. We introduced ourselves, explained our visit.

'Good of you,' the woman said dismissively.

'If you could just tell Martin we called . . .?'

An eyebrow was raised. 'You know my son?'

This then was the famous or infamous mother, the perpetrator of the original injury, and no doubt of others before and since.

'You must be Mrs Gibson,' I said. 'I see the resemblance.'

'Hayter. Elizabeth Hayter.'

'Mrs Hayter. I'm sorry we've called at an awkward moment.'

She gave in, collapsed into a chair, passed a worn hand over her careful silver-blonde hair. 'It's all awkward,' she said. 'I really shouldn't be here myself. I certainly can't stay any longer. My husband won't stand for it.'

'We just wondered if there was anything we could do,' said Wiggy, although we had not thought anything of the kind.

'If only you could,' said Mrs Hayter, who seemed all at once to accept our presence. 'Martin has completely collapsed. At least I think that is what he has done. Naturally he won't speak to me. It seems he won't speak to anyone. He's in bed. I think he must be having some sort of breakdown. Get us some tea, would you?' she said to the nurse.

'I can't really say I ever got on with my, with his wife,' she went on. 'She struck me as silly and selfish. And she made no effort.' This was rather what I had thought but in view of the woman's death the thought was now inappropriate. 'Not that Martin knew how to deal with that sort of woman.' She gave a brief laugh. 'With any sort of woman. He belongs in a book-lined study.' She made it sound like padded cell. 'And I really can't spend any more time here. My husband gets upset when I'm away.'

'But if he's not well . . .' said Wiggy.

'He's not ill,' she said, smoothing her hair again. 'He's sulking. To tell the truth there's no love lost . . .' She sighed. 'I've told the girl to stay on for a few days,' she said, as Sue entered the room with a tea tray. 'You'll stay for tea?' she asked.

'I think we should be going. You'll let Martin know we called?'

'I'll tell him, of course. I'm afraid I didn't catch your names.'

'Claire Pitt. And Caroline Wilson.'

'If you could just write them down. My memory is not what it was. It has all been a strain, as you can imagine. And I'm afraid I must get home. Just see if he needs anything, would you?' she said to the nurse. 'I'll get on to the agency in the morning, no, on Monday. I firmly intend to be at home by then. They can go on sending someone until he pulls himself together. Send the bill to me, of course, though my husband won't be best pleased. I'll leave you my address.' Pen and paper were produced miraculously from her bag, though there had been none to receive our names. 'Of course I'll be in touch. I just don't see that there's anything more I can do.'

I did not merely object to Mrs Hayter's manners. Her appearance also struck me as monstrously, inexcusably wrong. She looked like Cardinal Richelieu, or at least that portrait of him in the National Gallery, but a Cardinal Richelieu who had removed his moustache and beard and exchanged his crimson robes for a smart grey trouser suit. Yet the trouser suit itself seemed wrong, clashing as it did with the carved minatory features and the authoritative mouth. Here was a woman who would not hesitate to pronounce an anathema, who had no doubt pronounced many in her time. I did not wonder that she had objected to her poor self-indulgent daughter-in-law. Martin had said she was a snob. The scene at the wedding presented itself inexorably to my imagination: county brought face to face with trade. Mrs Hayter would have been discreetly over-dressed, Cynthia's mother indiscreetly over the top. Both would have been wrong, and a lingering but insistent sense of this would have made them react to each other more sharply than was wise.

Cynthia herself would not have noticed this; Martin certainly would have done. He would have felt, perhaps for the first time, that his wife needed his protection. Seeing her there, laughing and crying, in her extravagant white dress, he would have felt the dawning of a knightly quest. He would also have been conscious of a need to change sides, his own for that of Cynthia, with whom, he was beginning to realize, he did not have a great deal in common. Everyone except Cynthia would have felt ruffled. Complaints would have been voiced to the relevant husbands on the way home. I did not know any of this, of course, but Mrs Hayter's ecclesiastical features reminded me of the collapsing softness of Cynthia's face; both revealed social class, and the privations and indulgences that stem from antagonistic backgrounds. To Mrs Hayter's disdain Cynthia would oppose advanced hurt feelings. Neither would ever forgive the other.

Yet this adamantine woman was evidently in thrall to her husband – her second husband – who 'would not stand' for her being away from him, even to offer her son the meagre resources of her assistance. It was clear that this thrilled her. It occurred to me that what I particularly disliked about her was an unmistakable aura of sexiness. No wonder that there had been no room for Martin in that household. A boy, or a young man, whatever he had been, would have received disagreeable messages from this union, would have resolved to get away as soon as possible, would have made good his escape, and no doubt have been attracted in time to a woman who promised him the softness, the indulgence that his mother had denied him. It had not quite worked out like that. But then it seldom does.

What he had gained was excessive material comfort, which seemed part and parcel of his wife's attributes. He had replaced austerity with luxury, had exchanged his mother's neglect for his wife's affectionate mockery. He was the loser on both counts, as far as I could see. But he was a masochist; perhaps he felt at home in this new situation. Certainly, to judge from his behaviour, he was passionately committed to it. And he had demonstrated a devotion that was not in doubt. His inhibited utterances had been supported by a set of attitudes that were all ardour. Desire, that was it. He expressed desire, but it was desire for admittance to a world from which he felt excluded. Cynthia would have expected something more decisive in the way of manly behaviour. His yearning would have found no favour with her. Hence the bullying note apparent in some of her observations. It became more easy to sympathize with her once one became conscious of the background. Or the probable background, I reminded myself. In fact it became easier to sympathize with Cynthia than with her husband. What frustrations there must have been for that capricious woman, bewildered by her inability to impose herself in the only way that had any value for her! Yet all the time she would have been aware that his feelings for her were profound, as profound as any woman could wish, but inappropriate. What he felt for her was in fact pity. And fear.

'Who is it, Mother?' came a voice from the bedroom.

'It's all right, darling.' She might just as well have said 'Nobody', for that was evidently what she thought. I felt Wiggy stiffen beside me, and Wiggy is much nicer than I am. I was rather too fascinated by the contrast, the conflict even, between Mrs Hayter's impatience to be gone and her glacial manner. Even then I thought it about time that we were taken for granted as bona fide visitors. There had been no sign of welcome. The tea remained untouched on the tray. Maybe this was a hint that we should make ourselves scarce. It was clear that we were not to be offered any.

Martin materialized in the doorway, like Hamlet's father's ghost. He was wearing a dressing-gown over pyjamas. I knew he was the sort of man who would wear pyjamas. He looked thinner, older, but his face lightened briefly when he saw us.

'Claire! And Wiggy!'

'Wiggy?' queried Mrs Hayter.

'Caroline is called Wiggy,' I said firmly.

'We're so sorry, Martin.'

'How good of you to come,' he said.

'Now that you're up,' said his mother, 'you might as well get dressed. There's tea if you want it.'

'No, no,' he said. 'I'll go back to bed, if you don't mind.'

Mrs Hayter remained seated. Be a man, was her unspoken command. It went unheeded.

'So good of you,' he repeated, clearly keen to remove himself from his mother's presence. 'I'll let you know . . .' But what it was he would let us know remained obscure. He shook both our hands and went out of the room. His stance was leisurely, self-contained. There was a definite hint of assurance there, if one cared to see it.

We took our leave of Cardinal Richelieu, who made no effort to detain us, or even to find out why we had come, although I suppose that was obvious. No degree of affinity had been established between the Gibsons and ourselves, as I should have thought natural on such an occasion. Mrs Hayter evidently possessed the same sort of imperviousness to others as her former daughter-in-law had done. Sue accompanied us to the door. We stood in the dark hall, wondering who would speak first. We felt uncomfortably reduced to strangers, even to children.

'That woman!' said Sue, in a burst of indignation that set up a ghostly tinkle amid the milk-glass vases. 'You know she didn't even go out shopping? Sent me off to Selfridges with a list. As if I'm here for that!'

'Is he really ill?' I asked her.

'When I think of my mum! My mum would have been round here cooking things for the freezer. My mum would have been *baking*!'

She had an irritating voice, more noticeable when it was not interrupted by her habitual laugh. I was glad she was there, although I did not find it easy to take to her. I suppose it is difficult for women of my generation to trust other women, now that a certain loucheness of behaviour has become *de rigueur.* Loucheness involves betrayal, but that no longer seems to matter; we are all merry adventurers now. I was one myself. This rarely caused me discomfort, though I knew it worried Wiggy. She is alarmed for me; her own life is a model of loyalty and consistency compared to mine. For that reason we are rarely confessional about our intimate lives, though there is no one I trust more. She did not quite know how unsatisfactory I found my untenanted life, with only an aberrant imagination for company. Nor did she know how I hankered after simplicity, transparency. She found it safer to treat me as the joker I had become, but she is concerned for me, as if she knew that I was in danger, that I deliberately, from time to time, courted danger. Part of her could not see the reason for this. Indeed there was no reason, apart from a certain emptiness. I did not come up to her standards, that was all. Yet I regarded her dreary love affair as equally erroneous. Women could probably get on very well if it weren't for men. And men are jealous of women's friendships, which suffer as a result. That is why it is better to draw a veil sometimes. But it is a sorry business, and one's friendships never quite recover.

I put out a hand to steady the vases. 'How long will you stay?' I asked.

'Not long. Not at all, if she's coming back.'

'I don't think there's any danger of that. She seemed very keen to leave. Has he really had a breakdown?'

She shrugged. 'He's okay. Needs some time to himself, if you want my opinion. Cynthia was all right but she took up a lot of attention. Pity he hasn't got any friends.'

'I wondered about that. Has nobody been round?'

'You two are the first people I've seen,' she said, making it seem like a personal privation, which I suppose it was.

'We left our phone numbers. If there's anything . . .'

All at once she recovered her professional manner. 'We'll be fine,' she said, with a smile that revealed all of her teeth. 'Now, if you'll excuse me . . .'

We were outside once again, yet it did not seem like a true escape. 'Better leave it alone now,' said Wiggy. 'I doubt we'll hear any more.'

'Right,' I replied. But I remembered our telephone numbers,

hoped that they had been transferred to a diary, that we would be remembered. That, for the moment, was what I hoped. It did not seem too nefarious.

[9]

Two more unfortunate incidents took place in what seemed to me rapid succession, although in fact they were fairly widely separated. The first had to do with St John Collier, whose notebooks, alas, were still proving a disappointment. I had been worried by his increasing wordlessness, or decreasing wordiness; his pleasant philosophy seemed to have deserted him, and it was as much as he could do to consign to the page unrevealing comments such as 'Syringa. White petals scattered by rain,' or 'Elderflower. Stale nostalgic smell.' These were left undeveloped. Even more disconcerting was the fact that his walks seemed to take him no further than Hyde Park or Kensington Gardens, which I thought very banal. There was no reason given for this abandonment of the greater project. For a few weeks this mechanical joyless perambulation replaced earlier more hopeful excursions, hinting perhaps at boredom, disillusionment, hopelessness. I did not see how a walk in the park could satisfy one of his speculative disposition. I felt, with an odd tremor of sympathy, that perhaps he had had a sense of diminution, or seen the futility of keeping up a pretence of which he had recently become aware.

It must have seemed as if he were no longer taken seriously, or indeed could take himself seriously. Times had changed; his grateful readership of modest persons trying to lead quiet decent lives had given way to the pressures of the post-war era. Adults were replaced by teenagers, for whom 'Trust and hope' was a message addressed to the disappointed, the defeated. It struck me that this message had always made me slightly impatient, although it chimed in with whatever immemorial aspirations I might have had. These, however, I had discarded, as I thought appropriate. I lived in a millennial age; I had no need of faith. Catastrophes would be revealed without mediation, as they always had been. Trust would seem awkward in these circumstances, hope prove to have been misplaced. I could deal with this state of affairs, but what about those humble people whose one desire was to be soothed into acceptance? Besides, his former readers would be getting old, would have discovered that trust and hope were inadequate consolation for the inevitable ailments, the even greater afflictions that arrive in the fullness of time. St John Collier himself, with his tweed suit and his walking-stick, an old gentleman in the park on a Sunday afternoon, would have felt as out of date as he looked. I believe the old are lonely. If so he must have been lonelier than most, with only his girls and their invariable tea waiting for him at home.

And Kensington, where he seems, from the dateline, to have lingered! Who could find spiritual sustenance in Kensington? I had tried it myself, on empty Sunday afternoons, and had found the experience lowering. Only habit would have made him take a notebook out with him, for he had nothing to impart. He must have used these afternoons for rumination, and found his reflections, his observations not to his taste. His marriage was a distant memory, his daughters a responsibility. Some sort of belief had kept him buoyant, belief in the modest lives of others, and also their belief in him. These had done duty for a life which he had been denied. Therefore to be forgotten at an age when he himself had need of sustenance was doubly hard. And some iron must have entered his soul at the sight of those blank pages, with only the date and the place noted. And the weather: he was always scrupulous about that. That weather was not always benign: there were testy references to cloud, humidity, or alternately chill, rain, thunder. There was little I could do with any of this. It pained me that my work was ending. What would I do if I were to be banished from my basement? And would Muriel's filial piety be proof against the obvious sterility of her father's last years?

In fact the book which she envisaged – privately printed, and sold for a token sum in the shop – would be bought, if at all, as a curiosity, something to give to an unmarried aunt, suitable for a guest room, or worse. It was not necessarily to my credit that I took it seriously: it contained valid reflections that were not without an authentic appeal, a sweetness of intent. I would tell Muriel that the notebooks were incomplete (they were worse than that) and that the finished volume, in effect little more than a brochure, should contain only a judicious mixture of nature notes and such articles which had found so appropriate an outlet in the days when magazines were thought a suitable vehicle for uplifting thoughts.

It was not all bad news, I reflected: some of this stuff might strike a chord. On the other hand it was very bad news for myself. Without the shop to walk to every morning I should be left without a purpose. The prospect of looking for another job did not thrill me. Besides, I had little experience of normal work. In comparison with what films and television had shown me of office life Ex Libris belonged to another age, one in which I had spent contented days, and which had buttressed me against loneliness and a sense of futility. Life processes seemed to be speeding up: what St John Collier must have felt at the end I was feeling at an age he would have envied. It was only panic, I told myself. I could still attempt something in the way of an introduction. And that would take a month at most if I worked conscientiously, i.e. very slowly. Then I should be on my own.

The last page of the last notebook had been stuck down to the inside of the back cover, with dots of old-fashioned glue which had hardened. With my new-found assiduity I decided to see whether there was anything on the other side. I applied the steam of the kettle and the page came away quite easily. In tiny writing, on the ultimate page, were written the words, 'I cannot go on', and a name, Agnes. If there were anything else it had been obliterated by moisture (that is the trouble with this method). Since the kettle had boiled I made coffee and took a cup up to Muriel. 'What was your mother's name?' I asked casually.

'Ida,' she said. 'I hardly remember her. Hester knew her better than I did.'

I was grateful that Muriel had not made this particular discovery. At what point, I asked myself, had Agnes come on the scene? Evidently she lived in Kensington; the walk in the park would have been a mere pretext, the rest of the afternoon, or even the whole of it, spent in Agnes's company. Was this an affair of the flesh? I rather hoped not, but 'I cannot go on' hinted at amorous despair, even desperation. Much as I would have wished Agnes to be a lady, living in genteel retirement off Gloucester Road, she might equally well have been a woman of lesser repute. This I dismissed; St John Collier would not have understood a woman of lesser repute, a professional. I could, however, imagine him succumbing to a pretty plaintive widow who would be content with very little. And that would have been the end of it; he had the girls to consider. And Marchmont Street would have no attractions for someone used to the amenities of Kensington. I imagined a dewy-eyed woman with a palpitating throat, living her own idea of romance after long years of solitude. It was not the impossibility of having more that tormented him; it was the impossibility of wanting more. He was a man of honour; he had schooled himself in fine feelings. By a cruel trick of the beneficent fate which he had invoked with such confidence he had been trapped by the most subversive of instincts: untimely desire. And heroically he had suppressed the only instrument of pleasure that he knew: his ability to frame sentences. It was a stoic act of renunciation. He was not a young man; he had his dignity to think of. 'I cannot go on.' And all the while the widow or whatever she was would have been waiting for some sort of resolution. But there was no resolution, maybe not even a declaration. How could there be? There were no words left.

I stuck the page down again, and put the notebook at the bottom of the pile of others. In due course I would hand them back to Muriel and tell her that I had not found any new material in them. It was essential to save Muriel's belief in her father. Besides, I wanted to spare her unhappiness. The name would have haunted her, leading to futile speculation of an unwelcome kind. I wanted this family to remain as it always had been: spartan, upright, unquestioning. I felt far better equipped to deal with dubious behaviour than Muriel Collier. She was a protected species, whereas I was out in the world. Even I distrusted the world; that was why the Colliers had such a timeless appeal. Even if I was wrong in failing to give them credit for much intelligence I also knew that they were rare spirits, unique in my experience. I tested the page: stuck fast. I would suggest that the notebooks be kept in the safe. That way nobody would ever read them and capture their broken message. And Muriel would think this appropriate. 'Oh, yes, I still have his notebooks,' she would assure a purchaser, if one could ever be found. 'I keep them in the safe. One day, who knows? . . .' And she would be delighted by her part in the affair, perhaps discover that playing any sort of part, in any sort of affair, can be an enlivening experience. The only trouble was that I should not be around to witness this. I am ashamed to say that this affected me rather more than St John's putative affair. I half wished that he had got it together with Agnes and left some sort of record, which reflects badly on my character. Normally I make no apology for my bad character, but I do feel that others should be spared the sight of it.

The second unfortunate thing that happened was that Hester, making her enthusiastic way along Gower Street that same week, tripped and fell and landed heavily on her right wrist. A young man helped her up and brought her into the shop, to which I was summoned by a cry of 'Claire! Claire!' from Muriel. We put her into the chair which Muriel dragged from behind her desk, and she sat there, cradling her right wrist in the crook of her left arm like a new-born baby.

'She ought to go to hospital,' said the young man. 'I've got the bike outside, if that's any help.' He indicated a huge throbbing machine tilted against the kerb.

'Oh, how kind,' murmured Hester, then slumped back in the chair, her face ashen.

'An ambulance,' I said. 'I'll phone . . .'

'Oh, we don't want an ambulance,' Muriel protested, as much for her own sake as for Hester's. 'The hospital is just down the road. If you could find a taxi . . .'

Hester's eyes opened. 'A taxi, yes. So kind,' she gasped. Her good manners had not deserted her. The young man shot off and I was left alone with her while Muriel went to get the black coat which she wore winter and summer. I tried to get Hester to sip a little tea, remembering vaguely that tea is good for shock. I put my arm round her, and steadied the cup, but the tea ran down her chin on to the triangle of withered chest revealed by her still pretty print dress. I removed the cup, but kept my arm round her. 'So kind,' she said again, and winced.

The wrist was now twice the size. A difficult elderly tear fell from one eye.

'You'll be fine once they've bound it up,' I assured her, though I could see that it was broken. 'Nothing to it these days,' I added. Old bones crack without warning, and Hester was truly old, as was Muriel. It occurred to me that they were older than their father had been when he died; they had outlived him. They were bound together for life. What would happen if one of them were left alone? This clearly had not been envisaged. I think my shock was as great as theirs. I was relieved when the young man returned in a taxi. That was good of him, I thought. Few would have bothered.

Muriel thrust a bunch of keys into my hand. 'You'll have to lock up tonight, Claire. And perhaps open up in the morning. Do you think you can manage for a day or two on your own? Of course it may not be necessary.' We both knew that it would be.

'Don't worry about a thing,' I said. 'Go straight home with her after the hospital. I'll look in this evening, if that's all right. Just to reassure you.' And myself, actually. I had not liked the expression on Hester's face. The pain I could discount, but in addition, and overriding the shock from which she was clearly suffering, there had been a look of bewildered acquiescence that boded no good. That was out of character, an alteration in which it was possible to decipher an abandonment of her usual style. Hester, despite her age, had always struck me as the more viable of the Colliers. Now I wondered if her long life was beginning to weigh on her, whether the idea of total renunciation did not have a greater appeal. The thought had not yet communicated itself to Muriel, who still managed to live in the day-to-day present. Even now she was fussing over Hester as if this were merely a minor accident, which she in her austere competence was bound to put right. If she was worried about anything it was about entrusting me with the keys. She had never done such a thing before; she saw it as a delegation of authority, and this was upsetting, not only because she did not entirely trust me – I was of another age, I could not possibly have the Collier enterprise at heart – but symbolically, as if she too had momentarily seen the dangers of renunciation, for herself as well as for her sister. Though she must have been aware that they were both old she obviously thought that living was simply a matter of willpower, and so it had proved until now. Particularly unwelcome must have been the thought that willpower is not the deciding factor in one's continuation, that the wretched random accident might prove to be crucial, that the classical mythology of which she was so fond provided many examples of the fickleness of the powers that rule our lives. None of this was apparent in her controlled expression (but her lips were pale); I knew, however, that these reflections would come later, probably during the course of the first night she spent at home with an invalid, whose sleep might be broken, whose utterances might be discordant. Then I told myself that Hester probably harboured no such suspicions; she was the sunnier, the more cheerful of the two. Except that now she looked like a very old woman, collapsed, with a new trace of preoccupation on her face, as if factors had entered her life from the outside, and as if another sort of predictability had become apparent. Her valiant daily routine had been broken into. There would be no more cakes. As if to verify this fact she looked searchingly at her fingers, which were now blue. She leaned back against my arm and shut her eyes.

The young man who had been overseeing this operation helped her to her feet and told her to take it easy. The three of us manoeuvred her into the waiting taxi. I stood on the pavement, absurdly waving, until they were out of sight. When the young man returned he said his name was Bob and that he wouldn't mind a cup of tea, so I made another one. It was then that I noticed the absence of the cakes. I went out again, and saw the bag in the gutter. That too seemed symbolic.

The rest of the day was quiet. I put the chair back behind Muriel's desk and sat in it. To my surprise, at about half past five, a customer came in; to my even greater surprise I sold him a volume on Chinese and Japanese cloisonné enamels which he (fortunately) greatly appreciated. At six I locked the drawer containing the day's takings, turned off the lights, and closed up. I went round the corner to the Greek café and had a cup of coffee, thinking it only right to give Muriel and Hester time to compose themselves. When I judged that enough had elapsed I bought some peaches and a large bunch of grapes from a barrow and made my way to Marchmont Street.

It was a beautiful evening, yet the day's events had cast a shadow. I myself felt older as if awkward facts had intruded into my own life. I was somehow unwilling to enter the Collier household. I preferred it to remain in my imagination, where I could contemplate the family as not subject to change. I feared that I would come upon a scene of dereliction, or worse, Dickensian pathos: a house that had never known a man's presence apart from that of the father to whom they gave such exaggerated respect. They were virtuous women; they were also ignorant. Yet at this critical turn in their affairs even they must have spared a thought for the young men they must have known in their own youth, and wondered exactly why these young men had not stayed long enough to help them. They would not have imputed blame. But they may have thought, with puzzlement rather than with anger, that their lives should have taken a different direction, that they had ignored certain promptings which should have been addressed, and that the piety of their home rested on shaky foundations, that their father might have been responsible for their celibacy, that such bewildering ideas no longer had any justification, but that they had been brought to the forefront of their minds by the prospect of a long night, and perhaps even longer days to follow, in which they would no longer be two devoted sisters but an invalid and her nurse.

In fact the house in Marchmont Street was not as careworn as I had feared. It was dark, certainly, but comfortable; the room into which I was ushered seemed to contain armchairs and cushions and even a television. Hester was seated against several of the cushions in the largest of the chairs.

'Shouldn't you be in bed?' I asked.

'She says she feels easier sitting up,' said Muriel. 'But there's the matter of undressing her. We haven't thought that through yet.'

'I shall sleep in the chair tonight,' said Hester. 'In any event I shall be better in the morning. They gave me a pill. I think it may have made me a little drowsy.'

She looked as though she were passing from one life to the next, but at least she had not been kept in the hospital. I could now see that this would have broken her spirit, although I had cravenly wished it earlier.

'Claire has brought some fruit,' said Muriel, clearing her throat. 'Do you think you could eat a peach?'

'Don't worry about the shop,' I told her. 'I know what to do. And I sold a book this afternoon . . .'

'Which one?'

'Chinese enamels.'

'Oh, good. It was rather expensive. And I was hoping to look through it. Well done, Claire. You'll be there tomorrow morning?'

'Of course I will. You've no need to worry.' Glancing at Hester I saw that she had every need. 'And I can do your shopping for you. You'll have to eat. I'll come round in the evenings, shall I? Then you can tell me what you need for the following day.'

'It was Hester who looked after that side of things,' said Muriel. 'I'm not sure how we'll manage.'

'Marks and Spencers.'

'Too extravagant, Claire. And we eat very simply.' I ignored this, as perhaps she intended me to.

I could see that Hester was keeping her eyes open only with an effort, so, after some hesitation, I kissed her and followed Muriel out of the room. Now the real discussion would take place.

'You see what this means, Claire?' said Muriel.

'It means you can't leave her alone for a week or two,' I supplied.

'Exactly.'

'You could get a nurse,' I suggested. 'Yellow Pages . . .'

'Oh, no, I shall look after her myself. We have always been together, you see. I could not leave her in the hands of a stranger.'

'It won't be for long,' I lied. 'And I'll come round in the evenings to let you know how things are going.'

'You mentioned Marks and Spencers . . .'

'I'll see to that too. Now I suggest you both settle down for the evening. It's been a worrying day.'

I heard my new robust voice with some surprise. So did Muriel, who smiled faintly. I realized that I had been presuming, both on my own age and on Muriel's seniority, and stopped in some confusion. Muriel was more forbearing, and thanked me for my help. Yet when the door closed behind me I felt embarrassed.

I have to say that the following few days were delightful. I had been reprieved from unemployment. I sold a complete set of Batsford volumes, complete with dust jackets, and marked down all the review copies to half price. This was reckless and unprincipled but as they sold quickly I reckoned the enterprise had paid off. I was quite happy. The Colliers dined on poached salmon and haddock Mornay, and I sometimes ate with them. I felt competent, able to manage life. I was not at all surprised when one morning Martin Gibson appeared in the doorway. 'Give it a push,' I mimed. Then I sat him down, and made coffee, and concentrated on his well-being. And on mine, of course. But I can always be trusted to do that.

[10]

The summer, which had started so late and so uncertainly, became uncertain all over again, after a few misleadingly fine days. The glorious light dimmed; rain sprinkled down every afternoon, or so it seemed. When I walked home in the evenings there was a smell of damp, mingled with the scent of buddleia, which flourished even in the centre of town. Yet it was undeniably summer, though it seemed as though autumn were only a few days away. The nights were more convincing than the days. It got dark very late, so that I was reluctant to go to bed, although I was tired after a day in the shop. And when I woke, at three or at the most four, there was a stealthy secretive light in the bedroom, as if night had never truly fallen. The light broadened into a brief spell of sunshine, so that I ate breakfast in the promise of a fine day. When I left for the shop the sun was already obscured by the sort of generalized cloud that never truly dispersed. It was only at night that I was reminded that the invisible sun was at its zenith. The fact that I could not see it made it seem paradoxically more powerful, as if it knew its timetable, irrespective of what was demanded of it.

I was happy in the shop. When the door opened I looked up to see whether it was Martin who entered or just another customer, usually the latter. I could count his visits on the fingers of one hand: there had been precisely two, yet during those two visits he had made no pretence of looking for a book. He was there, he would have said, to express an entirely useless gratitude, though I had done nothing and now looked back impatiently to those curious visits. In fact he was there to talk about Cynthia – one subject leading quite naturally to the other – and it struck me most forcibly that he was talking to himself. I listened, of course, with every expression of interest. In fact I was interested in a way, although it was not a subject on which I thought he should dwell. But it was one he could not seem to leave alone, as though it was his sole reason for talking at all. It troubled him; that was obvious. It was as though he sought to banish the reluctance of those latter days, when his life had been so restricted, with memories of a happier time. Yet I, listening carefully, could discern only the ruefulness, and an effort to retrieve memories which, though faithful, seemed to disturb him. His life had taken a wrong turning, and poor Cynthia was the cause of this.

'She was so beautiful,' he would say repeatedly, and I would concur: yes, she was beautiful.

'But you didn't see her at her best,' he would protest. 'When I met her I thought I had never really looked at a woman before. She was so feminine, had such an awareness of me!'

This I could see had been the attraction for a shy and no doubt inhibited man: the luxuriant promise of care. He would not have seen the entirely innocent calculation behind such a display. Living alone, and working hard, he would have been impressed by the delighted exclamations that greeted him, would have succumbed gratefully to the lavish welcome of the parents, whose plans were already laid. They had been the astute ones. They were prepared to annexe him, knowing him to be inexperienced, and determined to give their daughter yet another present. And he would have seemed a suitable gift, his noble blond looks an invitation to some sort of takeover. He had probably never eaten so well as he did at that parental table, had never known such vigilance with regard to his tastes, his appreciation. Had he been another sort of man he would have been aware that what he had found was not a wife but a family, the complete antithesis of the only family he had ever known: lavish, sentimental, indulgent . . . That was how Cynthia would have made her mark, promising more of the same, for life.

Yet this may have been unfair of me. Even I had seen that Cynthia had the sort of corrupt exciting appeal that a man might find irresistible. And Martin in those days would have had around him an almost visible aura of innocence. Whatever fantasies had entered his head in adolescence would have been firmly suppressed. He would have shielded himself against the clumsy attentions of his students as if they represented abnormal temptation, a temptation he was bound to resist. Permission no longer to resist would have been Cynthia's gift to him, in exchange for his gratitude that he need resist no longer. She was cleverer than he was, but her form of intelligence was one he could not hope to understand. And she was furiously attracted. Endearments would have been deployed artlessly, tempting him to reply in kind. This would have been resisted for some time, yet once they were married she became 'Darling', rarely addressed by her name, as if 'Darling' were her status, as if this endearment, this accolade, which men bestow so carelessly, applied to her alone.

It was clear from certain expressions that crossed his face when he was purportedly telling me about her illness that he had, in those latter months, found her distasteful. The ardour of their early years (and I had no doubt that this had been authentic, all horrified excitement on his part, all confident boldness on hers) had not survived the change from his dependence on her to her dependence on him. This, in essence, was his tragedy. Although he looked like a man, and an exceptionally graceful man, he was as sensitive as a girl. It was the contrast between his looks and his apparent simplicity that had attracted her in the first place. I myself had had the same reaction. He would have had to revert to a position less of husband than of faithful servant, would have felt clouds of loneliness envelop him once again, as Cynthia, with the imperiousness of a sick woman, and something of the bitterness of a redundant lover, would have treated him with less than respect. And Martin was the sort of man who craved respect, knowing himself to be a timid character, less of a man than his appearance would lead one to expect. Because of that appearance, the tall lean figure, the slightly fatigued but regular features, the fastidiousness of gesture, the immaculate clothes, the dandyishness, it had been mistakenly assumed that he would know how to conduct himself. But I discerned a helplessness there that would have turned to misery once expectations metamorphosed into the sort of suspicions which a woman who had once been welcoming and was now both impotent and censorious had begun to exert.

He was healthy: his own body had not yet let him down, as Cynthia's had. In her presence he was faced with the realities of another kind of physical life: what my mother would have called little accidents, the progressive loss of control. He would have wondered how this had come about, not quite aware that this is the rule. I had learned it early in life from my father; I too knew that wincing distaste, and the guilt and shame that accompany it. I could and did feel for him as he traversed this unknown territory. And he no longer had the resources of his work to comfort him, for like the clever creature that she was and remained to the end Cynthia would have seen that his work was her enemy. A sensual and slightly hysterical woman would be more demanding than the more temperate company which might have suited him better (but he had not waited): she would have discerned attractions which she could not share. No matter that those attractions were literary, historical; she was thereby excluded. Her fear was that she might not understand what others might, would share as of right. Therefore she had effected a divorce, thinking that afterwards he would belong to her alone. He had done so but may not have been reconciled to this loss. Deprived of this comfort he had felt lonely, felt guilty at his quickly suppressed disappointment, had exchanged the library for the sickroom, for servitude, and had loyally made servitude his reason for living.

Thus they had both been unhappy, and like most unhappy and basically good people had not discussed their unhappiness. No wonder they relied on interruptions to their restricted way of life. This I could fully understand, although the sympathetic noises I was making were abstracted. I told myself that I knew nothing of his life, that my own construction had entirely taken over from facts which, as a gentleman, or rather just as a man, he would never divulge. It was I who discerned a darker tragedy behind his utterly routine reminiscences, which I did nothing to discourage. While he was telling me about a cruise they had taken round the Greek islands I was alert to the alteration in his voice that would let me know when the truth had broken through. None came. I made coffee, smiled pleasantly as various holidays were described for my benefit, and for his, as the legend was carefully reconstructed. The purpose of this was to negate the inevitable guilt that one feels after a death, and in his case the shame of those divided feelings which had preceded the death for quite some time. In fact for longer than he cared to admit. Again no curiosity was shown about my own life. And every time I tried to steer him back to the present another holiday was invoked, another rich person's diversion, as if he were guiding me through an album of illustrations to some sunny narrative, which only he was capable of expounding.

But I had seen the reality, the dark flat, and had heard the gilt clock ticking, the voice from the bedroom. He had no friends; I saw that too. Here again I could sympathize. My own home had been free of visitors, because they had upset my father, as indeed I had. 'Less enthusiasm, please, Claire,' he would say as I clattered in from school. I got used to the idea that he was easily upset at a very early age, an age at which children should be joyous, and after his death I felt it would be disloyal to my mother to treat the flat as if it were partly my own: she was so grateful to have it to herself that it would have seemed selfish to have destroyed her peace. No doubt she saw this, which was why she encouraged me to take holidays. No doubt she would have hidden from herself any knowledge of how I spent them. My mother was the least prurient of women. But this hidden life, or rather those private lives, mine and hers, explained why I was so much alone and had remained so, why I made up so much in default of direct contact with others, why I kept my own counsel, which was some compensation for the isolation I sometimes felt.

My experience of life with an invalid supplemented Martin's, although he was not to know this. I remembered the mournful inquiries: what sort of a day was it outside? Why had *The Times* not arrived? But I also remembered the querulous complaints, the heavy-breathing naps, the need at all times for his attendants to express concern. It had become impossible to invite my schoolfriends to tea; I knew the embarrassment they would feel. As his illness took hold my father became more and more eccentric, so that in addition to the physical burden to which he (and my mother) were subject there were sudden outbreaks of annoyance, peevish refusals, disquieting self-pity. I see now that he was not a very nice man or even a very good one, but then I had little knowledge of what had attracted my mother.

Indeed I refused to believe that she had ever been attracted, and this too made me impatient. Because my father was such a sad wreck I became more and more convinced that a man must possess a high degree of physical excellence. I told myself that I could deal with any moral imperfections that might become apparent, but in fact I gave them little time to become apparent. I perfected a discreet but unmistakable approach, and also the ability to make a quick departure. I believe that I was simply beguiled by looks and charm, qualities in which my poor father was notably deficient. He too possessed an invalid's caprices, demanding to know where we were, why we had to go out, jealous of those acquaintances to whom my mother said good morning in the supermarket . . .

I knew that the sick and the disabled exert a tyranny, that they nourish a grievance against the healthy and impervious, much as ill-favoured women resent the young and unmarked, thinking themselves justified in issuing verdicts of disapproval, yet at the same time unhappily aware of their own marginality. In an odd and reluctant sense I knew all this, was able to deplore my father's character and appearance without any thought for the unhappiness he caused, and, I think, intended to cause. I saw him as a prime example of the inequity of nature, or of God, but I also saw him as a mistake. My sympathies were with my mother, hers, I think, with me. Yet we both felt shame at what we perceived as the enormity of our reactions. Martin's reflections – urbane, wistful – taught me that he too felt this shame.

Naturally I said none of this. My part was to be careful and neutral, and above all appreciative, respectful, as he deployed his golden legend. I was there to help him to rearrange his story, to expunge the ugly memories, to cancel the inconvenient feelings. I knew about the retreat into fantasy, although for me fantasy is generally an advance, albeit an unreliable one. I was quite willing to play my part, for the moment. What slightly irked me was his continued lack of curiosity. I began to see that Cynthia, who had so sumptuously demonstrated her indifference to Wiggy and to myself, had passed on this virus to her husband, whose closed and secret nature would already have prepared the ground. Indeed when we were not talking about Cynthia there was very little to talk about. Cynthia was what we had in common, though I intended to change that. I excused his behaviour as the awkward stance one has in the world when one is totally constrained at home. I could have reacted differently, I could have distracted him with stories of St John Collier and the circumstances which accounted for my presence in the shop, but I was unwilling to do this. It would have seemed to me dereliction of a moral duty to deliver St John, who now appeared to me in a relatively noble light, into Martin Gibson's worried self-absorption. Martin, I could see, was now in the business of editing, much as I had been, but what he was producing was a version of the truth. St John Collier, vulnerable in his simplicity, had seen the truth for what it was, on that ultimate page, but had not thought to rearrange it. I was aware that he was the superior character, but I was not conducting a heavenly assize. St John Collier was without ambiguity, and it was ambiguity that excited me.

'Will you stay in the flat?' I asked him.

'The flat?' He looked at me blankly. 'Oh, yes, I'll have to stay. All Cynthia's things are there. Her beautiful things.'

I have a slight prejudice against beautiful things. 'You ought to get rid of her clothes, at least. Get someone to help you. The Salvation Army. Oxfam. They usually send someone round.'

'Sue might help. She's been awfully good, you know. She rings up sometimes to see if I'm all right. She's working at the Middlesex now. Quite near.'

'There you are then.' That at least was taken care of.

St John's reflections might do rather well, I was thinking. These slim aspirational tracts seemed to sell in millions. I had taken to glancing through Muriel's copy of the *Bookseller*, and was developing a new hard-headed attitude to my calling.

'And you're eating?' I inquired.

'Oh, yes, I'm doing all that.' He grinned suddenly. 'Who do you think did the cooking?' His face relapsed into mournfulness. 'Not that I have any appetite. I mustn't take up any more of your time, Claire. I may call you Claire?' He seemed unaware that he had been doing so all along. 'If I talk too much it's because you're such a good listener.'

'Talk as much as you like,' I said. 'Look in again. The morning's the best time. The afternoons can get quite busy.'

'Yes, I mustn't keep you. You've been a great help, both to Cynthia and myself. Yes, I'll look in again, if you're sure you don't mind.'

'Of course I don't mind.'

'I'll say goodbye, then.'

'Goodbye, Martin.'

Muriel reappeared one afternoon towards the end of the same week.

'It's all right,' she said. 'Hester's watching the tennis. I feel better about leaving her now. Only for an hour, of course. How are you getting on?'

I vacated her desk and prepared to retreat to the basement, though there was nothing for me to do down there.

'No, no, Claire. I shan't stop. I came to say that there's no need for you to sacrifice your evenings any more. We can manage quite well. I've been to Marks and Spencer. I shall take Hester with me tomorrow. She'll be very amused.' She looked round casually, carefully. 'Fortunately she's left-handed,' she said. 'So you can go straight home now.'

'If you're sure?'

'Quite sure.'

I accepted this, although my evenings would now be unoccupied. I also accepted the fact that the Colliers were closing ranks once again.

'Will you want a holiday?' she asked. This inquiry was the purpose of her visit.

'No, no,' I said. 'I shan't want a holiday.'

This was true. I had had enough of my solitary endeavours. I wanted something different now. I wanted someone to invest in me, to express curiosity, to ask me questions. I saw my summer as an affair of waiting for someone to do this. I thought of 'someone' with deliberate vagueness; at the same time I knew his face. I would ask him to dinner, I thought. I was no cook, but I could manage something. I was impatient for Muriel to leave, so that I could ruminate at my leisure. 'Give my love to Hester,' I said.

She rearranged a few books on one of the tables. She was homesick for the days when no domestic duties claimed her, when she could think of herself, with every justification, as a professional woman. She must have adopted this stance once earlier hopes had been relinquished. It would have been in order for a spinster, who knew she would remain a spinster, to present this dignified face to the world, to join the ranks of the virtuous pioneers, flying the flag for the liberated woman. They were brave in those days, braver than we are now. Now everything is a short-term contract. Muriel would have known that she had taken on a job for life.

After she had left, with expressions of thanks for my various contributions to her peace of mind, I was seized with a desire to be out in the street. The rainy weather had cleared, as it so often did in the evening, and the sun shone once more. I was in no hurry to get home. I thought of calling in on Wiggy but decided against it. For the moment I wanted no conversation other than that earlier one. This continued to occupy my mind, so much so that by the time I went to bed I felt as if it were still taking place, progressing indeed, beyond what had already been said.

[11]

When Wiggy called to say that Eileen Bateman had died I confess that my first thought was, Oh, no, not another death, but Wiggy was upset, so I put down the receiver and went round there.

Eileen Bateman was a fairly mysterious woman who occupied the top floor of Wiggy's building. When the café downstairs was closed they were the only two people in the house, a fact which bothered neither of them. Naturally they had got to know each other during the time that they had lived in such close proximity, but Eileen Bateman seemed entirely self-sufficient and had proved herself to be an excellent neighbour, if excellence is demonstrated by an ability to give no trouble, make no noise, receive no visitors, and be absent for most of the day.

We knew that she was retired, and that she had been a buyer for women's fashions in a department store. She was unmarried and always had been. Wiggy got to know her better when Eileen Bateman, in the throes of flu, had telephoned and asked apologetically if Wiggy had any aspirin. She added, hoarsely, that she had no belief in patent medicines, but she thought that aspirin might ease her headache. On her recovery she had visited Wiggy, and, with profuse thanks, had presented a bunch of flowers. They had got to know each other better, and Miss Bateman, or Eileen as she became, was, I suspect, the recipient of Wiggy's confidences with regard to her boyfriend, as I was not. I did not mind this, as I knew that Wiggy liked to maintain a certain tacit pride in the face of my scepticism, but when she mentioned that Eileen had read the tea leaves and promised her a late marriage I drew the line. Wiggy knew my views on this matter and henceforth remained prudent, but I rather thought that several of these sessions had taken place and that if I was spared the details it was because Wiggy herself was fairly ashamed of them. Thus, by mutual consent, the matter was not discussed.

Nevertheless Eileen Bateman was a feature of the landscape and a subject of discussion between Wiggy and myself. She impressed us as a woman who knew how to live alone. When she retired from the department store she had reinvented herself by buying a bicycle and continually planning excursions: Shakespeare country, the Gower peninsula, the Cornish coast. One summer, after extensive research, she put her bike on the ferry and went to France. Wiggy had in her kitchen a plate inscribed *Souvenir de Quimper* which Eileen had brought her after a tour of Brittany. Her bicycle was the subject of some altercation since it had to be kept in the passage. The café owners objected to this although they had their own entrance; against their fairly vociferous opposition Eileen won the day. I have noticed that single women sometimes possess these capabilities.

She was small, grey-haired, unimpressive but disarming, owing to her permanent expression of good will. I could not imagine how she spent her days, but Wiggy said she had once seen her cycling down Southampton Row, so I imagined her in perpetual motion from one place to another. She urged Wiggy to buy a bicycle herself and to emulate her own solitary movements: with singular tact she did not suggest that they team up. She was mindful of the difference in their ages, but evidently thought Wiggy less adventurous than she was herself. This may have been a source of some pride to her. Wiggy was used to brochures being thrust through her letterbox, which she then put into a drawer, not quite willing to throw them away for fear of hurting Eileen's feelings. And Eileen's feelings never seemed to be hurt. That was the nice thing about her.

She remained mysterious in that she made no reference to a family apart from the one she had known at work. Thus she appeared to have no antecedents, and we occasionally wondered what we should do if she were in any trouble; our own resources seemed to us too meagre to be deployed in this matter, and the people downstairs in the café would be no help since they had been the losers in the matter of the bicycle. I got to know her quite well: she was sometimes to be seen in Wiggy's kitchen, sitting at the table with a cup of tea. If I had not been there I am quite sure that she would have produced a pack of cards and told our fortunes, but even she had some misgivings about the propriety of doing this, although she maintained that she was protected by the hand of fate. This did seem to be the case; in any event she remained undiscouraged by the uncertainty of the time in front of her, and was not subject to changes of mood. As far as we knew she was always the same, out in all weathers, off to the public library or to some street market to buy her vegetables – naturally she was a vegetarian – or knocking a little bashfully on Wiggy's door to offer her a guide to the Lake District. She had if anything become bolder of late; she was thinking of tackling Holland and Belgium. We suspected that she collected all this literature in order to plan journeys she would never make; on the other hand there was the *Souvenir de Quimper* to show that she did travel quite far afield. She seemed indefatigable. Her eyes were bright, her cheeks pink. Her short rough grey hair, the only pointer to her age, which must have been about sixty-five, was offset by the odd stylishness of her habitual uniform of blue jeans and pullover. It was a comfort to

Wiggy to know she was there, above her head, listening to *The Archers*. She was someone on whom one could rely.

But evidently she was not, for Wiggy, infinitely distressed, told me that she had been found dead in bed one morning by the woman who cleaned the common parts of the building and who had keys to both their flats. It was the usual story: this woman, who was vigilant, had noticed a strange smell, had gone in, had discovered Eileen, had looked for a note or an empty pill bottle, had found neither, but had called the police anyway. Wiggy, returning from buying her newspapers, had had the horrifying experience of encountering the ambulance men with the body on the stairs. She became quite efficient after the initial shock; she too looked for a note or a pill bottle but also found nothing. It was then that the somehow incredible fact that Eileen had died of natural causes struck her, and this was corroborated by the inquest. Eileen had simply gone to bed one night and died, as obediently as she had lived. The police found that she had a sister in Cambridge. This sister now arrived to claim Eileen's possessions. She offered Wiggy Eileen's bicycle, but Wiggy declined. Nobody else could be found to take it, and it remained in the passage. Although this was something of a nuisance Wiggy could not bring herself to dispose of it. The pedals tended to snag our tights; we got used to this. Not doing anything about it seemed to be the only tribute we could pay.

For we were stunned by the fact that she had died alone, of a heart attack, it appeared, without crying out, without making a sound. A woman had lain dying above Wiggy's head and she had not known. Just as any death frightens one we were forced into unwelcome speculations. What if it had been Wiggy, now alone in the building? What if it had been me, in friendless Montagu Mansions? It seemed to us suddenly that we only had each other on whom to call, and that after our deaths few people would be notified. Uneasily we contemplated our prospective demise, and even more so our unpartnered lives. We were young and healthy, we assured each other – but Eileen, to all intents and purposes, had been healthy too. Old, of course, but not that old. Fearfully we speculated about her last hours, minutes. She would have known, I thought: I am sure there is always a warning. And suppose there had been other warnings, which she had faced down, convinced that she was armed by fate?

It must be a terrible thing to die alone, an even worse one to know that you will have to do so. Soldiers in battle have each other, but who will provide comfort in the stretches of the night for one who has had to make a virtue of self-sufficiency? Wiggy and I were entirely preoccupied with this matter. And Eileen had been the acme of common sense; she would certainly not have made as much of it as we were now doing. She represented a certain domesticity, or perhaps just a certain domestic busyness that would otherwise have been lacking, with her cards and her brochures and her reminiscences of life in the shop – but even these were curtailed, as if she had put a distance between her younger days and the time she was now obliged to live out. If there was sometimes a look of preoccupation in her eyes she was strong enough to dismiss whatever thoughts may have momentarily crossed her mind. She seemed entirely viable, armed against misfortune or disappointment. And yet she had died, and died alone.

Wiggy and I had exhausted the subject. I now wanted to discuss it with someone else, preferably Martin, whom I now sat facing across the table of an expensive restaurant. At least I assumed it was expensive: it was certainly not to my taste. It was the sort of formal meaningless place that gets written about, largely on account of the people who can be seen there. The owner, who is clearly some sort of character, greets them all by Christian name, and time is wasted in pleasantries before one is presented with a menu. Even Martin was addressed by name, and a lowered voice assured him of their condolences, both those of the staff and of the *patron*, who wore, I noticed, an engraved signet ring, before, in a lighter tone, inquiring if he could bring us an apéritif.

I had not wanted this. I had invited Martin for a meal, only to be told that, on the contrary, I must dine with him. I did not want to 'dine'; to me the meal was, or should have been, a preliminary, and this one seemed scheduled to last rather a long time. I did not like the look of the food on offer or the loud laughter of the party at the next table. I must have been the youngest person there. I thought with some feeling of our dinners, Wiggy's and mine, on Saturday evenings, and realized with a pang that I should now have to be the one to console her, as she had once consoled me. In fact we were both in need of consolation, a fact which was entirely out of context in this noisy fashionable place. Nevertheless I wanted to make my feelings known. I thought it about time that they were taken into account.

But Martin was being flattered by a waiter who stood by expectantly while he tasted the wine. Evidently this waiter remembered Cynthia, who had always struck him, if he might say so, as a perfect English beauty. Martin, his cheeks slightly flushed, agreed. The wine was pronounced satisfactory, and I was urged to try the spinach roulade and the *gratin de poissons*. I disliked this sort of show-off food, and anyway my thoughts were not on what I was eating. To be honest, and rather to my surprise, they were less on Martin than on Eileen Bateman, and on Wiggy, who would be obliged to spend this Saturday evening on her own. But I had apparently brought this *tête-à-tête* into being and I was bound to make the most of it, since, judging by what I now felt, there would not be another. I had lost interest in whatever Martin might have to offer. Rather, I was discouraged by the fact that he did not understand that some sort of signal should be given, some reciprocity established. Not that there was any awkwardness between us. The fact that I was rather silent probably suited him. His cheeks remained flushed. He seemed to be enjoying himself.

'You look better,' I said.

'One or two people have been in touch.' He blotted his mouth and smiled modestly. 'From the old days, you know. Jack and Angela Foster. They read about it in the paper. They said that if I wanted to get away from things for a while they would always lend me their cottage in Dorset. Extraordinarily kind of them, don't you think?'

'And will you take them up on it?'

'They also have a house in Italy,' he went on. 'Near Cortona. They offered me hospitality there as well. Cynthia and I went there once, overnight. Charming place. We planned to go again, but then . . .' He sighed and drank more wine.

I am not in the business of urging people to go on holiday. This was evidently to be my role for the evening, but in fact it made me rather angry. I put 'hospitality' in the same category as 'dining'; both struck me as unutterably pretentious. And I thought of Eileen Bateman planning to cycle through the Low Countries, her valiant legs pedalling through morose villages, and I knew that I was on her side. I had thought anyone would be, or should be, but apparently matters were to be conducted with more ceremony. The thought of introducing Eileen into the conversation now seemed ludicrous, and yet that was what I had wanted to do. Listen, I wanted to say, death can happen to anyone, at any time. It is always sad, but sometimes it is shocking, and now I am shocked and disorientated. What do you say to that? How much do you notice? He seemed to be eating heartily, which I thought both a good and a bad sign. He was evidently restored. But he was, as ever, incurious.

'Yes, we had very happy memories of that place,' he went on. 'The weather, the wine, the dinner on the terrace . . .'

'I thought you only stayed overnight.'

'Long enough to promise to go back. But it was not to be.' He shook his head and applied himself to his plate, which appeared to contain an entire horse's hoof but was probably something *en croute*. Stealthily I pushed my food to one side and concentrated on the wine. I was feeling extraordinarily unhappy. It was clear that for all my sympathy, no, my pity for him, I had nothing to set in the balance. My lonely wanderings did not stand comparison with evenings on the terrace. I was not apologetic about my holidays, or indeed my way of life, which I had chosen, but I was aware that it or they did not make for entertaining conversational exchange. Indeed the idea of exchange was what was noticeably absent, leaving a new area of awareness active in my mind. I was able to address myself to this, if only briefly, because Martin was now embarking on another discourse, about another holiday, this time in Saas Fee which, unfortunately, hadn't suited Cynthia so well. She was a luxurious creature, it appeared, was only happy in the sun, within reach of a very expensive hotel. They seemed to me to have lived a life consisting entirely of distractions, made possible by endless free time and a great deal of money. I found it unreal, and rather worse than unreal, uninteresting. I wondered whether I had been invited in order to listen to him reminisce, which he viewed as some sort of necessary activity, and one that would ensure my comparative silence. Silence and receptivity. It occurred to me that he might be slightly nervous. That was why he had chosen this glamorous restaurant, which was so crowded that I could hardly hear what he was saying. He took the fact of my leaning forward as evidence of my passionate desire to hear more.

'Well, there's nothing to stop you taking a holiday now,' I said.

His face fell. 'But it wouldn't be the same,' he said. 'Not on my own. Not without Cynthia.'

'Well, how will you occupy your time?' I asked, rather rudely, particularly as I almost had to shout.

'That's the thing,' he said, his face brightening. 'There's a piece of work I might tackle. Of course I'm very rusty. But a former colleague of mine wrote when he heard about Cynthia and suggested that I go back to the German Romantics.'

'Good idea,' I supplied.

'Don't you like your papaya ice cream?'

'It's delicious, but I think I'd just like some coffee.'

I was longing for a cigarette, although I rarely smoked. I wanted to add my contribution to the pall of odours that hung just above our heads. These were predominantly meaty, fishy: I felt as if I had tasted everybody else's meal. This evening was a palpable failure. Anyone could see that. Anyone but Martin, that is. An unlimited opportunity to talk was making him reckless, that and the surprise of being remembered by friends from a former life. He looked years younger, altogether impressive. A woman at the next table stole a glance at him, but fortunately he did not notice.

I was disheartened by the fact that he was entirely at home in this place, and furthermore in places where a certain opacity of behaviour was the norm – restaurants, luxury hotels, sojourns in other people's houses. There would be little room for spontaneity, for direct exchange, even for a kind of honesty. Everybody would be good-humoured, insincere, subject to flattery, like the assiduity of the *patron* who was now wandering from table to table offering and receiving compliments. Money would have schooled these people, and the others, no doubt, those friends from the past, in the sort of behaviour one exhibited in public, and it would have been money, rather than anything so vulgar as class. Money creates acceptance of manners, of unanimity of taste, which would be for the best of everything. It struck me that all the people in this restaurant looked rather alike, wore the same clothes, had the same air of good living, of high expectations. In this gathering only Martin manifested any appearance of refinement. He was markedly at ease, as I had never seen him before. I looked at my watch, which was not gold. It, like the rest of me, signalled my difference. I was young, well-dressed, and reasonably attractive, but I was out of place. This was not remarked upon because glances were exchanged to the right or left of me or above my head. Attention was focused on Martin, who had recovered a sort of worldliness. He had the right patina. I did not.

'What was Cynthia's background?' I inquired, anxious to define this matter.

'Oh . . . manufacturing,' he replied.

'What did her people manufacture?'

'They were very well off. Factories, you know.'

'And what did these factories manufacture?'

'Some kind of hair preparation, I believe. I don't know the details.'

'And your background?'

'The church. My father was a minister. My stepfather was in shipping.'

'Hence the boat trip.'

'Oh, well, that was his hobby. I suppose he was decent enough. But we saw little of him, or indeed of Cynthia's parents. They had a house in Malta. Strange choice.'

'So you were very much on your own?'

'But that was how we liked it.'

'Yes, I see.'

Despite the wine I had drunk I was stone cold sober, Martin

slightly less so. This if anything enhanced his appearance. I could no longer hide from myself that he was an extraordinarily desirable man. But I did not want him like this. I wanted him on my territory, on my terms. I told myself that this was all I wanted, but it was not quite true. It was all I wanted for the moment. I had no other ambitions, or so I told myself. I did not want, had not ever wanted, what is smugly defined as a long-term relationship. I had other appetites, other plans. What these were I did not know, but my way seemed preferable to his, for all the memories that had been served up to me so unstintingly throughout the evening. And this was not simple male display – see how happy I have been! – but a genuinely sexless monologue, such as a child might offer after a party, an outing. That irked me. But I was also dejected on my own account. I had failed to make an impression.

Getting out of the restaurant proved to be as lengthy as getting in had been. Every transaction, paying the bill, collecting his umbrella, provoked new congratulatory remarks. 'We shall be seeing more of you, I hope,' said the owner, rather unnecessarily, I thought. Martin seemed refreshed by these bizarre attentions.

'Do you know that man?' I asked, when we were safely on the pavement.

'Slightly. His family comes from Norfolk.'

I was anxious to get home, back to reality, grateful for the taxi that had presented itself. I had been out of my depth. This surprised me; the situation had not come up to expectations and I felt that this was my fault. I blamed the setting, with which I was unfamiliar. But really I blamed us both. Martin's relentless nostalgia had excluded me, but I was the more at fault. My usual directness had failed me, which made me all the more determined to retrieve it.

'That was lovely,' I said, holding out my hand. 'You must come to me next time.'

He took my hand, then, greatly daring, gave me a peck on the cheek.

'Goodnight, Claire. And thank you once again. For everything.'

When I got home I phoned Wiggy, to see how she was getting on. She sounded mournful, as mournful as I felt.

'I keep expecting Eileen to come down with her cards and read my fortune,' she said.

'Just as well she couldn't read her own.'

'Maybe she did. Who knows?'

'I've just had dinner with Martin,' I told her. 'It was awful.'

'He's not your type, Claire.'

'I know.' There was a pause. 'Actually I haven't got a type.'

'I should let it go if I were you.'

There was another pause. 'You're not too lonely?'

'Me? Not really. We might do something tomorrow. I'll ring you in the morning.'

'Good idea. Sleep well.'

'You too.'

What was it about the flat that reassured me? The plain furniture, my very bedroom, put an end to my misgivings. I too could impose, if the circumstances were favourable. And despite the evening's experience I knew that time was on my side.

[12]

The streets emptied and then filled again with strangers. It was summer, and yet it was not summer: the weather consistently failed to come up to expectations. I took to leaving home very early, much too early, so as to have the city to myself. Besides, the sun shone briefly every morning, between six and seven, before clouding over into the inevitable humid dullness. Sometimes I got to the shop before the cleaner had left. I made her a cup of tea, then locked up again and went round to the café for breakfast. The day then stretched before me endlessly. By the time I opened up, at half-past nine, I felt as though I had already done a day's work.

Somehow I was able to get rid of this feeling, so that I turned imperceptibly into what customers expected the manageress of a bookshop to be: useful, tactful, helpful. But a heaviness settled over me and I wondered how long I should have to continue like this. In the afternoons Muriel came in for an hour. Her manners were always restrained, but now I saw that she regarded me with something like suspicion, as if I had taken over from her, was filling the place where she had elected to spend her life, had ousted her, in short, although without me she would have had to shut the shop or even sell it. She would look round the shelves, almost disappointed that nothing was amiss, then take the money round to the bank. This I saw as the first sign of distrust on her part, for I could easily have done so myself, and indeed had done in the past. Those customers who remembered her greeted her absently but came to me with their purchases. When she had gone I resigned myself to those long empty hours before I could close and sat at my desk with a book in front of me which I did not read. I walked home through now dull and dusty streets, eating at the café where Wiggy and I had gone, and reached Montagu Mansions at about eight o'clock. It was too early to go to bed but sometimes I did so, feeling heavy and disappointed, though without cause.

Every time the door of the shop opened I expected to see Martin, but he was absent for what seemed a long time, though it was really only a couple of weeks. I told myself that he was staying with those friends of his, either in Dorset or in Cortona, and this caused me an odd feeling of displacement, as if it were I who had gone away and was homesick in unfamiliar surroundings. His absence was not entirely unexpected. I felt as if I had ruined my chances, although I knew I could retrieve the situation when he returned. I would conduct the affair this time, leaving him no opportunity for pious reminiscence: I would confront him with the actual, with the business in hand. For I thought that my rights in the matter had been ignored, overlooked, and I was determined that my failure, or what I thought of as my failure, should be eradicated. It was up to me to redress the balance. When I thought of that evening in the restaurant I grew hot with indignation at his opacity. No man, I thought, should behave like that, delivering himself to a woman's attention with no hint of a suggestion that he should do more. I blamed myself as well; I had been too impatient for the conclusion of this affair – I would not use the word relationship for there was none. I knew what I wanted and I thought that he should want it too. That was the heart of the matter and I could not see what was wrong with it.

Sometimes, after Muriel had gone, I indulged in a little make-believe, of which I was mildly ashamed. I was overcome with a longing for a normal life, one as filled with diversions as the Gibsons' had been. Again, I thought that some attention was due to me, but instead of making me indignant this reflection made me wistful. I too should like a holiday, but again it was up to me to engineer one, and now I was tired of those buccaneering excursions, tired of ecclesiastical details and the less than ecclesiastical behaviour in which I indulged. Now these holidays appeared to me in a morbid light, and I felt secretive, shameful. The fact that I could never discuss them with anyone made matters worse. My mother of course had chosen a wilful ignorance, and was probably right to do so, yet now, looking back, I saw this as not quite straightforward, as if my entire inheritance had consisted of the obligation not to disturb others, or rather to give as little offence as possible.

Wiggy knew something of my activities without my having to tell her. Wiggy is a romantic whose illusions are still in place. She is steadily, consistently faithful to her lover, whom she never discusses with me. Our mutual exchange in this context is confined to a fairly routine, 'Are you seeing George this week?' to which the reply is, 'Yes, tomorrow,' or 'Probably not. He's very busy.' And yet he telephoned her every day, which gave her life a settled aspect, and it was this that I began to crave. Stealthily it became clear to me that I had somehow forfeited respect, that I had failed to conform to what a woman should do and be, even in this unregulated age. I knew few people. This was not the reflection induced by Eileen Bateman's demise but something quite different, though possibly related. I wanted a proper setting.

It was useless to remind myself that I had felt this before, that it was something to do with summer, which I regarded as the equivalent of the empty quarter, when everyone was away and I was left in the desert. This year I was not even able to make plans on my own account, owing to Hester's accident and Muriel's reliance on my presence in the shop. It was not even as though I particularly wanted to go away, or at least I did not want to go away on my own. Wiggy would be staying with her cousins in Scotland, as she generally did both in August and December, but I did not even have that resource. What I wanted was some sort of mutuality, some sharing of plans, some utterly banal interlude of walking hand in hand with someone devoted to me, in whose affections I was absolutely secure. My companion, whom I would not allow myself to identify, would address himself to my well-being. Only a husband would fit the bill. I made excuses for Martin, which I should have realized was a departure from my normal intolerance: he had suffered a bereavement, he was inhibited, unworldly, glad of a sympathetic ear. At the same time as I dismissed his performance as inadequate I began to question my own knowingness. What if he had been genuinely devoted to Cynthia, so that even to follow where she led had made him happy? And he was a man who followed because he was content to be the passive partner, disposed of by the will of another, obedient to another's decree.

Where I was not wrong, I thought, was in considering the odd, even perverse attraction of this passivity, as no doubt Cynthia had done. There was about a man as simple as Martin an urge to violate that he would inevitably awaken in a woman like Cynthia, whose every gesture was predatory. And his response would have been her secret, hers and possibly his as well, if he had allowed himself to dwell on it. His seemliness would soon have reasserted itself; he would want to believe in his own continued decency. So in fact it was up to his wife to make him love her. This struck me as my own situation, for I was still sufficiently in charge of myself to calculate my chances. In fact the element of chance was absent: I was thinking of a foregone conclusion. I felt an odd sympathy for Cynthia. She was not stupid; she would have known his hesitations. I excused her from understanding them; perhaps few women could. One has been fed stereotypes; perhaps they are a genetic inheritance. One knows how a man should behave, or one thinks one does. And if his approach is lacking in fervour one will do one's best to inspire it. Poor Cynthia, on what was to be her deathbed, had been divested of her powers, worse, had become a burden, no longer capable of joining in the game of perpetual courtship at which they both excelled. And both, in their respective ways, would have known that the time for holidays was past, and only the grim present and the even grimmer future bound them together. When the present is satisfactory it is natural to seek diversion. When present comfort fades one is more inclined to think of flight.

That was my situation and I could hardly make myself believe that it was undeserved. But what I wanted was precisely undeserved in another sense. I wanted to be overwhelmed by pleasant surprises, to hear people exclaim in my wake, 'What a delightful girl!' That this wish was puerile did not disturb me unduly. What did disturb me was the knowledge that none of this was likely to happen, that I should continue to leave the flat in the early morning, continue to encounter the man attempting to walk his ancient shuffling dog, continue to spend my days in the dusty shop, even continue to attempt to put Muriel's mind at rest. I suppose it was inevitable that she should think of me as a usurper. Her settled expectations had received an unwelcome jolt, and her no doubt inadequate domesticity revealed for what it was, an uninteresting set of tasks to be performed for as long as the future lasted. Her dignity had been impaired, and with it her status. Seated behind her desk she had felt at one with those early pioneers, those rigid but welcome reminders of the conformist past, so soon to be discredited. Muriel was as much a victim of the emancipation of women as

I was. She had thought to do without love, only to be shown that love was on offer to those who knew how to deal with it. The climate of sexual liberation which succeeded her middle years, possible as long as she was not forced to contemplate a life of unbridled hedonism, had moved her into the age of exclusion, of disqualification. Old, Muriel would have seen that the young enjoyed a monstrous freedom, one that she had been denied through sheer goodness, by the example of an upright father, a devoted sister with whom she was condemned to finish out her days, ever more restrained by good manners, ever more taciturn, ever more bitterly reflective.

I of course had been empowered by what must have seemed to Muriel as inordinate licence. Now she had become aware of this and perhaps began to dislike me, not only in the matter of my assiduity in the shop but for my youth, and all the advantages she imagined I enjoyed. I did enjoy them, but even young people can be lonely, whereas children can be very lonely, as I well knew. I wanted to reassure her that this was out of the question. What she wanted was myself back in the basement, attending to poor St John's papers. Even at this late date she wanted to believe that his simple but admirable codes had held value, not only for himself but for others. She did not know, or did not wish to know, how wistfulness had overtaken him towards the end, would no doubt maintain that 'Elderflower. Stale nostalgic smell' was a perfectly valid observation, ignoring the forlorn aspect of the expanse of white paper surrounding this particular notation and the other empty pages that succeeded it. The one good thing I had done was to stick that last page down again, for Muriel, I believe, would not have accepted that her father was a man like other men. She probably believed that all men were like her father, and that it was perfectly possible to deal with them in a professional manner, respecting their differences, which one was bound to take into consideration, but too proud to make the necessary concessions. Duty, stern daughter of the voice of God . . . It had served well enough, but now perhaps it threatened to serve no longer.

There was little I could do about this. What she would like me to do, I reckoned, was to resign as soon as she was able to put in a full day once more. That might be a couple of months, if Hester were to maintain her progress. Hester, I thought, was the stronger of the two, largely because she was innocent of Muriel's regrets. Hester had somehow remained an eager girl who had no knowledge of defeat. When those suitors Muriel had mentioned had disappeared, a little puzzled, perhaps, she would have been as undamaged as when they had made her acquaintance. Thus she was not a victim in the sense that I imagined Muriel to be; rather she was unawakened, in her case a blessed state. It was eating of the tree of knowledge that did you down, since innocence was then pronounced to be irretrievable. I, who believed that everything was retrievable, and who behaved as if it were, was no longer so sure.

I called on Wiggy on my way home and said, 'It looks as if I ought to be taking a holiday. Any suggestions?'

She opened a drawer and extracted a handful of leaflets. 'Take your pick,' she said. 'These are what Eileen kept urging on me. I kept them because I couldn't bring myself to throw them away. Not that they're much use to me. But you never know, do you? Might as well put them to some use. Tea?'

'Thanks.' I spread them on the table. Barcelona. Budapest. A tour of Georgia and Armenia. Various spa towns, Biarritz, Vichy. Who on earth would want to go to Vichy? Apparently it was much in favour with the ladies of Napoleon III's court, who thought that the waters eliminated the ravages inflicted by the chocolate of which they were so fond. I thought of whalebone compressing those inflated diaphragms, all fizzy with gas.

'Did she intend to go to these places?' I asked.

Wiggy sat down. 'This will interest you, no doubt. No, she didn't. The farthest she ever got was that journey to Brittany. You know? The plate?'

I nodded.

'She hated going away. It was after Brittany that she was ill. I thought it was flu, but now I'm not so sure. She was constantly nerving herself up to be a traveller, but she was really only happy when she was on her bike, on her own, in control. She knew that she ought to be more adventurous; that was why she collected all these brochures. Besides it was something to do with her day. I'm sure she consulted travel agents, made extensive inquiries. But when she had the leaflets in her hand the whole enterprise somehow expired.'

'Did she tell you all this?'

'No, I guessed it. I didn't want to upset her. I went on pretending that she might take off at any minute. We even discussed the best routes – you can see, there are train timetables there.'

'Probably out of date.'

'Almost certainly. When I heard her overhead I said nothing. It seemed wrong to inquire.'

'She was frightened.'

'But she wanted to live up to the pretence. She wanted to think that at any minute she could be a world-class traveller. All it would take was a little courage. But her courage consisted of accepting that she couldn't manage it.'

'She never struck me as lonely.'

'I don't think she was. I think she had come to terms with it. She just knew she had to stay within limits.'

'Do you honestly think something dramatic would have happened if she had gone to Budapest or Biarritz?'

'I think it would have killed her.'

'You're not serious?'

'Perfectly serious. The odd thing was that when she was

working she did go away. She took her three weeks like everybody else. The difference was that she had something to come back to, something to tell the girls, as she called them. They all got on very well, apparently; they used to tease her, pretend she was a woman of the world, likely to spring surprises. I dare say that suited her. Whereas the reality . . .'

I knew the reality, which I had fought with the weapons at my disposal. For Eileen those lonely days amid the tourist sights would have been unrelieved. The preparations would have been enthusiastic; no doubt she had bought new clothes from the shop. And the destinations would have been ambitious, fashionable, whereas she would probably have been happier in some modest English seaside resort, changing for dinner, exhibiting her sunburnt face in the bar, inquiring after the children of the other guests, not too conscious, in that incurious company, of her solitude. Whereas the sharp eyes of the French, the Italians, would have found it out immediately. Pride sent her to the demanding south, in her new clothes which proved to be somehow not quite right. Pride accompanied her home again, with assurances that she had had a marvellous time. She would have had as much of a marvellous time as she could endure. She had done this for a number of years, no doubt thought that she could do it again. But on her own she was not so sure. She could drop the names of glamorous and beautiful places, but that was why she had gone there. They had served their purpose. And besides she no longer had an audience. I knew what a difference that made.

I merely said, 'How sad.'

Wiggy gave me a thoughtful look. 'I hope you're not going to waste the summer, Claire.'

'Well, the shop, you know. I'm a bit tied there for the moment. But no, I'm not going to waste it. When are you off?'

She made a face. 'Friday. I don't want to go, actually. I want to stay here and see George.'

'Remember Eileen,' I said.

'But she was different.' We pondered the nature of this difference, but said nothing. We smiled apologetically at one another and agreed to have dinner in ten days' time.

'Same place?'

'Same place,' I said. I was unwilling to say goodbye. I think she was too.

The following morning Minnie, who cleans the shop, announced that she was going on holiday.

'Where are you going?' I asked.

'Cuba,' was the answer. This did not surprise me; she comes from there. I gave her two weeks' money and resigned myself to going round with a feather duster. Muriel had evidently forgotten about Minnie, she who was so vigilantly attached to every transaction that took place. I wondered whether she was beginning to be a little vague, whether her watchful eye simply hid a desire to hang on for as long as possible. I should have to deal with this too, as tactfully as I could. I did not want to get embroiled in what I thought of as old people's problems, but I was extremely disheartened on my own account. In fact I succumbed to an entirely uncharacteristic depression which lasted for most of the morning. When Martin appeared, at about midday, I was released from this state as if I had been restored to my own youth.

'I've been to Dorset,' he explained.

'Excellent,' I said. 'I'm so glad you looked in. I've been wanting to invite you to dinner. To repay your hospitality,' I added, as if this were the only term he would understand.

I was no longer surprised at my lightning change of mood. In fact it seemed as if my early unhappiness had merely prepared the way for the enthusiasm I now felt. This did not surprise me either. After all, everything is connected.

[13]

The desire and pursuit of the whole was the only instruction my mother gave me, and I never knew what she meant. I think I related it to her own disappointment, spending dull days with an almost immobile husband, or possibly to the courtship she had entered into half-heartedly after her friend's wedding. Who knows what went through a girl's mind in those conformist days? I saw, and maybe she had too, some very slight betrayal of honesty in her friend's desire that she should not be left out, that all weddings should prepare the way for other weddings, so that the newly married woman would not have to pity her unmarried friend, and that some semblance of complicity could be restored.

But in fact the friend would have been conscious of the distance between her own eager husband, so proper and so desirable, and the shy widower towards whom she had directed my mother. Perhaps she had not liked to see her alone, on the outskirts of the wedding party, her untouched glass of champagne in her hand. In any event she had dispatched her, knowing what she was doing, hoping that she was acting in all good faith, but hiding from herself the knowledge that her high-minded and innocent companion would accept the arrangements that she was making for her.

Her only error, and she may have perceived this at the time, was to believe, or to make herself believe, that this partnership would make my mother happy. She would have been too happy herself to make a balanced assessment. She may even have thought that my mother was in any case too unawakened to be able to seek her own happiness for herself. Yet even in those prelapsarian days when nothing was supposed to occur after marriage, at least to the girls they were then, she must have felt some misgivings. The man in question was clumsy, inhibited, well-behaved; no doubt she told herself that he would be kind, as if this fact would cancel out all the others, in particular his physical dullness, not caring in that moment of joy that she herself would never settle for anything less than perfection, which, to her mind, she had found in the subject of her choice.

The desire and pursuit of the whole was what my mother cherished, had always cherished, and had never known. This ideal, which went with her vaguely Arthurian beliefs in chivalry, in knightly quests, had remained unrealized. She had told me that a man's major quality was courtesy. No doubt at that distant wedding she had been relieved to have been rescued from her faintly embarrassing position. I imagined them both, my father and my mother, standing a little straighter, discarding their champagne, and joining in the festivities, the congratulations, in slightly better heart. And she would have appreciated the fact that he had taken her arm to guide her away from the garden as the guests were leaving, for if a man did not know these gestures what virtue did he possess? She had probably thought that he would serve as a companion, and she was newly deprived of company. And he, a widower, would have embraced the possibility of a second chance, particularly with one so untouched, so obviously inexperienced. He had escorted her home, had asked if he might be in touch, and after various decorous diversions they had become engaged. The long engagement was no doubt in consideration of his sad bereavement. But this was the part that had always remained unclear. Why was the engagement so protracted? I see now that although events were moving inexorably to their foregone conclusion that my mother knew, no doubt in the course of his embraces, that this was not what she wanted. Thereafter she issued this vague – to me – ideal as if it should contain not her own disillusionment but rather the illusion to which she still clung, a life's journey with the perfect partner, a union so complete that it left no room for doubt or regret or dashed hopes. This last she was not to know.

Maybe I am wrong in this (but misgivings of this kind would open the way to all sorts of reflections). Maybe this was simply a maxim that fitted in with her art school studies, with her taste for plain furniture, her slightly bewildered sympathy with my unexpected antipathy to the man to whom she was still indebted. In any event she had, in her oblique way, instructed me, or rather given me permission to seek something different, and in so doing had confused me for ever, as it seemed. My own desires, once I became aware of them, were easily satisfied. I did not think beyond them. But now I did. Now I began to see some virtue in the life my mother had lived, whereas before I had avoided dwelling on it. There is something horrifying in speculations about one's parents' intimate life, which should always remain discreet. Yet now I saw something correct in my parents' union which seemed out of reach for one of my disposition. They had behaved faithfully, even through the long years which I had experienced as frustrating, even shocking. They remained courteous: even my father's complaints were easily appeased. What was unmistakable was his disappointment in me, not simply because I was more rebellious than he thought fitting but because he saw that I would never be as fine a creature as my mother.

In my defence I could assert that I had no wish to be. I was aware that I had grown up with something less than perfect in my background. However well they behaved, and they did behave well, I knew that they were both disillusioned. My mother in particular had attained adult status without ever knowing romantic ardour, would have schooled herself to believe that companionship was a worthy substitute for love. Her hopes for me would no doubt have remained unformulated. Of my own rash behaviour I am still convinced that she knew nothing. Thinking me to be intellectually curious, and entitled to legitimate diversion, she gently urged me to spread my wings, knowing instinctively that I would always return to her. As I had done. And that maybe was the flaw that united us. There is no rule which says that a daughter should be faithful to her own mother, yet we loved each other and our closeness was no hardship. No doubt my mother believed that her own ideals would instruct me to pursue that whole which remained mysterious. But I was impatient of ideals, and besides I did not know how to identify that particular one. Who does?

Now I think it is simply a metaphor for love. Desire and pursuit I could understand; there was no problem there. But anything abstract defeated me, or had until now. Now I saw it as the miracle that removes one from lifelong loneliness, that puts an end to expectation. If it formed an image in my mind it was a vaguely pre-Raphaelite one, like the Burne-Jones I had seen with Wiggy at the Tate. I had not understood the picture, which was dreamy but explicit: a procession of girls descending a staircase. They had low foreheads, wore white dresses and garlands in their hair; one carried a flute. What they were doing, whether they were virgins or some kind of enclosed order, was not made clear, but I had known, for all of a split second, that my mother had wanted to be of that company, surrounded by others of her kind, all with the same level of unknowingness but confident that their strange beauty would bring them within reach of their goal. It was not the painter's intention to show that goal; I thought him something of a virgin himself. But the picture put my mother into context for me, and I was grateful to it. Looking around the other pictures in the same room I saw that the men were exactly the same as the girls descending the staircase. They had the same high-nosed features, the same inviolable innocence. A union between the two would produce no offspring, would probably never even be consummated. Yet there would have been total compatibility. In this way I understood my mother's maxim, which was, as I thought, delivered for my benefit. Now I see that like Burne-Jones's maidens it was the ideal she had once embraced, but betrayed, that she was not entirely guilty in having done so because it had taken her a lifetime to understand it. It was to remain an ideal – that was its function – but it would gain in desirability from having secret adherents. They would never be any kind of elect, but they would remain true to themselves. It had always struck me as odd that my mother preferred the Tate to other museums. Now, retrospectively, I understood.

The man sitting opposite me in my own kitchen surely belonged in the Arthurian or Burne-Jones category. His unusual fairness – the hair and skin having the same blond tint – relegated him to some distant age before cosmetic embellishment, of which he was all too obviously unaware, as if he had just left school. Yet here was a man of forty or perhaps a little older, I thought, as I noted the fine lines that bracketed the mouth, who could hardly have spent his life in ignorance of worldly matters. No one can do that, however aspirational they may remain. There are women who have a singular faculty, who are unthinkingly, unstintingly kind, as if in ignorance of the world's cruelty, as though no other form of behaviour existed. Even I had been the recipient of such random kindness, from the owner of the café near the shop, who always smiled and asked eagerly, 'All right, love?' whenever I looked in, as if she genuinely wished me well. I think of this faculty as being in the gift of women. I had never yet experienced it from a man. Besides, kindness, of the same undiscriminating sort, is not what one is looking for in a man, though perhaps it should be. One rather looks for its opposite, a certain combative excitement. Now I had captive in my own home a man who had almost certainly never understood this. He had probably accepted this invitation as coming into the approved category, that of 'entertaining', and therefore legitimized. He was in fact 'entertaining' me with an account of his bird-watching activities in Dorset, an old hobby of his, he said, one that he had practised as a boy in Norfolk, where the birds were quite different. I made noises expressing interest, while serving the fine pineapple I had bought earlier at Selfridges. I had let it get warm on the windowsill; the scent hung over our plates, bringing illusions of southern warmth, though there was none of that here. He was at one with the virtuous austerity of our furnishings, as if he had been designed by the same hand. I watched his fastidious gestures with fruit knife and fork and wondered whether he had any idea of what was passing through my mind. He was talking rather a lot, as a guest is supposed to do. I even caught sight of an ordinary male response in his eyes, but that too was part of the procedure, the appreciation due to the hostess, permitted, even expected, in the absence of other guests.

There was something chaste about the man that excited my worst instincts, the ones I had formerly ascribed to Cynthia, with whom, now that I found myself in the same position, I was entirely in sympathy. I saw that in order to arouse his interest, or rather to dispel his lack of interest, one would have to . . . What, exactly? A normal approach seemed unthinkable. At the same time his obvious good behaviour, with its fussy formulae, his refusal to see a woman as anything but an appropriate dinner companion, aroused a certain respect. Here was someone outside my experience, dull-witted and fine, who would never discern an ulterior motive, a man so sexless that he took me entirely at face value. I got up to make coffee, asking him if he would like a cigarette. But smoking was apparently another thing he rarely did.

'I went back to the college,' he said. 'Of course I can always use the library there.'

'And will you?'

'Yes, I think so. It's a way of filling the days, you know.'

'I envy you.'

He looked surprised. 'But your days are full, Claire.'

'Not quite. The shop is my way of filling the days. Most people are conscious that there is a gap to be filled, you know.'

'But in your case . . . I should have thought that you were quite content.'

'Why would you have thought that?'

'Well, you're young, attractive . . . You always seem to be in such good spirits.'

'The one doesn't preclude the other.'

'The other?'

'The gap to be filled.' I got up. 'Shall we go into the other room? It seems quite a nice evening. And there's a better light in there.'

My earlier mood had shaded into a sort of resignation. I was well aware of the undercurrents of my remarks, yet he knew no better than to adopt a tone of bluff reassurance, as if I were a child. There was nothing to be done about any of this. I must consign him to the German Romantics, whom he intended to pursue, and with whom, I dare say, he had a lot in common. He would have been quite at home in a neckcloth and a tailcoat, standing on a bluff, one foot braced on a rock, giving birth to a small but perfect verse. I told him this and he laughed, the first sign of spontaneity of the entire evening.

'I'm much too spoiled to be a romantic,' he said.

'I can't see how.'

'To begin with I like my creature comforts. That was an excellent dinner, by the way. Thank you so much. You must be my guest next time.'

'What else disqualifies you?'

'I'm wary of causes. And I'm not young enough to be an idealist.'

'To be an idealist you don't have to be young. You have to be passionate.'

'Well, those days are over for me.'

'Are you lonely, then?'

'Yes. Yes, I am, of course. Once I liked living alone. Now I can hardly bear it. When the telephone rings it almost shocks me. And yet people are kind, the Fosters and so on. Even Sue. Unfortunately I can only tell them that I'm all right. That's what they want to hear.'

'And are you all right?'

'That's it. I don't know. My whole life has collapsed, and yet I appear to be in excellent health. I enjoyed looking at those birds, breathing a fresher air. Yet when I got home I could hardly bring myself to put my key in the door. Every morning I wake up believing that I'll hear Cynthia's voice. Then when I don't I get up and make tea and behave as though I were in one piece.'

'Maybe you are.'

He looked at me then. 'Oh, no,' he said. 'I'm marked for life.'

His words hung in the air. They seemed entirely believable.

'People ask me out,' he went on. 'Kind people. Like you, Claire. They even invite a woman friend of theirs, as if I might be interested. As if I could go through the motions again. Dinner. Polite conversation.'

'You haven't done too badly this evening,' I said. 'Was it awful?'

He smiled sadly. 'No, it wasn't. But then you knew Cynthia. It's different with you. She was awfully fond of you, you know, you and Wiggy. We never had children, you see.'

'Did you want them?'

'I did, yes. I wanted a daughter.'

'You could still have one.'

'I know,' he said, surprising me. 'But I shan't.'

'You could marry again,' I suggested. I thought immediately that this was a fatal thing to have said, but no doubt others had said it before me, in a clumsy attempt to cheer him up. But he took it as a kindness on my part, though still without a thought for myself. 'If you're lonely,' I supplied. 'It seems the obvious step to take.'

'One doesn't marry simply because one is lonely,' he said.

'I'm quite sure some people do. That's why they go to dating agencies. It seems easier to take a chance, trust a stranger, anything to avoid confessing that one is lonely.'

'I can't imagine that.'

'Yet some men do it. And rather a lot of women.'

'I've been boring you with my troubles, I see.'

I was startled. 'No, not at all. Why did you say that?'

'I thought you looked sad,' he replied.

I was in fact sad, yet I hardly knew why. I wanted to be comforted, made up to. Attention should be paid! I felt like many a woman after an unsuccessful evening, anticipating the tired exchange of thanks and protestations. I hardly had the energy to proffer another kindly suggestion, as if I no longer had any kindness in my nature. I could have been kind in another context, hardly in this one. In fact all at once my loneliness seemed greater than his, with these Fosters on the phone to him all the time.

My face must have reflected my passing distress, for he said, 'I've been very selfish, talking about myself. Now, what about you? I know hardly anything about you.'

This was a little failing he had shared with Cynthia, but now was hardly the time to tell him so. In fact it was the one thing I should never remark upon, although I am sure he would have taken it as a compliment to their closeness. I should phrase it differently, of course. 'You are very like her,' I should have said. 'You share the same characteristics.' Instead I tried manfully to give an account of myself, aware of all that must be left out. I made it as amusing as possible, knowing that that was what was required, although I did not require it myself. I served up my life in the dusty second-hand bookshop as if it were a genuine calling, rather than a temporary assignment that might soon come to an end. I was aware of the light fading, but did not move to switch on the lamps. Soon, I thought childishly, it will be too dark for him to go home.

'I had assumed you were a partner,' he said, of the shop.

I then told him about St John Collier, feeling no sense now of betrayal. They were both part of me, I reckoned. It was time they got to know each other. I felt sombre, and some of this may have shown on my face, for he leaned over and took my hand.

'You know that you can always call on me for advice,' he said.

We sat for a while in the dusk. Then, with a sigh, he straightened himself and looked at his watch. 'I mustn't keep you up any longer,' he said. 'As always you've been more than kind.'

That was what brought me out of myself, or perhaps restored me to normal. I no longer had any desire to be patient, or, as he would say, kind. I did not feel kind. I felt as if I had briefly succumbed to a mode of feeling that was entirely foreign to me. Now that I had engaged his interest, or what he was willing to spare of it, I was reluctant to let him return to his own way of life, which was in fact entirely opposed to mine.

'Don't go home, Martin,' I said. 'You can stay here tonight.'

He looked shocked, as I knew he would. 'You don't know what you're saying,' he protested. 'I couldn't possibly take advantage. Besides, I must get over this sadness about going home. Think about what you're saying, Claire . . .'

Once more I felt the predator's instinct. With the shock still mirrored on his face he let me guide him into the bedroom. I took off my clothes and watched his eyes narrow. He did not disappoint me. Later that night he uttered a single rueful laugh. That contained matter for further reflection. I promised myself that I should examine this, together with his very slight look of aversion before he kissed me and left.

Somehow, at the back of my mind, there lurked an awareness that I had done something quite serious: I had interfered with his image of himself as a righteous, even a self-righteous person. But at the same time I knew he would be back.

[14]

'Sit down, Claire,' said Muriel. 'We need to talk.'

It was what they said in television sitcoms. Even Muriel, I reflected, was becoming susceptible to contemporary influences.

She was wearing her off-duty uniform of trousers and an unconvincing blouse. Instead of making her look more up to date these garments showed her for what she was: a gaunt old woman. Not even a lady: dignity had been shed with the skirts she habitually wore in the shop. She looked thinner, more disturbed than I had ever seen her. She pulled out a handkerchief and wiped the corners of her mouth.

'You can probably guess what I'm going to say.' She stared at the handkerchief for a moment, but kept it clutched in her left hand. 'I've sold the shop.'

I should have been prepared for this, but in the event it took me by surprise. In my head I was saying, 'Sit down, Martin. We need to talk.' With an effort I concentrated on Muriel.

'A friend of mine in Long Acre is interested,' she said. 'He is looking for an outlet for his son. Oh, I know what will happen. The son is not interested, but he has been a problem to them since he left university. He will amuse himself for a time, and then sell it on. Probably to a patisserie or some such. But I can't worry about that any more.'

'What decided you?' I asked.

'Well, Hester. I can't take risks with her any more. I can't leave her. I might as well tell you the rest. We are going into sheltered accommodation. That's what they call it, don't they? A perfectly ordinary flat with an emergency cord in every room and some kind of warden on the ground floor. It will kill me, of course. But there will be someone to look after Hester when I've gone. I'm eighty-two, Claire. I can't carry on any longer. I persuaded myself that I could but events have outstripped me. I bought this place – in Bournemouth, I'm afraid – after only a morning. I went down there with Hester and we more or less decided straight away. At least, I did. Hester was more interested in the car journey. It was the farthest we had gone for months. Years, probably.'

She applied the handkerchief again. 'Of course I'll put in a good word for you, although this young man will probably want to make a clean sweep. On the other hand he may want someone to tide him over, in case he wants to make bookselling his career, which I doubt. As I say, he has been a problem. But I shall recommend you highly. This might carry more weight with his father, who is also about to retire. He has hung on, you see. He might be persuaded to keep an eye on the place, although he is a keen fisherman and will want to spend most of his time in the country. He has a cottage on the Test.'

'What about Marchmont Street?'

'Oh, we'll have no trouble selling that. In fact it's all worked out quite well. Of course it was a painful decision. One's whole way of life gone in an instant. I think Hester is unaware of the implications. She loved the place, but you know how optimistic she is. She probably thinks we can come back when we want to. But I'm afraid there'll be no coming back.'

'I can see how serious this is for you,' I said.

She smiled painfully. 'I doubt it. This has been my life, this business. Father handed it on to me like an inheritance, a trust. He knew I wouldn't let him down. I acquiesced quite cheerfully. I loved the shop. But lately I've had more time to think. Perhaps Father shouldn't have done that. Perhaps he should have done what I'm doing now, settled a bit of money on us, and sent us out into the world. I'm not accusing him of selfishness, but I believe he preferred us as we were, inexperienced. Innocent, if you like. Who knows? We might have married. Hester certainly. Whereas he made sure we were married to each other. I don't think that was fair. Not that this occurred to me at the time. I was obedient, you see. And I thought the world of Father.'

'What will you do with his papers?'

'I'll take them away with me. No one will want them now. I can't see young Peter giving them much consideration. He'll probably throw them out. That's why I'll keep them. You've finished with them, haven't you, Claire?'

I nodded. I was appalled at this destruction of so many lives, in the space of a single morning.

'I'll call for them another time. At the end of the week, perhaps. Perhaps you'll put them in some kind of order for me?'

'They're all ready. I shall miss him,' I said.

'Yes, I believe you will. You took him to heart, didn't you? This surprised me in a young person . . .'

'I liked his philosophy of life. It seemed to me encouraging. And peaceful.'

'Of course no one instructs the young these days. That's how we were instructed, Hester and I. We abided by his tenets. Lately it has occurred to me that we were wrong to do so.'

'Does Hester feel like this?'

'I don't think so. She is more his daughter than I ever was. Hester has the gift of gladness. My temperament is more sombre.'

'Shall I make coffee?'

'That would be nice, Claire. We have both grown very fond

of you, you know. I don't suppose many people have been in recently?'

The tide of American academics had receded, leaving the shop virtually unvisited. Although the stock looked the same I was aware that it would soon need to be replenished. This was a matter which had never been discussed with me, naturally enough. Now it was no one's responsibility, unless this were to fall to the new owner's father, the mysterious friend in Long Acre who had never been mentioned before and who in any event preferred fishing.

'I've known Geoffrey for years,' she said, as if divining my curiosity. 'We were friends for a time. It was only natural, being in the same trade. We used to meet at book fairs, have a cup of tea together.' She smiled. 'No doubt this seems very quaint to you. But I think we got on well. I certainly thought so. But nothing came of it. Now that he is doing me this favour I'm not quite grateful to him. It seems like a consolation prize.'

'Was he married?'

'Oh, yes. Most people are, aren't they?'

She spoke as one to whom marriage is a great mystery, one to which others are admitted but from which she had been disbarred. There had been no wrongdoing afoot with this Geoffrey. When she had said that they were friends she had meant just that. A friend means anything these days. 'My friend', as often as not, implies a partnership. I imagined Muriel dressing with more care than usual to go to these book fairs; I imagined the anticipation, which would have been entirely virginal. In the ruins of her face and figure could be seen the handsome girl she had once been. Yet a man would have perceived an unreadiness about her and would have been careful. Encouragement might disclose an error, or worse. Although I had no doubt that Muriel would have made an excellent wife she would have leapt ahead from gauche girlhood without giving much thought to her youth and expectations. She would have seen herself as an adult, taking her place on an entirely respectable female ladder. Fulfilment had been denied her, at least in this role, and the other was unthinkable. But as the years passed she had no doubt thought about it. Virginity is a rotten endowment. In the magazines in the basement, which I no longer consulted, it is referred to as self-respect. I felt a little upset at losing this store of archaic wisdom, for the magazines would be the first things to be thrown out. Muriel had no doubt grown up with normal expectations, only to find that these could be ignored, even by those with whom some sort of bond existed. And worse than her own disappointment, borne no doubt with the utmost dignity, would have been the speculations of others in the trade, witnesses at those book fairs, viewing the *mésalliance* with amused comments, the sort of comments with which unworthy candidates in the romantic game are usually dismissed.

A lifetime of humiliation had not soured Muriel. She had remained an utterly decent woman. But I had credited her with too little perception. It was true that she had come to resent me, but only as a reproach to her younger self. My freedoms must have been more visible than I knew. She was not much interested in me as a person, found me vaguely good-hearted and congenial, but desired to know very little about how I spent the rest of my life. Outside the shop she probably relinquished me automatically. I had been useful, but I was not wanted on any further voyages. My fate at the hands of the new owner probably left her completely indifferent.

'If you want any help with the move,' I offered. There were many questions I wanted to ask. When was this handover scheduled to take place?

'When do you want me to leave?' I asked.

She looked shocked. 'I hope you weren't thinking of leaving

immediately, Claire. It may be a little while before contracts are exchanged. Then Peter will want to take stock, I suppose.'

'Does he know the trade?'

'Well, his father has always been a bookseller. And Peter has helped in the holidays. So if you could stay on until he decides what to do? You may not have to wait long, I'm afraid. But, as I say, all that is now out of my hands.'

'I'll keep in touch,' I promised. 'You'll give me your new address? What's it like, this place?'

'Oh, quite pretty, I suppose. Flowerbeds, that sort of thing. Frankly it's of little interest to me. I have a sense of endings, Claire. And Hester is going to be eighty-five. We have both outlived our parents by many years. That alters your perspective, you know.'

'I know,' I said.

'Yes, of course you do. But you're young, Claire. You must make the most of your youth. Fortunately you are a well-balanced girl.' The handkerchief was applied once more, and then resolutely tucked up a sleeve. This conversation was now over, and she would no doubt regret her confidences. This would be an additional reason for not seeking out my company. For she had let down her guard, and she would not forget this.

'I'll bring the papers round to Marchmont Street,' I said. 'I'm sure you're going to be busy.'

'Oh, I'll look in again,' she replied. 'Though it won't be the same. Have you seen *The Cherry Orchard*? The new owner, you know, though there's really no comparison. I was a most . . . conscientious worker.' Her voice broke slightly. 'He will no doubt be able to fix that door at last. I never got round to it. Neither did Father, now that I come to think of it. Oh, good morning,' she said, in a new agreeable tone of voice, as Martin made his way in. Not a word, said her cautionary glance at me.

'I was just leaving. Claire will look after you. Now, if you'll excuse me . . .' She left, her rather wide trousers flapping round her thin ankles. She had definitively lost weight.

'She's selling the shop,' I said without compunction, as soon as Muriel was out of sight.

Instead of the resounding 'No!' of protestation, which he must have known I should have welcomed, he merely said, 'How very unexpected.'

Wiggy would be the ideal recipient of this news, but Wiggy was still in Scotland. Wiggy would be aghast for me, would devote a whole evening to mulling over Muriel's story. She would not be so precipitate as to ask me what I should do. I had decided nothing; it had all been decided for me. This was what held me up. I had hitherto been convinced of my own autonomy, had made a virtue of it, had told myself that I valued it. Now, in one important context, it had been taken away, but the implications of this had not yet sunk in.

In default of Wiggy Martin was proving inadequate. In fact as a confidant Martin was unsatisfactory. His confidences only went in one direction, his own. As long as I was willing to listen he was willing to talk. Yet in spite of the information he had divulged I knew very little about him. His confessions were like press releases: utterly predictable, and available to all. He had never told me anything that revealed the inner man. I thought I knew something of the inner man, which could only be revealed in secret circumstances and was therefore taboo. No words had been exchanged about our other meetings, on which he remained resolutely tight-lipped. As I did. I did not make love to him in the ordinary sense, knowing that he would find this unacceptable. Sometimes I would have welcomed a simple exchange of question and answer. This impulse I suppressed. I knew that I embarrassed him, that I represented all kinds of wrongdoing on his part, of which he had not quite managed to exculpate himself. The woman tempted me. Strange how the Bible comes back to one at the most inconvenient moments.

'The shop will still be open,' I said, with commendable restraint. 'It will be under new management, that's all.'

'You'll stay on, I take it.'

'Probably.'

'That's a relief. I shouldn't like to lose sight of you.'

I stared at him. 'You know how to keep in touch, Martin. I shall be at home this evening, by the way. About eight o'clock? Bread and cheese and salad, if that's all right.'

Evidently I was being too familiar. The only way he could justify our meetings to himself was as a heartbroken widower seeking consolation. Yet I had noticed that his grief, which had been intense, was now abating. I did not think that I was responsible for this. Rather I put it down to his rediscovery of a former freedom. He was less a widower these days than a bachelor. There was no one at home to interrogate him, and I would never do that. I knew how it felt to be the conduit of a sick person's longing, that doomed eagerness to take in the outside world again. I knew what a burden it was, and I did not grudge him his liberty. What I grudged him, ever so slightly, even then, was the distance he maintained from his own bad behaviour, as he no doubt thought of it, and hence from me. Only when talking about Cynthia did he feel restored to something like purity. But I knew his other face and told myself that I had the best of him.

'Who's the new owner?' he asked.

'Someone quite young. A man. Peter. I don't know his other name. His father is a friend of Muriel's.'

Some sense of what was fitting prevented me from telling him about Muriel's friendship with the man in Long Acre, those long-ago book fairs that had amounted to nothing but the acquisition of her property. No doubt this man, whom I disliked without ever having met him, would have put in a bid for the house in Marchmont Street as well, so that the son would be adequately endowed. And Muriel would be staring at the flowerbeds in Bournemouth, aware of all she had forgone. Out of unreadiness, lack of drive, of curiosity, whatever it was that kept women at home. Out of fear, too, no doubt. And the example of parental virtue, the potential shame of parental disappointment. No one lives like that now, fortunately. Yet my sorrow on Muriel's behalf was unshadowed by contempt. I knew that she was aware of all that had happened to her, or rather had not happened. I also knew that she would give me little further thought. I did not resent this. I knew that her grief was enormous. At that moment Muriel's tragedy seemed more serious than Martin's. He had been left behind, but not abandoned. Not noticeably deprived, to judge from his present immaculate appearance. He could hold his head up. A period of mourning is nobler than run-of-the-mill sorrow. Others will sympathize, will console. But there is no consolation for those who have missed their chance.

'I may be going off to Italy for a few days,' he said.

'With those friends of yours?'

'Jack and Angela, yes. They've been extraordinarily kind.'

This was what he had come in to tell me, not because he wanted me to know so much as he felt the need to be accountable, in the clear. That this was a subterfuge was obvious to me, if not to him. It was up to me to deal with his unavailability. When he returned his unannounced presence in the shop would once more indicate renewed access. He never telephoned. Neither did I. The thought of the phone ringing in Weymouth Street unnerved me. Besides, I knew he would not welcome it.

'I'll see you later then. About eight.'

He did not know the correct formulae for expressing anticipation. It was therefore up to me to ambush him. He preferred it this way. I did this without prejudice. After all, I was in control.

After he left I had no customers for the rest of the day. At four o'clock Doris, who sells the *Big Issue* outside the café, looked in and said she could murder a cup of tea. Doris was perhaps the first sign that I had let things slide; at least she had the sense to stay away if she saw that Muriel was in the shop. She is quite an interesting woman, of gipsy stock, who prefers life on the streets to living with her erstwhile common-law husband. She has a council flat near King's Cross and is always on duty when I arrive and sometimes when I leave. I imagine she makes enough for her needs; she seems quite contented with her way of life. Sometimes I congratulated us both on being so gainfully employed. When you came down to it I was as unqualified as she was. Of the two of us Doris was the one with street cred.

'So she's selling up?' she now said, one leg crossed over the other, one foot on the opposite knee.

'How did you know that?' I said, startled.

'The word gets out. Someone in the caff mentioned it last week. Going to be a wine bar, isn't it?'

'No, it isn't. It's going to remain a bookshop. Under new management.'

'Don't like the look of the new owner,' she said.

I was even more puzzled. 'You've seen him?'

'Came in on Sunday, with an older man. Looked like his dad. They had a look round.'

This was disconcerting. Plans were evidently far advanced. Muriel had no doubt lent them, or perhaps given them, a set of keys.

'I shall be staying on,' I said firmly, though I was by no means sure of that.

'Might not be up to you, though. They usually bring in their own people, don't they?'

'After all, I am acting manageress.'

She looked sceptical, as well she might. 'Where's she going, then?' At least she had the grace to ask after Muriel, whom she disliked, largely because Muriel, in her opinion, belonged to an ancient land-owning class with whom her ancestors and what remained of her family were in conflict, purely as a matter of principle. It was true that Muriel carried about with her a fine air of disdain for those who did not do a proper job of work, but that was because she had striven so hard herself. Cheerful failure, of the kind represented by Doris, was simply unknown to her. Looking at Doris's fat legs, so generously displayed, I began to have an inkling of how she felt. But it was I who had given Doris that permission to look in. That made me some sort of accomplice, a traitor to Muriel's standards. I told myself that the new man could sort this out. And Doris, who was sensitive to atmosphere, would know without being told that her presence was no longer welcome. A pity: I should miss her.

After I had locked up I went down into the basement and rescued the folder containing St John Collier's collected works. Then I took a valedictory look at the magazines before consigning them to a black plastic bag. A winsome female face appeared briefly before I dumped the rotting newspapers on top of it. It seemed like the end of an era, as if I personally were burying the 1950s, and in addition immolating the entire Collier family. My work had been for nothing. I did not doubt that Muriel would read and re-read the articles I had so carefully typed. But they would never reach a wider public, as she had hoped. Maybe this was just as well. Such innocence should not be let loose on the streets. After the day's events I knew that acceptance is a dubious commodity. Whatever desire I had for certainties was likely to be frustrated. I knew that as well as I knew anything. Nevertheless I wished that I had brought my father's old briefcase, so that St John Collier could be respectfully interred.

[15]

I did not have long to wait. When I got to work on the following Monday the door was unlocked and there were piles of books on the floor as if some gigantic upheaval were under way. I wondered briefly if there had been a break-in; some of the shelves were almost empty, and Muriel's desk – and mine – had been moved. A young man emerged from the basement, and said, 'You must be Claire.'

'And you must be Peter,' I replied.

He smiled and held out his hand. He wore a tie loosely draped round the collar of his bright blue shirt, the sleeves of which were rolled up. He looked sunny, effective, and unreliable. People do not want to see this sort of character in a second-hand bookshop. They prefer someone austere, preoccupied, preferably reading, paying them no attention. They prefer a person like Muriel, in short. This man looked too managerial, as if he worked for some sort of organization. And the smile and the handshake were a little too ready, a little too falsely convivial. I could see that there was no longer any place for me here.

'Muriel gave you the keys, then,' I stated. Clearly this arrangement had been made some time ago. I had been told only when there had been no possibility of concealing the facts from me any longer.

'Yes. We're more or less ready to start trading,' he said.

Trading. It was what they did in the City, young men like him. He clearly did not belong in this context. I felt a belated proprietorial indignation. 'You're moving the books?' I queried.

'Just putting them into some sort of order.'

'Muriel preferred them as they were. I think you'll find that the customers prefer them that way too. After all, we're not Waterstone's.'

'You can say that again. Dad!' he shouted down the stairs. 'Come up a minute, can you?'

The head of an older man, that of Muriel's hoped-for intended, appeared slowly as he emerged from the basement. He too held out a hand with alacrity. 'Miss Pitt?'

This appellation seemed to relegate me to the role of office drudge, faithful, uncomplaining, the sort who can be relied upon to oppose change, hold up progress. 'Claire Pitt,' I told him. 'You've moved in, then?'

'Yes. We shan't be needing you much longer, you'll be glad to hear. We thought we'd close for a couple of weeks and re-open on a Monday. Of course, if you'd like to give us a hand moving the books we'd be most grateful. And Muriel left this for you.' He handed over an envelope. I studied it for a moment, then put it in my pocket. There was a moment of hesitation.

'Could Claire make us a cup of coffee, do you think?'

This question was addressed by Peter to his father. Evidently something in my face prevented him from asking me directly.

'If you're sure there's nothing else I can do,' I said pointedly, 'I think I'll leave you to it. If you see Muriel would you tell her that I'll bring her father's papers round to Marchmont Street this evening?'

They looked at each other, briefly alarmed.

'Papers? She said nothing about any papers.'

'These would not interest you,' I said. 'A project I was

working on. An idea of Muriel's. I don't suppose she said anything to you about it. There was no need. Now, if you'll excuse me . . .'

'Lovely meeting you,' said Peter, his corporate manners pressed into service once more. I could have managed him, I reckoned. It was the older man who was the stumbling block. I could see why Muriel had had no success with him. He had not smiled once. He was handsome in an obdurate sort of way, the sort of man who relents only briefly, lapsing into a concession as if it damaged him in some way to do so. And Muriel, so maidenly, would have admired this, thinking that it indicated strength of character. The father, then, was a bully, and the son was a weakling. The 'problems' to which Muriel had alluded all stemmed from the inevitable conflict between a heavyweight parent and an inadequate offspring. I saw this Peter as a child (it was not too difficult) larking about at the breakfast table, trying to amuse his father with his antics, resorting to ever more frantic pantomimes until it all ended in tears and he was sent to his room. His face was a pale reflection of his father's, with all the character left out. Only the all-purpose smile remained, a guarantee of willingness to please. He was smiling now, revealing faultless teeth, which reminded me of Cynthia Gibson's former nurse. They would have got on famously, I reflected, whereas I, who was so clearly failing to respond, would have no further place here. He would begrudge any disagreement I proffered: he could no doubt sense the disapproval I was making an effort to conceal.

'There's a café round the corner,' I told him. 'And an electric kettle in the basement. There's nothing else I can do here, I see. You'll want my keys, of course.' I laid them on the desk.

'You've got your P45?'

'Oh, we didn't bother with that. I was paid on a part-time basis. I didn't earn enough to make it worthwhile to tax me.'

They both looked shocked, as well they might. But this had never bothered me. My little envelope of money at the end of each week had been quite enough for me. Now I had to give some thought to how I would manage without it.

My needs were simple. I lived at home – and here I realized thankfully that it was now mine entirely – only rarely went to the theatre or the cinema, ate frugally from choice rather than necessity, and never 'entertained' in the Gibsonian sense. I had not been away since my mother's death; some instinct bound me to Montagu Mansions, which I was loath to leave. Perhaps that enforced separation had made me aware of the shallowness of my roots, which I felt now were exposed. The silence of the flat which had so frightened me when I became newly aware of my solitude was no longer inimical: besides, I had those rare evenings to look forward to when my solitude was replaced by an enactment of some sort. Collusion? Certainly not quite intimacy. All this was manageable, even desirable. I was not aware that money was needed for what Peter and his kind would inevitably refer to as my lifestyle. At the same time my complacency had received something of a jolt. I should have to look for another job, and I was not foolish enough to imagine that I could find another one anything like so congenial as working for Muriel. And she had telephoned me after my mother's death, I remembered, with a flush of gratitude: she may even have been fond of me. I resolved to put my affairs in order, go to the bank, see what assets remained. My mother's will had left everything to me, but I had paid no attention to it, holding on for dear life to surface normality as I had been, as I was now. There was probably enough to tide me over, although I instinctively shied away from the idea of unearned income. If there was any. I preferred the feeling of the envelope in my hand at the end of the working week. I liked that feeling of solidarity with the homegoing crowds. This, I suppose, is characteristic of those who find themselves alone through force of circumstance.

I could almost certainly last out the summer, I reckoned. Then, when the skies began to darken, I would think seriously about the future. I might even take a brief holiday, like a normal person. If Martin could go to Italy I could go to France. The point of this would be to have views to exchange. Instantly I saw that this was an illusion. He was far more self-sufficient than I could ever be. Ours was not an affair, properly speaking, even though I had a desire to attach myself which I knew was dangerous. That was why I was so upset at being dispensed with by Peter and his father. I could have made myself useful to them if I had been a different sort of character. But I was too stiff-necked to ingratiate myself, and, being men, albeit men who had not known me until I had walked through the shop door, they knew this instinctively. It was my awkwardness, my unclassifiability, that made me unwelcome. They, or at least Peter, may have had some confused awareness that I was being summarily treated. But because I was evidently ready to leave they made no move to detain me. And I had proved tellingly uncooperative in the matter of their coffee. This, it was clear to me, had been a test case. I had proved that I was no collaborator, so it was only natural that I would not fit in as an employee. This was more or less out in the open, except that we were all still smiling. Even the father had forced a grim smile to his lips. This would be described as a decision arrived at by mutual agreement. I wonder who thinks up these terms. They must have come in useful time and time again.

It may have been the thought of the coming autumn and winter that kept me lingering in the shop long after I had received my cue to leave. It was only August, but the summer was virtually finished. Thick cloud was rarely pierced by anything resembling normal sunshine, and what heat there was was excessively humid, spoiled. Only that morning I had found a large moth spreadeagled on my bedroom wall, with no tremor at my approach. This attitude seemed to mirror my own inertia, although inertia now seemed to me something of a luxury I could no longer afford. I felt an uncomfortable mixture of emotions as I turned over a couple of books, deliberately taking my time. I felt anger, of course, but also some satisfaction at the uneasiness I was causing these two men to feel. They had no way of making me leave, as we all knew. I also felt fear. My fear was of the primitive variety; quite simply I did not know how to fill the rest of the day. And there would be days to follow about which I did not permit myself to think. In a few moments – since this scene, in which I briefly held the upper hand, could not be prolonged indefinitely – I should find myself on the pavement, as hapless as any monoglot tourist. A shadow on the window behind me alerted me to the fact that Doris had come along to see what was happening, no doubt in order to inform the others at the café. I waved pleasantly, then offered the same hand to Peter. The father retreated to the desk and began ostentatiously to examine the contents of the drawers. My quarrel was with him, I told myself. For myself and for Muriel. I believe he may even have sensed this. He was the sort of man who pours scorn on feminine intuition, knowing it can be used to his disadvantage.

'Doris will make your coffee,' I told him. 'She knows where everything is kept. She is, so to speak, a regular visitor.' Doris was wearing her usual uniform of shorts and baseball cap. The panic on their faces was my sole reward. After that I was on my own.

It was only ten o'clock. As I retraced my steps – for it seemed as if I had no alternative but to go home – I felt ashamed that I could think of no way of passing the time. All the tourist attractions were open to me, I who now felt as uprooted as the tiny Japanese girls and the bulky Americans who had taken over the streets. Martin would not know where to find me; that was the thought that was uppermost in my mind. The scrupulously uncommitted nature of our arrangement would now be at an end unless I could think of some other way of establishing the same careless contact. His avoidance of any reference to our meetings was now going to be an obstacle, whereas until now it had seemed almost amusing. At least it had amused me to witness his mournful dignity collapse from time to time. I took a sort of pleasure in the suspicious, almost resentful, face he showed me when his guard was down. Now I did not see why, of the two of us, he should assume the mantle of outraged virtue. I too had wishes. I shrank from the word needs, but it was true that I had a need for something that was not contained in this affair, for some sort of friendship. I too was vulnerable. My future was uncertain. I was only grateful that he had not been present when I had been dismissed, as I now saw. He would have been of little help, but I should have felt more dignified, less exposed. I had the sense to realize that I was fantasizing in a peculiarly unhelpful way. Martin would never protect me. It was I who protected him, against all sorts of failings, against smugness, complacency, a falsely flattering view of himself. For none of this did he thank me: rather the opposite. I kept him in a state of creative indignation at my audacity. I had made a man of him, as he had been all too willing to prove. After years of good behaviour I had awakened him to the pleasure of slipping below his own knightly standards. I had given him a great deal to think about. Unfortunately this left little room for thoughts of a more generous nature. But when he could spare the time and the attention to take a broader view I knew that he would acknowledge this. Then my turn would come, and I should be ready for it.

I would drop him a note, I thought. Surely that was permitted?

A note, rather than a telephone call, which still seemed like an intrusion. He would find it on his return from Italy. I was strong enough not to go round to Weymouth Street. I had always been scrupulous about not dropping in. In a curious way I respected his life, though I could spare little respect for my own. He had humbled me too. The thought of the letter, which I should write that afternoon, cheered me a little, and I made my way to the National Gallery along with all the other transients. I would have something to eat in the restaurant, I told myself, and only look at one picture. But in the event I was so discouraged by the crowds that I did neither. Unemployment was making me apologetic. I did not even have the patience to walk home. Instead I took a taxi, as though I had run out of strength. In a way I felt I had.

That afternoon was one of the strangest I had ever spent. The flat was filled with a hazy milky light that was unfamiliar to me. I could hear distant traffic sounds from Baker Street, but otherwise I was conscious of being alone and undisturbed. There were no telephone messages. This disappointed me, though I had not expected any. My main priority was to get in touch with Martin, but even this proved difficult. I might have been trying to make an appointment with a doctor or a dentist, with whom one is on cordial but inhibited terms. I stared at the paper, then pushed it aside and lit a cigarette. This too was a departure from the norm. In the end I wrote, 'Dear Martin. I have left the shop and will be spending the rest of the month at home, so you can contact me here. I shall probably go away in the early autumn.' (In fact I had decided none of this; the idea had only just occurred to me.) 'Naturally I hope to see you before then. I am longing to hear about Italy. Perhaps you will come to dinner on the 15th. You should be back by then, but if not give me a call when you have read this. It seems very odd not going to work, and I wonder if I shall ever get used to it.

On the other hand I shall be glad of a chance to make further plans. Let me know if the 15th is all right. If not, do suggest another date.' I thought this sounded reasonably well-balanced, though it might have been strategically better not to write at all. But I was tired of all that: I only wanted to see him again. I hesitated over the ending, and finally just signed my name. Then I sealed and stamped it and posted it straight away. That meant that I could expect a letter. I thought this was preferable to not expecting one.

At six o'clock I picked up the briefcase to which I had consigned St John Collier's papers and set out for Marchmont Street. I realized that I had never encountered workers heading for home: I was used to being one of their number. Those last weeks in the shop seemed like a lost haven of calm and safety. Now that I was out in the world again I did not quite know how to deal with it. My situation was fairly grave for I had found the ideal job and lost it. This occasioned a few thoughts on chance and serendipity. After all the job had been secured without difficulty, and through it I had met Martin. Cynthia I now consigned to the past, hoping that Martin would eventually do the same. I could help him to do this. I reckoned I had made a fair start.

Muriel answered the door, looking tired and flustered. It was all too evident that I had come at an inconvenient time. 'Come in, Claire,' she said. 'We were just eating. Hester,' she called. 'It's Claire.'

Hester was seated at the table, a meagre plate of scrambled eggs in front of her. It was obvious that a vast change had taken place. Her mouth, which was moist from the eggs, was open, almost sagging. Her chest seemed concave, or was it that the bodice of her dress looked empty, as if there were no one inside it?

'Claire,' she said thoughtfully. 'Claire.'

'Sit down, Claire,' said Muriel. 'You don't mind if we finish this, do you? I'll make some tea in a minute. Or coffee. You prefer coffee, don't you?'

'Don't bother,' I told her. 'I shan't stop. I came to bring you these.' I handed over the briefcase. 'And to tell you I've left the shop.'

'I rather thought you would. You are an independent person. As I am. It was all taken out of my hands, you know. Once I'd lent Geoffrey the keys – lent, as I thought, not given – I realized that I should have made a few conditions. When he came back to return them he said that he might as well hang on to them, in order to get another set cut. I thought nothing of it. Then I realized that as he would have two sets of keys he would naturally give one to Peter. Which he evidently did. I realized my mistake only after he left. Then he telephoned later in the evening to say that they'd be starting on the work as soon as possible. The work! As if there were anything to do! Everything was left in order.' The handkerchief was brought out again. 'So it was a virtual takeover.'

I nodded. 'They were there when I got in this morning. Moving books around.'

'I didn't expect Geoffrey to be so ruthless.'

'Maybe it was Peter . . .'

'Oh, no. It was Geoffrey. His mind was always very acute. He always knew what he wanted.'

Or did not want. Neither of us said anything.

'So when are you moving?'

'He's buying the house, of course. He said it was to spare me any further worry. I confess I was quite pleased when he made the offer. Now I'm not so sure. I acquiesced because it seemed simpler to fall in with his plans. Hester! Leave that food, if you don't want it. In any case it must be quite cold by now. You can watch television for half an hour. Claire will come and say goodbye to you when she leaves.'

Slowly Hester negotiated her way from behind the table, looked at the napkin in her hand, then dropped it. We both watched her snail's progress out of the room. 'I'll just switch on the television for her,' said Muriel. 'She'll fall asleep as soon as she sits down.' She smiled painfully. 'Don't look so concerned, Claire. It's what happens to old people.'

Left alone I could hear only Muriel's voice, and then a burst of canned laughter. That sounded even more sinister than Hester's silence. When Muriel came back I realized that I no longer knew what to say. I was anxious to leave, even more anxious not to let this show, though it was clearly what she wanted.

'You see how things are, Claire,' she said. 'There was nothing else I could do.'

'If I can help . . .' I suggested.

'You've been very good, Claire. You could have been quite angry with me.'

'Oh, no, I could never be that.' There was a pause. 'Do keep in touch.'

'Oh, I will.' We both knew that this was untrue. 'I'll tell Hester that you said goodbye. I'm afraid she must have dozed off.'

'Of course. Goodbye, Muriel. I hope it all . . .' All what? Goes well? How could it? They were finished, that was manifest. And they had done so well! Such spotless lives, shipwrecked at the last, when they had not expected it! Even Muriel had now given in, or rather given up. Applause erupted from the television. 'Don't see me out, Muriel. You must be rather tired.'

'Yes,' she said. 'I am tired. Thank you, Claire. Goodbye.'

'Goodbye,' I said. But she had already turned away.

[16]

I had a problem: how to deal with the time at my disposal. Ordinary time is spent working, but I had no work, and therefore this was not ordinary time. Exceptional weather – a heatwave, say – would have made such leisure acceptable by others, but this summer was not conforming to normal standards. It remained dull, except for that promising show of sunlight in the early morning which soon faded behind cloud, so that the effect was always of a slight mist or even of impending rain. I still left the flat purposefully, as if I had engagements, appointments, only to return an hour or two later, at a time when the ladies of the neighbourhood, some of them from Montagu Mansions, emerged with their wheeled baskets to do their shopping. They expressed no surprise at seeing me, or perhaps they were too polite to inquire what I was doing at home. They may have assumed that I was on holiday, or sorting out my mother's affairs. In a sense I was doing both, but I should have made a bad job of explaining this. I felt in a sense illegitimate, even shameful, though I had committed no fault. Yet I could not have stood up to the kindly interrogation that these women would not deny themselves, no matter how it would have been received. I knew that excuses had been made for me when I had been constrained by my parents' poor health, even more when my mother began her long slow descent into illness. Now

I began to see even that illness as a way of occupying time. I was healthy: I had no use for this. But I saw that despair, which my mother must have felt, can eat up the hours, with all the little routines one devises to distract one. I did not feel despair, only a slow bewilderment, with which I suppose despair is associated.

I went to the bank and discovered that I had been left nine thousand pounds which was in a reserve account accumulating interest. This money seemed not only unreal but somehow unavailable, as if it did nothing to fulfil my everyday needs. Those had been served by my own personal salary, which seemed to me infinitely more respectable. There was, however, in that unreal account, an assurance that I could continue as I was until some other form of work presented itself. At the back of my mind I suspected that in a month or two I should go back to the shop, ostensibly to see how Peter was getting on, and if I were desperate enough, which I reckoned I should be by then, would ask if he needed any help, offering to cover for him at the weekends, if necessary, or at any other time. This should not be too difficult, although the prospect was humiliating. But I, who had always sidestepped humiliation, now began to make its acquaintance. And in the coming winter (for personal disorientation always makes one dread the winter) I should be glad of some occupation, however much of a come-down it represented. And the shop was in a sense my true home, now that the empty flat seemed so alien. Brought to this pass I made an inventory of my advantages: solvency, for the time being, headed my list. I was perfectly entitled to waste a few days, at least until I saw Wiggy again. And Martin, who had not replied to my letter. When I thought of him in Italy I grew both indignant and wistful, but there was nothing I could do to prevent him from enjoying his liberty, of which I told myself I was a part. It was just that my surroundings were the opposite of picturesque: Baker Street, at all times of day, is noisy and clogged with traffic, and I could not summon the energy to go far afield. In fact a lethargy was beginning to envelop me. At least I still got up very early and began vigorously enough to prepare my day. It was just that the preparations seemed to peter out at about nine o'clock, by which time that early sun had disappeared, so that the time in front of me stretched out endlessly, as if both the day and I were under a cloud.

I felt older, as if I had recently qualified for adult concerns. I shopped conscientiously, thus gaining the tacit approval of the other shoppers, my neighbours, who smiled kindly when they saw me with my basket over my arm. If I were not very careful I should become one of them, and spend days like theirs. I had no idea what they did with themselves, but I could dimly foresee hours spent on trivial pastimes, on telephone calls, on library books, on family visits. None of these was available to me: I became newly aware of my isolated position. What had seemed like my own liberty was now an illusion of sorts; perhaps it always had been. Liberty is defined by constraints, and when these are removed liberty is aways a little disappointing. It does not coincide with freedom, which is what everyone craves; rather it is a guarantee of a certain social position, which I did in fact enjoy. I was a householder; I had money in the bank. What I lacked was a consciousness of my own entitlements, which I took to be an endowment conferred by liberty. I should have preferred a wild surge of possibilities, of desires, no doubt anarchic, which would have convinced me that I was free. I could not understand how, if I were free, I was not free to envisage an alternative to the life I was living. I seemed to be in abeyance until that alternative presented itself. In that way I was not free, was in fact subject to circumstance. I was too wary to examine this, knowing that danger lay in that direction. My enemy was fantasy. The rest I could just about deal with.

On one of my shopping expeditions I caught sight of Sue on the opposite side of the street, just going into Selfridges. I hesitated, then went in search of her. I did not particularly want to see her, but I was in need of conversation, however anodyne. Out of uniform she looked healthy and banal, as I had always seen her. It was the white coat that lent her distinction.

'Hello,' I said. 'Do you remember me?'

She looked doubtful, standing there with two mangoes in her hands. The doubt was absolutely genuine, although it seemed exaggerated. She was in a hurry, I told myself, with my new lack of confidence: she was due at the hospital, had bought these two mangoes for a patient perhaps.

'We met at the Gibsons,' I reminded her. 'I was so sorry for them both. I'm sure you were the most marvellous help.'

'Oh, yes,' she said. Her tone of voice did not encourage further reminiscence. In fact her previous boldness seemed to have vanished, as if she too were under the same edict of dullness as I was myself.

'What are you doing now?' I asked. 'Still private nursing?'

'No, I'm at the hospital. I've been seconded.'

'And do you prefer it?' I persisted. 'I don't suppose you've got time for coffee? I'm on holiday,' I explained. 'I shan't be going away just yet, though. What about you?'

I was having to make extraordinary efforts to detain her. She volunteered nothing, still seemed anxious to move on. Yet she examined me with a curiosity which I assumed was purely professional. I wondered if she could detect some hidden morbidity of which I was not yet aware, but my face obviously revealed nothing. She seemed uneasy, as if she would rather not have seen me, as if I had interrupted her day, much as I had hoped that someone would interrupt mine. Yet she was not grateful for this interruption, as I should have been. This puzzled me, and finally made me a little indignant: surely this girl had no right to make me feel an intruder? She had not replied to my suggestion of a cup of coffee, but looked down at the mangoes as if they might answer for her.

'Those look delicious,' I said tamely.

'I'd better get on,' was her reply. Yet this was reluctant, dragged out of her. 'I'm on duty in half an hour.'

'Nice seeing you,' I said. 'Maybe we'll bump into each other again. Next time we really will have coffee.'

She smiled, with relief, it seemed, but perhaps she was just not used to dealing with impromptu conversations, as I had learnt to be in the shop, and before that in the encounters I cultivated, and even in my odd habit of making up people's lives for them. I had had no success here. I told myself that the girl's awkwardness had nothing to do with me, that she felt divested of authority when not in her uniform, that she was no doubt performing a kindness for someone who was in her care, that she genuinely found it difficult to remember who I was. Yet her scrutiny had been intense. Was this due to the half-light in the hallway in Weymouth Street, in which it had been difficult to see anything except her white coat and in which conversations had been conducted in a whisper? And yet she had seemed to know me, in a way that precluded any intimacy between us. This saddened me, not because I desired to make a friend of her, but because it seemed symptomatic of my new condition. It was only natural that I seemed uninteresting; I was even uninteresting to myself. The proof of this was my new inability to speculate. This had always been such a resource, an endowment, even a gift, that its disappearance, however temporary, however ephemeral, however rationally explained – my change of circumstances – left me desolate. I could no more penetrate this girl's defences, as I once could have done, than if those defences did in fact exist. Yet I had no reason to suppose that there was any personal dislike involved, only that curious scrutiny, and as its accompaniment, a certain reluctance to engage, even in such a conversation as I was having to provide.

'I'll let you get on,' I said, aware of being something of a failure where I had once felt myself to be an expert. 'Goodbye. Have a nice day.' As I heard myself utter this formula, which had never passed my lips on any previous occasion, I registered the depths to which I was sinking. I watched her make her way to the till, pay for her mangoes, and leave. By the door she looked back, saw me, and gave a brief wave of farewell. That cheered me a little. Sometimes a gesture is more eloquent than words.

The odd incident disconcerted me, as though I were responsible for the other's wordlessness, her stare, her lingering indifference that was not quite oxymoronic: she was indifferent, and she had lingered, considering me as if she knew that we had met yet did not remember me. It was her opacity that shocked me; her eyes had searched my face, but without interest, and if she hesitated it was because I was blocking her path. She volunteered no information apart from the fact that she was shortly on duty, and all the time she weighed the mangoes in her hands, as if they, and only they, explained her presence in that place. I realized that I had not told her my name, and that I would not expect her to remember it, if in fact I had ever given it. We had met in circumstances that were extraordinary to me but no doubt not to her. I wanted to ask her how Cynthia had died; this became a matter of supreme interest to me, particularly as I had never heard an explanation. Again I was back in Weymouth Street, in the darkness of the vestibule, while beyond, in the bedroom, that strange drama was taking place. I worried about those missing details, which to her must have been without mystery. If I had been the nurse, witnessing those terminal events, I should have been willing to unburden myself, indeed anxious to. And I was not in one sense an outsider; I had been something of a friend. Yet those events remained a secret. Something prevented me from asking a direct question: I did not want to offend her professional discretion. It was for her to offer information, and this she refused to do. Indeed I wondered whether Cynthia was to be distinguished from any of her other patients, whether she had in fact remembered her with any exactitude. Certainly she did not remember me. And yet she had waved her hand at the door, as if some memory had struck her, too late for any exchange. This worried me, together with my inability to imagine her out in the street, the mangoes now in a bag, no doubt to be presented to a grateful patient. An ordinary girl, attractive in her no-nonsense way, with whom it had been demonstrated that I had so little in common that I felt a disconnectedness that had something uncanny about it, as if I were deprived all at once of the ability to sympathize, to comprehend, to invent, even to feel anything over and above a generalized confusion, as if I had committed an offence.

I dismissed the incident once I was out in the street, although this offered little in the way of diversion. Crowds moved slowly, in search of bargains. I had a sudden longing to get away, to some more noble place, even thought respectfully of those French cathedrals that I had once got to know so well, in particular of Rouen, which was perhaps my favourite of them all. But, stranded as I was in Baker Street, France now seemed unreachable, and worse, alien. I remembered Eileen Bateman, and how she had left bravely on her summer holiday for as long as there was a context into which she could be re-absorbed, and how she had given up once she was on her own and had no one to whom she could recount her adventures. This had now happened to me, although I knew that the comparison was false. And my surroundings were so mundane that I would willingly have embraced another cathedral. But I also knew that an effort of will would be needed if I were to make the journey. I also knew that the journey was necessary.

In this way I formulated a half-hearted plan. I would go away, and when I returned I would drop into the shop, just to see how they were getting on. I should by then have found the right form of words – they escaped me now – which would let Peter know that I was willing to return. If he did not respond then that chapter was closed. Somehow between now and then I should have worked out the formula that would have him rise gratefully from behind the desk and ask me to stay. There was no reason why this should not be entirely possible. Reason also told me that he was not ready for me to offer my services. Let him pass a few boring weeks in the shop, staring longingly through the door at the outside world, and he would be only too eager for a break. Strange how the shop had never struck me as a place of constraint; rather the opposite. If anything it emphasized the freedom I possessed to walk out at six o'clock and resume my own life. In that way it was like school, which I had enjoyed, particularly the last hour of the day, when my movements would reassert their independence. I had had the same feeling of physical optimism when Muriel, and latterly I, had locked up for the day, no matter what my plans were for the evening. It was enough to be out in the air, the darkness left behind me, but within that darkness the assurance of a familiar welcome on the following morning. I had thought it would last, against all the evidence to the contrary. I had grown so used to it that I regarded it as my normal setting, rather more so than the flat, which I no longer saw. Yet it was the flat that was waiting for me now and would continue to do so. The flat was now my only home. I was not easy with this thought; the flat seemed less mine than the shop had done. In the flat I was alone; that was why it seemed inimical.

The second post brought a card from Wiggy but no letter

from Martin. The card showed a view of the cousins' house in Scotland; it looked imposing. Wiggy was due back on the 12th, when the house emptied to receive another lot of guests for the shoot; I should see her on the Saturday. I longed for this, as if she were my only contact with the world. Also Wiggy, who spent her days alone, painting her rather good miniatures, would understand my new isolation, and also the reasons for it. These reasons were not confined to my fortunes at the shop but had more to do with Martin's absence. It was difficult for me to accommodate a sensible view of his holiday, for I knew that he would be a favoured guest, and that his hosts, who seemed to have his well-being at heart, would do their utmost to rehabilitate him, having no doubt discussed his unfortunate condition between themselves. He would represent an interesting problem, one with which they would sympathize, having kept away tactfully while Cynthia was alive. Perhaps they had originally earmarked him for one of their friends; perhaps friends of that type were already gathering. These friends too would be sympathetic; in fact he would be in receipt of much sympathy and attention. He would be perceived as dignified, worthy of discreet indulgence. The contrast between his status and my own was difficult to understand. I could only judge this matter from afar, using my well-worn and suddenly offensive powers of visualization. This was more like envy, or perhaps the contrast between a house party and an empty flat was too strong. Predictably the weather had clouded over again, and the flat was filled with a dull white light far removed from the Italian sun. It was the peak of the holiday season, when families decamped, no doubt to other families, to resorts of their choice. It was a season for easy companionship. I even envied Wiggy, who had a family of sorts, and whose relations, those cousins, remained faithful to their obligations. I seemed to be the only person I knew who was not similarly endowed, as if my antecedents had failed in some genetic task. Thus I was doubly deprived, of a family, preferably not my own – for my own family seemed too sad, even tragic – and of Martin, who might provide me with a family in the future.

I had not considered this in any depth before. I did so now. Perhaps it was the silence of the flat that encouraged these thoughts, but the fact was that I longed to feature in another's plans, even if I had to manoeuvre my way into them. My own independence had been fashioned in response to the neediness of others, of my parents, who, for their respective reasons, desired always to know where I was, where I was going, when I would be back. I had accepted this all my life, together with an awareness that I might have to have recourse to concealment. I had been conscious always of their wish that I remain at home, at hand. My contact with the Gibsons had brought to mind the tedium of those similarly burdened. And yet the life I had fashioned for myself was inventive, certainly, but not fulfilling. I saw that now. That was why Martin, who was allowed out on sufferance in the daytime, inspired in me such a depth of fellow feeling. I recognized that this was not the only explanation for what threatened to become an *idée fixe*. But it did seem to me that what I had to do was to point out the parallels in our lives in order to awaken him out of his self-absorption, to make him see that further depths of understanding could be reached.

Part of me knew that this was excessively sentimental, and, what was worse, out of character. All the hard work I had put into myself over the years was threatened. I had thought that I had won a victory over those softer feelings that undermine one and which deserve to be repressed: loyalties which were once in order but which no longer obtained, pity for those unresolved conflicts which would now never know any resol-ution. I had refused to be enrolled among the defeated, to know the hapless resignation which my mother so dutifully disguised.

Gradually I had hardened, always seeking out the easy solution, the easy compensation. This I had considered worthy work; now I was not so sure. I had eliminated certain responses, notably that of genuine understanding, even of the sort of compassion that I despised, and this may have been more noticeable than I was able to appreciate. I had become as self-centred in my way as Martin was in his, and no doubt for good enough reasons. What was now both untimely and inconvenient was my new desire to break this pattern, and even, dangerously enough, to become fallible, vulnerable, appealing even in my weakness. Cynthia had been all of these things, which I had seen as unsatisfactory. Now they seemed merely sensible. Anything demanding hardness, boldness, courage I thought I could manage. I even took a measure of satisfaction from my ability to put these qualities to the test. I had made myself into the sort of independent character that qualified me for inclusion among today's women. I knew the opprobrium that is visited on those who do not make the grade, spinsters like Muriel and Hester who come to a tragic end. What sort of end is reserved for determined women like myself is never mentioned, as if women of my type can be relied upon to save their own lives, or at least make a decent job of trying to. Yet we too will be subject to change, to shock, when the verdict is unfavourable, when we are shown the X-rays after the final diagnosis. Then no doubt the virtues of dependency will manifest themselves, and it will be too late to cultivate the softness that might have brought them into being.

I spent the afternoon in the Wallace Collection, listening to my footsteps on the shining floors. I saw little, but merely noticed a remote excellence. This was a place of virtue, perhaps the only virtue I should ever know. My mood was sad. The incident in Selfridges still puzzled me, as if my contact with others had been abruptly terminated. That night I slept badly, though I was not troubled by dreams. Perhaps I was not sufficiently asleep for dreams to occur. I got up very early, made tea, read an old copy of the *New Statesman* until the arrival of the post. There was a card. 'I will be with you on the 15th. Regards, M. G.'

[17]

'Wonderful countryside round there,' he was saying. 'And the sunsets! We would sit on the terrace until it was quite dark. And we were out all day, of course.'

'It sounds marvellous,' I supplied.

'It was rather. Extraordinarily kind of those people.'

'Was it a big party?'

'We were eight. One or two people I hadn't seen in years. And they had cars, so we could get out and about.'

'No wonder you look so well.'

He did look well. He looked tanned, which was not surprising, but there was a new readiness in his movements which spoke of freedom, as if he had drawn a line under past events and relegated them to history, his history. Cynthia, in her dim bedroom, was now a creature of memory, on whom he was not inclined to dwell.

'Do you know that part of the world at all?'

'No. No, I don't.'

'You should go. Cortona itself is a fascinating place. But it is the surroundings which constitute the real Italy.'

'Good weather?'

'Oh, yes, marvellous weather.'

'And you'll go again?'

'Yes, at Christmas. We've all been convened for Christmas.' He laughed deprecatingly. 'Not that I want to wear out my welcome.'

'I'm sure you won't do that.'

None of this was of much interest to me. Our exchanges were not half so fascinating as the conversation I was having with him in my head. Listen, Martin, I was saying. Let me tell you about yourself. He would have brightened: every man likes to hear about himself. You are a very attractive man, I should have said, but you are not a whole human being. You lack empathy. There is no feminine side to your nature that would enable you to understand women. Women seem to you totally unreasonable. From time to time you allow yourself to surrender to them, but you give the impression that you surrender against your will. The way to capture you is to torment you, as Cynthia did. Intemperate demands seem to you to be part of a woman's nature. Once you are miserably in chains you feel that you are doing all a man can do in the way of love and devotion. And to do you justice you play your part honourably. It does not occur to you to do more. In the act of love you behave like a man, and yet you express subtle reservations of which I think you are aware. These you accommodate by holding up your behaviour to the scrutiny of some terrifying tribunal, as if you will be excused if only you remind that tribunal how very noble your standards really are. And you are wordless afterwards, as if absorbed in the task of making your way back into a state of grace. You offer a great deal and withhold a great deal at the same time. You offer your attributes, your looks, your grace, even your social position. Women succumb eagerly, and are in turn baffled by your withdrawal into a sort of solitude. Everything you say – are saying – is of an extreme banality. You offered more information about yourself when you were legally tied. You find it more comfortable to operate under restraint. When Cynthia was alive you were dutiful, which pleased that same tribunal. I will not ask you how you feel, because you would not tell me. Your masochism, or perhaps it would be kinder to call it your impermeability, supplied your psychic needs. You were doing your duty; that was enough. The more overbearing the demands, the greater the spiritual satisfaction.

Now let me tell you what a woman wants. It may surprise you to know that you have never supplied this. Cynthia made the demands and you submitted, perhaps because it was time for you to do so. A woman wants more than that, wants ardour, an erotic eagerness that goes beyond the physical. The desire and pursuit of the whole. And also an unmasking, so that it will become possible to meet on every level. They call it commitment these days, but that sounds too legalistic. A woman does not want to be left alone to calculate her chances. All those clichés about waiting by the telephone are unfortunately true. There is perhaps an atavistic desire in women to be mastered, taken over, or at least to arouse some passion, if that is what passion is, if that is what you felt, or indeed feel, for you are here now. It was left to Cynthia, and no doubt to others, to enact the other half of the equation. I was always aware that there were satisfactions to be gleaned in pursuing this path, even though it is not really in a woman's nature to do so.

What I am saying is politically incorrect in the highest degree. I should be expelled from any women's co-operative for even thinking it. Your apparent virginity is your strongest suit. The more untouched a man appears to be the stronger the temptation to touch him, not only physically but emotionally. You no doubt hoped to find a woman as inviolate as yourself, but I'm afraid that is no longer on the cards. You may once have envisaged an angelic union, but even you are not proof against experience. Cynthia acted simply, in accordance with her eager curiosity. A kind of arrest took place; you shook your head ruefully and submitted. But you were not always comfortable until you were brought into line by your sense of duty. Imprisoned, you gave more of yourself. That has now come to an end: you are free. That is why I am hearing so much about the Italian countryside and the sunsets. You know why you are here, but something in your make-up refuses to acknowledge this.

If I were to love you I should be utterly defeated. Whatever you suspected – but we are not talking about feelings here – you would be careful to treat me as the merest acquaintance. If and when the danger were past, if you were to remarry, say, you might allow your reticence to subside: as virtual strangers once more we might become friends. You would feel no compunction in not caring for me, in not asking if I needed more than the very little you are prepared to give, or rather to lend, for however long it suited you. And I think that this arrangement does suit you for the moment; after all, I have asked for nothing, and you are therefore quite safe. It might also surprise you to know that when you are with me I feel lonely. Are we not two civilized grown-ups? Perhaps only one of us is civilized, and I can't yet decide which of us it is. You dismiss my complicity as unwomanly, not quite up to your cloudy standards. This gives you permission to be quite ruthless, in a way that once surprised me, but no longer does. No doubt you see me as a fallen creature: as I say, my transactions are simple. What I perhaps understand, as you do not, is that it is your behaviour that is aberrant rather than mine. I meant you to become a man once more, and I succeeded. But because you were not interested in understanding me, as I have tried to understand you, I am left with the feeling that I have comprehensively failed, simply by allowing you to succeed on your terms, within the very narrow parameters you have unilaterally allowed yourself to observe.

Naturally I said none of this. I had the wit to observe that it could not, perhaps should not, be said. I offered him more lemon tart, which he ate in a deliberately refined manner which effectively detached him from my presence. For some reason I kept my gaze lowered to the table: to look at him seemed indelicate. When I was sufficiently in command of myself I suggested lightly that we move into the other room. Here I looked out of the window, as if searching for some mythical evening star, which in any event could not be seen through the cloud, although that cloud was suffused, even slightly red, as though preparing itself for that brief episode of sunlight which would manifest itself early on the following morning. I wanted to be out in the evening air, under that timidly optimistic sky, before the darkness took hold. It was no kind of a sunset, unlike those convivial sunsets he had experienced in Italy, but it seemed more realistic, indecisive like myself, troubled by indistinct currents of acceptance and denial. It was the time of day when I reconciled myself to nothing further happening. If I took a walk, which I sometimes did, it was to prepare myself for the night, to put the day behind me, to participate in that general slowing down in which I could imagine the weariness of others, their desire to be at home. I willed myself to share this, as if there were some communality in observing the onset of the hours of rest. So strong was my wish to be alone that I even stood at the window, looking out, until the scrape of a match told me that Martin was lighting a cigarette, and that the main business of the night was still to come. Still jaunty from his recent holiday he seemed more at ease than I had ever known him to be, but in a way that excluded me, as I was now excluding him. The atmosphere in the room took on a certain tension. We both knew that he would stay, that he was not even in a hurry to leave, but that his mind was not on the matter in hand. And outside the window the bands of cloud seemed lit from below, shading from rose to a dark grey, as if anything could be expected in the way of weather, either some sun, as it was meant to appear, or a thorough drenching of rain, as was more likely.

'Do sit down,' I said. 'I'll make some coffee in a moment.'

'Thank you. That was a delicious meal.'

'I'm glad you enjoyed it.' My voice was as lifeless as if I were playing the part of a polite hostess in a bad play, and not playing it very well. 'You must tell me more,' I said, moving back towards the kitchen. 'I shan't be long.'

In the kitchen I noticed that my hands were shaking slightly, and it was with an effort that I reminded myself that I had not uttered those indiscreet remarks which would have utterly condemned me. Indeed I was behaving as he wanted me to behave, that is to say self-effacingly, betraying no resolute or challenging inclinations, enabling him to convince himself that he was not obliged to say or do anything that might sully the uncommitted evening. That it would end in the usual manner, safely in the dark, we both knew. What was required of me was that I should not allude to this. It did occur to me that he seemed more relaxed than usual; he was not offering any paternal advice, as he had once promised to do, was not even taking the trouble to furnish the silence that had inexplicably descended on me. I could hear him walking about the room, examining the books, as if he were in command of any situation that might arise. This new confidence puzzled me. I wished that I could feel the same. I wished that I could find the words to put us both at our ease, for although he seemed comfortable enough I was not. Again it was as I had thought earlier. Either he had no notion of what was required of him, or, if he had, had decided – quite equably – that he was under no obligation to me, or indeed to anyone else.

The smell of coffee restored me somewhat, and I drank mine gratefully and far too quickly, scalding my mouth. I almost wished that he would leave, or rather that I could disguise my general disappointment with the whole evening. The subject of Italy had been thoroughly exhausted, and there arose in my mind a memory of the tympanum of Autun cathedral, a photograph of which my mother had pasted in her album. The photograph was not very good: there had been a blanket of cloud even then. But my mother had been delighted. This almost pious memory was thoroughly out of place. Nevertheless I heard myself saying, 'I was thinking of taking a holiday myself.'

'Good idea,' he replied. 'It refreshes the mind, you know. I myself feel quite different.'

'You certainly seem different.'

'Do I?'

'Yes. Less burdened. Less sad.'

'I've come to some important decisions. The first, of course, is to get back to work. Everyone seems to be in favour of this . . .'

'And the others?'

'Well, Claire, this may be difficult for you to understand.'

'I'm listening.'

'I intend to live more . . . lightly.'

'You mean more selfishly.'

'If you care to put it that way.'

'A wise decision,' I said. 'Although it doesn't always work when the going gets heavy. When true emotion breaks through.'

'In my case true emotion died with Cynthia. I could never entertain those feelings again. Nor do I want to. No, the way ahead is through lightness. Seizing the moment.'

As he was now. This oblique reference to his presence here, in my company, was supposed to put an end to my inquiries.

'You'll marry again, of course.'

'I don't rule it out,' he said judiciously. 'I'll consider the possibility. It's not good to live alone.'

'I know. I live alone.'

'It's different for you. You're young. You'll find someone.'

'Maybe I have.' This, I knew, would not please him. As it did not.

I was acutely unhappy. An antipathy seemed to have sprung up between us which I had done nothing to provoke. Perhaps I provoked it simply by being myself. This is the hardest thing to bear: the knowledge that one has been found wanting, because one is simply one kind of person and not another. He would continue to visit me for as long as it suited him; from time to time I would receive a postcard in his tiny, almost furtive writing, or worse, I should have to write a letter, in an airy fashion, filled with routine observations, manufacturing news in which I now knew he would not be interested. Yet I could see that he would be the one to keep his comments light and neutral, that we should never have a decent conversation – for what we were engaged in was not a conversation; it was a statement of intent. He was moving about the room as if newly energized, as if some secret enthusiasm were being entertained. I wondered briefly if he was thinking of a member of that Italian houseparty. That would make sense: a woman friend of the host, or rather of the hostess, detailed off to cultivate him, to sympathize. She would have been intrigued, as most women would be intrigued, by his appearance, his sensitivity. I saw now that this must have happened. And she would have had the wit, which I no longer had, to treat him with comradely effervescence, since that was what he wanted, so that they would have parted on excellent terms, promising to meet from time to time, with no obligations on either side. That was why he had so enjoyed his holiday. Eulogies to the sunset and the delights of Cortona were neither here nor there, though I did not doubt that they had enhanced the pleasure.

'Tell me what you look for in a woman,' I said.

'Oh, I'm no judge of women. I've always had a certain

amount of difficulty with women. Until I met Cynthia, that is. She seemed to me so entirely feminine.'

'But she can't have been the first woman you knew. There must have been others.'

'I suppose so. But I lived on my own for quite a while, you know. And I had my work.'

'Which you still have. Or rather which you will have once more.'

'Yes, I'm looking forward to that. In a week or so I'll start going through my papers again. They're still in the same box files in the flat.'

'Will you stay in the flat?'

'I'm not at all sure. It was Cynthia's flat, you see. So many memories. I could hardly bring anyone else there.'

So he had got that far, I saw. He had outdistanced me. There was no point in my hating him; it was already too late for me to do that. The woman in Italy had obviously operated some miracle cure, or perhaps it was the complicity of the host and hostess, indeed of everyone concerned, that had shown him another kind of compliance. I looked around in despair. The plain furnishings of the living-room mocked me with their very plainness. A sort of life was possible within these confines, but it was a life that could hardly attract others. It had a certain appeal, but that appeal was modest. It was a room in which everything had fallen short of expectation, a room still imprinted with the presence of my disappointed father, my disappointed mother. Suddenly I was filled with love for them both, and this was new to me. I saw that they had made the best of things, had done their duty, that theirs were tame lives, but lives that they had managed for themselves. No one had removed them to an idyllic setting and slyly proposed an alternative to their undoubted celibacy. Although their minds were troubled by the burdens that had been laid upon them their consciences were clear. Or rather their collective conscience, for there were no interlopers. Their marriage was so utterly unpromising that it had forged them into a sort of partnership, in which resignation and recognition formed a not altogether ironic bond.

I should never know such simplicity, but then again neither would Martin. I could see that he was ready once more to be preyed upon, to be acquisitioned. Other women would have Cynthia's skills, although hers had been strikingly old-fashioned. No doubt these had been updated. I felt at one with the room, plain, underfurnished, making no claims, offering no attractions. I became newly self-conscious, pulled down my skirt, wondered why I had not changed my shoes for a smarter pair.

'Do sit down,' I said again. 'You are very restless. You were telling me what qualities you looked for in a woman.'

'You mean you were asking me.'

'All right, I was asking you.'

'I don't think it would be right for me to tell you.'

'Why on earth not?'

'Because I know that whatever I said would bring back the memory of Cynthia.'

'And you're trying not to think of her so much?'

'Her memory never leaves me.'

'So anyone else would have to be different?'

'Very different. That way I should never be disloyal.'

'Make no mistake, Martin. You will be disloyal in the long run. Everyone is.'

His mouth tightened with anger. I looked at him with dismay. Why was I ruining my own chances in this way? Perhaps because I saw those chances dwindling, because I was no longer that disinterested friend but was newly revealed as an adversary. And it was true that I now wanted to goad him, to wring some sort of confession out of him, to have all his weakness for myself rather than see it so lightly displayed. Men always want to start again with a clean slate, as women never do. I should have had the confidence I had gleaned from previous affairs; now I was obliged to consider the faulty nature of my own position. He had not perceived my true nature, my inconvenient and quite undisclosed longing for permanence, for the permanence of someone's affections. I did not know how to deal with this newly defensive man who, as if to demonstrate his defensiveness, was sitting on the very edge of his chair. Throughout the evening he had not asked me a single question about myself. This was what his emancipation amounted to, an ability to ignore another's expectations.

'She will have to be very young, your ideal woman,' I said, collecting the coffee cups. 'No woman with normal experience could meet your demands.'

'But I have no demands. I make no demands upon others. I am merely not ruling out possibilities. I intend to have an orderly life. I shall work. I hardly think that is a punishable offence.'

'Not the work, certainly.'

I heard these words with horror, as if I were now openly reproaching him. Yet he seemed if anything energized by the prospect, or perhaps the prospects, open to him. It was as if I had served my purpose as a transitional object or system, and, having proved unsatisfactory, had given him tacit permission to move on. He even seemed to me slightly manic in this new manifestation, while I sank into a dullness from which I could only be rescued by another's generosity. I even wondered whether I liked him. But perhaps all women feel this spurt of antagonism towards a partner who excludes them.

'You go through,' I said. 'I'll just wash these cups.'

I lingered in the kitchen, even looked longingly out of the window, although it was now quite dark and there was nothing to be seen. I was conscious that I had embarked unwittingly on something like self-exposure. I had said nothing that was overtly revealing, but I had been unsympathetic; I had withheld approval. Worse, I had said nothing that was not true, but in return I had encountered a form of dissimulation which had made giant strides since our last meeting. I thought again of the woman in Italy, and gave a brief instinctive shake of the head. The explanation did not lie in this incident, whether or not it ever took place. It lay in something much more present, something that had not yet been enacted. What this was I could not make out: the connection was missing. Perhaps my dismay was more general than I supposed. I was disheartened, to the point of dread, that I could no longer see my way ahead. I thought I had lost him, as if he were in some way mine to lose. The display put on for my benefit was unmistakable, yet I had done nothing to provoke it. I had not gone beyond the role he had written for me. Maybe I should have been coarser, but such behaviour was anathema to me. Part of the awful fascination of Cynthia was that she was a bully. That kind of bullying can only be practised successfully within marriage, and I dare say it has its own satisfactions. These remained, and would remain, unknown to me. All I could present was a smiling receptive demeanour, not so much forgiving of a behaviour which I now saw as unconscionable, so much as mildly interested, no more than that. Lightness, he had emphasized, but he was really stating his terms. I wondered if it were already too late to take note of this.

Later, in the middle of the night, I said, 'You really hate anyone to see you with your guard down, don't you?'

Incensed, he turned on his side, his back to me. When I woke up again he was gone.

[18]

In late August the leaves begin to fall; the darkness sets in earlier; the mornings are more shadowy. My bedroom smelled of sleep, although I still got up at an unnecessary hour and cleaned the flat vigorously, as if expecting a visitor. I spent most of the day in one park or another, putting off the time when this would no longer be possible. It occurred to me that one could spend an entire holiday in Hyde Park, emerging perhaps for lunch, only to relinquish the crowded streets gratefully for a long uninterrupted afternoon which would, eventually, make some sense of going home. Instinctively I avoided art galleries. Art is supposed to console, although it does nothing of the kind. Religion, I suspect, is merely an unhelpful comment on the circumstances in which I now found myself. One might, if one were a believer, and even more if one were not, be inclined to complain, to send up even more vain petitions in the hope of receiving a word of affirmation that one were not hopelessly adrift. That this would never come, had never come, would induce a bewilderment which was surely not in the scheme of things, or indeed in anyone's interest. Even the most subtle explanations could not convince me that some lives, and not others, are destined to be unfulfilled. One hears of charmed lives, and may even have witnessed them: a friend blessed with looks, and intelligence, and determination, and a reasonable endowment in the way of family background that will cast doubt on one's own poor efforts. Such characters bring out the worst in one, and perhaps the worst realization of all is that there is no consolation.

One day I walked, almost idly, to the shop, only to find it closed and a notice on the door which read: 'Under new management. Re-opening in September.' I knew that I should present myself then, but I began to doubt that I should ever be able to summon up the requisite insouciance. No matter: I was not in a position to choose my effects. I should humbly and straightforwardly ask for a job, and perhaps they would take me on. I reasoned that the father would have retired to his fishing activities, leaving the son in charge. I should have to work on the son, which should not be too difficult, although I suspected that the father would be a different proposition altogether. The trouble was that I had no means of knowing about any of this. There was no one I could ask. I telephoned Marchmont Street more than once and got no reply, from which I concluded that Muriel and Hester had already left. Doris, outside the café, could no doubt have filled me in, but I was not yet so desperate as to seek her out. Nor could I face the café itself, which would already have forgotten my early morning visits, so regular, for so long a time, and so abruptly terminated.

I felt a hesitation that amounted to shame that I had no decent excuses to offer that kind proprietor: besides, all I could supply was a lame explanation that the shop was in effect under new management – which they already knew – and that I might be going back in the autumn, which commercial shrewdness might incline them to doubt. I had the uneasy sense of having been outmanoeuvred by everyone in the case, even by Muriel, whom I instantly forgave. Muriel was too tired, too stricken to worry about a maverick such as myself, whose youth was thought to protect her against the blows of fate. I thought a lot about fate in those long afternoons in the park. The scheming restless gods of Olympus, preoccupied by their love affairs, seemed to me a far more accurate reflection of the world as we know it, than a deity who purports to be benevolent but who is in fact indifferent, unreachable, at least by those who feel they have no claim other than their own human need.

Little by little I was becoming accustomed to my own strange idleness. I made no attempt to find a job, having fixed my sights on the shop ever since it had become unavailable to me. In the same way I became accustomed to Martin's absence, while all the time keeping myself in readiness for him. I was aware that I had not behaved well, had, ever since we had met, exerted undue influence. I had no real business in his life. Everything separated us: his age, his status as a widower, his utter refusal to question his own motives and behaviour. I did not even answer his needs, for he repudiated me at the same time as he succumbed to that undue influence. I did not even blame him: that was how bereft I felt. And yet I knew, unhappily, that what I had been denied was part of his strategy, so that I should not come to rely on him or expect anything in the way of help or support. Even expectation was thereby ruled out. Such prudence disgusted me; such dishonesty puzzled me. He was perfectly entitled to stake his temporary claim, as I had done so often, but to do so, and to deny that he was doing so, effectively reduced me to less than nothing, to someone who was perhaps useful in a very limited capacity but who could be discarded, without prejudice, when life proposed other opportunities, other invitations, other partners. I represented the shabby side of his nature and was therefore unpalatable. It did occur to me to resent this from time to time, but in fact I was so preoccupied by my own failure – my inactivity, my solitude – that I accepted this particular failure as of right. I blamed myself for imposing my own expectations on him, although those expectations were inalienably mine; presumably I was free to dispose of them as I thought fit. But the sad truth was that those expectations had not been met, and while Martin had remained in character I had somehow slipped out of mine, so that I was now wistful where I had once been energetic, uncertain where I had once been sceptical, and apologetic where I was accustomed to feeling confident.

I went over my remarks and judged them tactless, as he had. I had already reached that point at which the other's opinion of one seals one's fate, so that imperceptibly one agrees with the other's reactions, joins in the other's faint responses to one's own identity, discards or loses that identity for the foreseeable future, or until one's common sense alerts one to the danger. In this state of mind reason is simply unavailable. I told myself that it would be better if I never saw him again. In some ways it was a relief that he had not got in touch; his absence in a way concealed my disappointment. That was why I spent so much time away from home, in the park, where no one would find me or think of looking for me. When I got back to the flat I would make a cup of tea, and sit down and drink it quite normally before picking up my messages. In that fashion I could persuade myself that all of this was unimportant, that shortly I would put my life back on the right track again, go away, return to the shop, and pick up where I left off. I also knew that an unsatisfactory or unfinished love affair can banish normality for some time, and that it was incumbent on me not to indulge in speculation but to dismiss the whole episode as one of those aberrations that unfortunately afflict one from time to time and for which one is hardly responsible, since the gods, or the fates, or the furies, are merely going about their usual business of disorganizing human affairs according to their inscrutable remit. Nevertheless, when I looked at the clock I would see that it was time for me to have my bath and wash my hair, so that I could be found, should anyone care to find me, in my usual place, at the usual time, and perhaps for something more than the usual exchange. Friendship, some sort of trust, was what I wanted, and I was prepared to spend the evening on my own, entertaining thoughts of what such friendship might lead to, until it was time to cancel such fantasies for another day and go to bed.

I said none of this to Wiggy. I knew she would be dismayed, even as I was dismayed, and I still had enough pride to behave as I had always behaved, that is to say flippantly, uncensoriously, tactfully. We had long ago adopted tact as the right way to go about things. We did not confide in each other in the way women are supposed to; we each knew the other's cast of characters, and that was enough. We informed each other of our prospective absences; we kept in close touch, and I dare say we knew each other as well as two people who had never exchanged a single guilty secret could do. Wiggy's life was more populated than mine; she had these dutiful cousins who seemed to welcome her each year with something like proper affection, the familial kind, and above all she had this lover, whom I had never met, of whom I disapproved because I thought she deserved better. And yet she was happy enough with his visits, kept a bottle of wine always ready should he drop in, was reassured by his telephone calls, seemed content to paint other people's children all day at her kitchen table, and to exchange news with me when I visited her. I had fallen into these visits as a more satisfactory way of keeping in touch; in my mind the telephone was being kept clear for another's call. Besides I was always out and Wiggy was always in, so what more natural than my haphazard visits? She knew of my worries about the shop, which formed the main subject of conversation; like myself she knew the value of work. But I said nothing about that mournful conviction I had that I had failed where so many others had succeeded, nor did she know about my empty evenings, when some sort of vain hope surfaced, as if I had always nurtured such a hope, and was still, even now, not entirely discouraged by the fact that it had not yet been met.

I found Wiggy in her usual place at the table, studying the photograph of a hopefully smiling little girl of about three. The child seemed to be baring her teeth more in obedience to some offstage urgings than from personal conviction that this was a happy occasion.

'One can see,' said Wiggy, 'that all is not right with this child.'

'How so?'

'The desperate glint in her eye. The fatal desire to please already apparent.'

I studied the photograph. All I could see was that the child was overweight, a fact emphasized by the fat legs stuffed into lace tights and the velvet dress bunched round her nonexistent waist.

'You'll have a job doing that lace,' I said.

'I'm only doing her head. Just as well; she's going to be large. This is an attempt by her grandmother to remember her as she always was, or rather as the grandmother would like her to remain. I see trouble ahead for them both, misplaced love on both sides.'

'Why misplaced? Surely at that age love is not self-seeking?'

'I'm not sure about that. There is already a fatal gleam of knowledge in that child. Her name is Arabella, by the way. And her grandmother, Mrs Corbett, intuits it in a way that the parents perhaps do not.'

'Maybe Mrs Corbett objects to her daughter-in-law. Maybe there have been unwise criticisms.'

'Exactly so. It was Mrs Corbett who got in touch with me, of course, recommended by one of her friends. We had a meeting. She was very proper, very formal, but her hands trembled. She said she didn't see the child as much as she had hoped, because the child's mother didn't wish it. After that she spent half an hour telling me that perhaps – she said perhaps – they had different views on child management, that Arabella needed a more stable background than her mother was able to provide. She became quite agitated as she said this, although as far as I could judge the mother's only crime was to go out to work. Mrs Corbett had offered to look after Arabella in the daytime, but the offer had been refused. "I bought her that dress," she said. " And the tights." I told her I only did the heads, and she was a bit disappointed. Then she said, " Just as long as you capture her lovely smile." She clearly didn't want to part with the photograph, but she knew, she said, that the portrait would keep her company, even during those days when the child and she were denied access to each other.'

'Poor little girl,' I said. 'She has been introduced to family dissension. She has learned that one must love all equally, but some more equally than others.'

'I shall do my very best for her,' said Wiggy. 'For them both. Tea?'

'Thanks. I feel even more sorry for Mrs Corbett than for Arabella,' I remarked. 'Anyone could see that that dress would be dead wrong. She will probably go on buying her unsuitable clothes and unsuitable presents until the girl goes to school, to university, gets a job. These gifts will be acknowledged, but no more. All this will be laid at the mother's door; the original dislike will be intensified. And the child will throw off this inconvenient love; she will have to if she's not to be a family hostage. In time she will train as a psychotherapist, simply in order to explain all this to herself.'

'Oh, really, Claire. I doubt if it's as bad as that. She's only three, remember. You don't look all that well, if I may say so, despite your afternoons in the park.'

'Or possibly because of them. I feel at one with all the pensioners and the unemployed who probably spend the same sort of day as I do now.'

'It's the shop, isn't it?'

I agreed that it was the shop that was making me downcast. Arabella's hopeful face, all teeth showing, gazed insistently into mine until Wiggy removed the photograph and set down two cups of tea and a plate of chocolate biscuits.

'I'm sure the situation can be retrieved, particularly if you time it right. If you go in looking carefree and capable they'll jump at the chance of having you back. Just don't plead. Be offhand, as if you might be in a position to do them a favour. Look as if you don't need the money, as if the last thing you want is a job.'

'Easy to say.'

'But it works, Claire. Indifference puts people on their mettle. People who set out to please don't know this. One must put on an act. And you don't even have to, which should make it easier. After all . . .'

'Yes, I know all that. How anyone would jump at the chance of having me.' I managed to smile as I said this, and hoped that my smile was convincing. 'I probably need a break,' I said. 'Although I don't really want to go away. My place is here, with all the other unemployed. Very few children in the park, incidentally. I suppose they're on holiday. And yet you'd think that some children would love the freedom of the park, boys, probably, living in flats. Their mothers could send them out in the morning with a packet of sandwiches and their bus fare, and they'd probably do as well as children transported to Italian villas, like all those politicians' kids, and look just as healthy when it was time to go back to school.'

'You need a proper holiday, Claire. You're not exactly down and out, even if you pretend to be.'

'Have you still got Eileen's archive?'

'Certainly.' She went to the drawer and produced Eileen's travel leaflets. 'Take your pick.'

One could trace Eileen's trajectory through the diminishing claims of the brochures, as Shakespeare's country (by coach) replaced Biarritz and Budapest. Both were wrong for her, but she had not gone there anyway. Instead a valetudinarian preoccupation had crept in, as if her health must be catered for should anything go wrong, as she may have suspected. That was how Vichy came to be there, either because it promised an almost nursing-home regime, with plenty of doctors in attendance, or because the brochure contained recommendations from English visitors who had come back rejuvenated. 'Hotel Victoria, rue des Carmes,' ran one comment: 'a haven of tranquillity. English spoken. Evening meal not provided, but café next door. Hire of bicycle possible.'

'That's probably what attracted her,' I told Wiggy. 'I feel I know the Hotel Victoria already. And the rue des Carmes, which is considerably off the beaten track. The haven of tranquillity is disturbed in the early morning by the rattle of the shutters going up at the café next door, and no doubt by the motorbike of the owner's son. The room itself will be a distillation of all the hotel rooms one has ever stayed in, that is to say that the last occupant will have left his imprint on the atmosphere. There will be an adjoining bathroom, but no soap. And the owners, so happy to welcome English visitors, will no doubt manage to convey a wish that those visitors do not loiter in their rooms but get out into the town or in fact anywhere where they will immediately become invisible. Walks by the river, the Allier, will be recommended. And of course the waters may be taken.'

The sheer tedium of such a visit exerted a perverse appeal. 'I'll go there,' I said.

'Don't be silly, Claire. Go to Paris, buy yourself some clothes.'

'No, I mean it. I feel too provincial for Paris. Not outgoing enough. I should appreciate some sort of backwater.'

'You're depressed about the shop. Don't be. I'm sure it'll all work out.'

I stopped only because I sensed Wiggy's impatience. I swept the leaflets and brochures together and said, 'You might as well get rid of these. Nobody is going to use them.'

'What will you do?'

'I'll go to Paris and get the first train out, it hardly matters which. I'll go wherever it takes me. That way I'll have done something positive.'

She brightened. 'You'll let me know what you decide?'

'Of course. Don't I always?'

But I was conscious of a lack of candour, although Wiggy, I think, did not perceive this. I did not tell her about Martin, for reasons that had more to do with instinct than pride, or its converse, shame. As far as Wiggy was concerned Martin was an acquaintance whom we had once encountered in bizarre circumstances and with whom we had not kept in touch. I did not want to unburden myself to her, as if we were fellow conspirators in the mating game. I did not even want to talk to a woman, however close. I thought that only a man could explain me to myself. I wanted one of those conversations that women like to initiate and which men tend to dismiss. Such conversations are usually unwise, but one embarks on them with a dreadful eagerness, regardless of the other's closed expression. With Martin, of course, one would have to battle with his own self-absorption before such a conversation could take place. He would feel that his dignity was impugned by the mere fact of listening. He had established that his feelings were paramount, whatever they were. He had issued a policy statement to that effect. I did not want to tell Wiggy that I was bewildered, and in any event I doubt if I could have found the words to describe my condition, which was basically regretful, as if I had been found out in a fault. The fault was undoubtedly mine, but I wanted to have it explained to me by the only person in a position to do so. I should have listened respectfully; probably the words once spoken would be fatal, terminal. Silence, maybe years of silence, must follow such an exchange. But if it does not take place the alternative is worse. One may ask oneself questions for the rest of one's life, and still receive no answers.

I felt a sense of disloyalty to Wiggy, for I knew that this was a friendship that would last, whereas others might fail, might indeed already have failed, but the instinct that makes a woman want to attach herself to a man was uppermost. I wanted to explore that instinct, to embrace it, until it was time to face the world, triumphantly partnered. This is where women part company; friendships are never quite the same when affections have been redistributed. I wandered home, rather regretting my visit. I should have stayed in the park, where no one suspected me of duplicity. And then it went against my nature to be indifferently honest, not to present an open mind, which meant a mind open to all. Candour is a primordial virtue, though it can lead one into difficulties, as I well knew. I felt physically uncomfortable with anything less, which was why I made so many disastrous mistakes. Strange how what is recommended by all the authorities can prove to be one's undoing. Different values should no doubt be taught, for if they are not one learns them too late for them to be of any use to one. Those gods of Olympus, with their enviable lack of conscience, are probably the ones to emulate. Their reputation has not noticeably suffered from their unashamed preoccupation with sex and influence. We who have been taught to love our enemies, sometimes to the detriment of our friends, will always be sunk in a morass of self-questioning, timorous restraint taking the place of robust self-interest. Wiggy had thought that I was depressed about the shop. Indeed I was, but I had other concerns. She may have sensed this, but had had the grace not to probe. In time I should probably tell her everything; the time might come when I should need to. For the time being, however, I preferred concealment. Perhaps for the first time in my life I did not understand myself. Nor did I altogether want to.

The air in the streets seemed heavy, stale, as if everyone had breathed out at the same time. Maybe it would not be a bad idea to go away, to catch that first train standing at the station, to end up in Venice or in Madrid, carefree and unprejudiced, as I had once been. A few days' absence could hardly affect my chances, my ultimate goal. And then I could write to Martin – I still avoided the telephone – and tell him that I was going on holiday, like everyone else. This would provoke some response or other. Eventually my traveller's tales would match his, put me on a new footing. This seemed so obvious that I wondered why I had not thought of it before. On the following morning I would consult my continental timetables. The pain of leaving, which I always suffered, was already slightly mitigated by the anticipation of arriving. I was on my way once more.

[19]

Every day that elusive sun stood lower in the sky, in the brief interval before it disappeared altogether. Every day the trees in the park appeared more immobile, solid blocks of dark green, as if they were not subject to change, despite the evidence of leaves fallen on to the ground beneath them. The summer was over, and as if to demonstrate the fact familiar faces began to reappear in my neighbourhood. I thought that I should tell some of these people that I was going away, knocked on a few doors in Montagu Mansions, and announced my imminent departure. This information was more or less kindly received, although as I was habitually out all day there was a slight air of surprise that told me that my absence would not be remarked upon. This exercise was undertaken mainly to convince myself. I went about my preparations as if for the benefit of a whole army of observers. I collected foreign currency of all denominations – who knew where that phantom train would be taking me? – and half-heartedly put a few garments aside to take to the cleaners. I was not concerned with my appearance. I knew that in that foreign city, wherever it turned out to be, I should pass unnoticed. I did not really wish it otherwise, for this was a calculated absence, undertaken merely in relation to a convincing return. What plans I made were for that return, rather than for days in which I should wander among crowds like an ordinary holidaymaker, not even sightseeing, but attaching myself to any group of people who seemed to know where they were going.

None of this mattered, for it was being done for a purpose. Fixed firmly in my mind was the notion that this was necessary apprenticeship for a kind of reinstatement. I could do nothing with the time at my disposal, but in the darker days to come I should somehow have recovered a sense of intention, of busyness, and above all of pleasure. I calculated that within a few months – or weeks if I were particularly fortunate – I should have secured my old job. This did not seem impossible. Rather more problematic was the question of Martin, from whom I had not heard. I accepted this: I knew somehow that the pattern had been set, that he would recognize my overtures as coming from myself alone, leaving him utterly free of calculation. His conscience demanded this, whereas my own conscience was troubled only slightly by the conviction that such precautions were totally unnecessary, were in fact aberrant, and that affection (I used that word even to myself) had no need of such artifice but should spring from a natural desire for company, for conversation, and finally for closeness. I put it no higher than that, not even to myself.

But one night I had a disquieting dream. I was in a wide street which I could not identify. Some paces in front of me was Martin, but a Martin whom I did not know, Martin as a much younger man, with dishevelled hair and a livelier step. I could see him quite clearly: he wore an open-necked shirt, which was out of character, and he appeared to be skipping along and humming to himself. I managed to catch up with him and put my hand on his arm; he shook it off, but I took no notice. I was trying to engage him in some sort of colloquy. Do you remember so-and-so? I said, but he looked at me as if I were a stranger, before taking off again, with that curiously insouciant step. He soon outdistanced me but I kept him within my sights, so that we both made our discordant way down that broad street, Martin ahead, myself following vainly behind. From time to time I flung out a question, but received no response. I was as impressed as if he were some exotic stranger whose presence I had been appointed to monitor; he meanwhile appeared to be in genuine ignorance of the fact that I was in the vicinity, as he made his curiously youthful way along the edge of the pavement, like a boy playing a game. A wind ruffled both his hair and his shirt but left my own hair untouched, as if I had no corporeal body, or at least not one like his. We were both invisible to other passers-by, from which I concluded that this was indeed a dream. Yet when I finally awoke it was in a state of some agitation, as if I could still see that untroubled skipping figure in front of me, his fair looks quite familiar and unmistakable, but somehow translated into a past to which I had no access, as if he were a boy again, while I had grown older, older than the age I was now, in the present, and obliged to keep a watch on him and to work out the enormous conundrum of his good humour, as revealed by his carelessness, a physical carelessness which in fact was against his nature, and his self-absorption, so great that it prevented him from responding to my overtures.

Somehow, as I bathed and dressed, I knew that this lack of response had a cause, and that cause was even more worrying than the dream itself. I saw that his preoccupation occluded my presence altogether. Even my hand on his arm had had no weight; he did not so much shrug it off as cause it to disappear, and my questions met with no response because he quite naturally could not hear them. My conscious mind furnished the dream with more detail, as if it contained evidence that I had only to examine in order to arrive at a full explanation. Thus to the open-necked shirt and disordered hair were added grey flannel trousers and brown leather sandals, such as schoolboys used to wear, so that I knew that this was a genuine survival of his younger self. I had seen no signs of this in the straitlaced and immaculately presented person I thought I knew, but I recognized this younger self as somehow authentic. As was his deafness to my questions. This I did recognize as coming within the realm of fact, although in real life my questions had been anodyne enough, if not particularly well received. My final impression was that Martin in the dream had proved untouchable, since his thoughts eluded me, were in fact his own, jealously guarded, and therefore unknowable.

But this explanation did not fully convince me, since the figure in the dream had had a vague smile of pleasure on his lips, so that whatever took place in his untouchable head had to do with anticipation rather than with recollection. I had no reason for arriving at this conclusion. It was simply that, throughout the morning, I remembered my hand being shrugged from his arm, and my feeling of surprise that this was so easily accomplished, not so much from a lack of scruple or delicacy, as entirely naturally, as one might brush a hair from one's face. There was no human importunity in that gesture of mine, nor was there any motive behind his rejection of it. And indeed the whole dream had been so brief, resolving itself into an image of disconnected progress along a street which was unknown to me, that I had no clue as to its final significance. And yet when I had woken I had moved my head uneasily from side to side on my pillow, as if to eradicate it. It proved difficult to dislodge. Yet in the daytime, with the assistance of that brief shaft of sunlight, I castigated myself. If I were now to become superstitious, in addition to all my other preoccupations, I was in a bad way. The hour and a half it somehow took to book my ticket put paid to this. Reality, it seemed, still had enough power to put fantasy to flight. A woman trod heavily on my foot as I was leaving the travel agency. On that sort of reality one could always rely.

The letter that I wrote to Martin was brief, airy, and non-specific. It merely stated that I should be away for a few days, but that I hoped to see him before I left. For a few moments this letter seemed to resolve various problems: it set the seal on my departure, and it signified a forthcoming meeting with Martin, not the boyish contented Martin of the dream but the fearfully divided man whose mentality now began to trouble me. I should almost have preferred him to have the characteristics of the early dreamed figure, although I knew that this was impossible, and that the earlier Martin would not have known me anyway. Posting the letter gave me an access of energy, as if I could now start anticipating a future which would bring him once again into my orbit.

I had planned to leave on the Wednesday of the following week. If I had heard nothing by Saturday I should overcome my reluctance and telephone him. There was no good reason why I had not done this before, apart from my suspicion that he would do his best to avoid anything like direct confrontation, that he was a man who was at a disadvantage when interrupted, and that he genuinely disliked the privacy of his home being disturbed. With this last I could sympathize: the flat was only truly mine when it was silent and preferably empty, ready to receive me when I returned in the early evening, and maintaining its own mysterious integrity while I was absent. Also it seemed entirely in keeping that this cautious and exploratory approach should suit both of us, for I had become more tentative since knowing him, while he would, for reasons of his own, prefer to exert control in the matter of accepting or refusing an invitation. It occurred to me to wonder whether his other friends – those Fosters, for example – observed such restrictions. I rather thought not. He had come to them with a clean record, whereas his association with me was unwise. At least that was how he saw it. I found such behaviour absurd. I was unhappy that my calculations outran his, that was all. I had hoped that we might meet at the weekend, spend time as other people spent time, although I was not quite clear on this point. I might have envisaged a holiday together had I not foreseen the utter impossibility of this ever taking place. I castigated my imagination for misleading me, as it sometimes did. My mind, like most people's minds, was a mixture of instinct, information, and ignorance, all entirely characteristic. And in addition there was that intriguing area of detritus that came to the fore in sleep. Such dreams as I had, and I had very few, proved surprisingly difficult to dislodge, though this did not persuade me that they were in any way meaningful. I marvelled rather at the images than at what they signified. I myself had only a shadow existence in these dreams, whereas those of whom I was dreaming were endowed with an alarming distinction, as if enjoying another life of which I knew nothing but into which I had somehow gained an unnerving insight. Thus the characters who people one's dreams are revealed as strangers, and strangers, moreover, who have no interest in oneself, even though one is the agent behind all their movements. In the act of dreaming it is impossible to consider oneself the prime mover. More often one is the victim of circumstance, unsuitably dressed, missing the train, enrolled in the wrong examination, vainly requesting help that is not forthcoming, whereas those who make a random appearance seem to enjoy a more substantial existence. I tried in vain to repeat my dream but was not able to do so. Again reality proved too strong: I had received no answer to my letter and I had not made my telephone call. I told myself that the following day, Sunday, would be more propitious, since time is different, more permissive, on a Sunday. Perhaps I was even enjoying the anticipation. In any event I held back.

But when I eventually made the call and still received no answer I told myself that he was away for the weekend, probably in Dorset, and set out once more for the park. This was to be a valedictory occasion since I should not care to repeat it in the colder days to come, in which other, more superior activities might be adumbrated. This had one unforeseen advantage: it turned England into a foreign country which I should soon leave in search of other heartlands. In fact I paid little attention to what I saw, merely noting the preponderance of decorous Asian families, and the curious effect of silence from the unmoving trees standing sentinel over the seats on which few people took their ease. A light rain came on half-way through the afternoon and I retraced my steps thankfully, for I had had enough of the tired grass and the stony paths. My ability to envisage other lives had more or less deserted me, vanquished perhaps by what seemed the stronger reality of my disturbing dream. At least I had registered it as disturbing, whereas in fact it was merely dreamlike. On waking I had instinctively and uneasily moved my head from side to side, before abruptly turning over as if in search of further sleep. No sleep had come, and I had remained uncomfortably wakeful for the rest of the night. Only the act of writing the letter had provided some relief, and I could see that letter now, on the mat in Weymouth Street, where there was no one to pick it up, open it, and read it.

In an instant, and without any warning, came the conviction that I could not, should not, contact him again, that it was not in my gift to solicit his company but merely his to grant it from time to time. My letter was explicit enough: he could respond to it or not as he thought fit. This caused me some confusion, but also a better recognition of the circumstances. I had somehow failed to make the transition from acquaintance to familiar, and further eagerness on my part would be counter-productive. I did not know myself in this new manifestation, but recognized it as appropriate. Want is not always met; only an empty Sunday afternoon intensifies one's own emptiness, as busier more ordinary days do not. I was eager now to leave in order to come back and start again. The intervening time seemed utterly devoid of interest. Cultural pursuits must now fill my brief horizon, and if I paid them little attention, as I knew I should, I should nevertheless appreciate them for furnishing information which I might yet put to advantage. In this way I could provide the sort of conversation best indicated in the circumstances, with no reference to more personal inclinations, and, even if I were given a further opportunity, no leading questions.

As I went up the steps of Montagu Mansions loud jocose laughter heralded the downward approach of Mrs Dilnot, one of the neighbours whom I had warned of my impending departure. She was one of my favourites, a tall commanding elderly woman with a face enlivened by various carelessly applied colours. She was accompanied by her niece, who usually put in an appearance on a Sunday, largely to monitor and report on Mrs Dilnot's progress into an increasingly eccentric old age.

'Ah, Claire, there you are. Not gone yet?'

'No, I go on Wednesday.'

'You know Rosemary, don't you? My sister's girl.'

The girl in question was probably in her late fifties, with grey hair and a pleasant lined face. If I were not mistaken she viewed her Sunday attendance as less of a chore than a stimulant. Mrs Dilnot was uninhibited, verging on the outrageous, a woman who had seen off three husbands to whom she made no reference.

'We're off to our usual gambling hell.'

'Your bridge club?'

'Yes. The delights of old age, bridge and the telly. Mark you, old age has something to be said for it. You can ignore all health warnings, for one thing. You can drink, smoke, take pills, eat butter, lie in the sun; it doesn't matter a damn. My life took on a new meaning when I decided to devote it to idle degeneracy. And do you know, Claire, I didn't hear a word of criticism. Which proves what I've always maintained: it's the virtuous who get it in the neck.'

'True.'

'So you're off to the south of France?'

'Well, no, I thought . . .'

'Oh, I could tell you a thing or two about the adventures I've had, but I don't want to shock Rosemary.'

Rosemary smiled patiently, having heard it all before.

'Juan les Pins, Cap Ferrat, Antibes – I know them well. I'd take off, just like you, after my first divorce. I went alone, but I didn't remain alone for long, I can tell you. There was always someone with a yacht, always someone to bring my drinks, someone to stay up all night with, if you take my meaning.'

'I don't suppose I . . .'

'Oh, make the most of it, why don't you? You're young, nice-looking. And you were so good to your mother. You deserve a little fun.'

Mrs Dilnot had, as usual, drunk a few glasses of wine with her lunch, unlike Rosemary, who was presumably present to make sure that her aunt did not commit any indiscretions that would go down badly in Montagu Mansions. In the mornings Mrs Dilnot was entirely presentable, supporting herself on her stick, her brilliant poncho concealing her imposing bosom. After her regulation excursion to the shops she was more or less invisible for the rest of the day. What she did was no concern of mine or indeed of the rest of the tenants, although the day could not be far off when she would pass out in an inconvenient place, when a rescue mission would have to be mounted, an ambulance called. In hospital, deprived of her usual beverage, and with no one to listen to her reminiscences of the Riviera, she would die. I reckoned she must be the same age as Muriel Collier, and the comparison did Muriel no favours. Interestingly, she looked as ruined as Muriel, which proves that no regime, however hedonistic, protects one from the outrageous depredations of old age. My mother, who had lived an entirely spotless life, had looked like a girl well into her sixties, but during her last illness her face had collapsed inwards, less from pain than from consciousness that she had wasted the time allotted to her. I had been told that I looked like her, information that contained a warning that only I could appreciate. Mrs Dilnot, in her violently patterned tunics, her trousers, her scarves, and her broad-brimmed hats, was evidently not going gentle into that good night. One could only silently applaud, and resolve to follow her example.

'Buy some new clothes while you're away,' she was saying. 'You must make the most of your looks while there's still time. I'm always telling Rosemary the same thing.' She looked disparagingly at her niece, and shook her head. 'Not that it's any use. There's a man at the club who's made it quite clear that he'd like to know her better but she takes no notice. I told him he'd have better luck with me.' She gave a coarse laugh. 'Well, we mustn't keep you. Enjoy yourself, whatever you do. Come along, Rosemary. We might as well start burning the midnight oil.' This time the laugh was slightly more bitter. 'When I think,' I could hear her say, as Rosemary manoeuvred her into the street. 'Juan les Pins. Cap Ferrat. Antibes. Now it's as much as I can do . . .' Fortunately the rest of the declaration was interrupted as the street door closed, though I could hear her loud agitated voice, could imagine the discreetly helping hand under the elbow, before a taxi drew up and bore them away.

I went into the flat and made tea. There was a message from

Wiggy on my machine but I did not particularly want to talk to anyone. We frequently telephoned each other and got no answer; it was a way of keeping in touch. Each would register the call and know that the other was at home, ready with a listening ear should it be required. We exchanged little information, but we nevertheless counted on that wordless companionship, which serves us in default of relatives, descendants. Latterly I was conscious of deliberately concealing information from her, but short of making a full confession, which I instinctively rejected, I had precious little to tell. We relied on each other to recount an amusing anecdote or two, to warn of a change of plan. We knew each other's movements, trusted each other with spare keys, were confident that plants would be watered in our absence. The one disadvantage of this holiday (but there was more than one) was that I should not have Wiggy to talk to at the end of the day. To telephone from Venice or Madrid was something I should only feel entitled to do in an emergency. But in fact the emergency had already presented itself in the form of that dream which was still clear in my mind, and everyone knows that however vivid and important a dream appears to the dreamer it is of no conceivable interest to anyone else.

I spent the following day, Monday, discarding various clothes I knew I should never wear again. I wondered how on earth I had ever thought myself presentable. In the shop my appearance had hardly mattered. In any case book buyers are usually short-sighted. Now I compared myself with those elegant women, or perhaps one elegant woman, in Italy, and felt ashamed. And I had hoped to make an impression simply by being myself! I dispatched naïveté for ever, consigning it to a prelapsarian time before doubt had set in. There was of course no letter, no telephone message. I told myself that the weekend in Dorset had been prolonged. Despite myself I could not entirely banish a feeling of extreme scepticism. Such mental activity as I allowed myself was suitable only to the simple-minded; in fact I had embroiled myself in something that stretched my calculations at the limit. Somewhere I had failed to find the key to a personality which was not mysterious in itself, but merely contained the complexities of which everyone is formed. I was still fearful of making contact, even walked stealthily about the flat, so as not to miss the ringing of the telephone. Part of me knew that I should not be disturbed. I even felt a relief that I should soon be on my way, free of this tension that would not cease to mount.

On the Tuesday evening, my bag packed, my newly empty cupboards mute witnesses to my departure, I phoned Wiggy to say goodbye. A mild exhilaration had replaced my earlier perplexity. The past weekend now appeared strange to me, as if I had suffered a passing illness, with all the disordered thinking that illness brings in its wake.

'You've got everything?' said Wiggy. 'What time are you off?'

'The nine o'clock Eurostar, then lunch at the Brasserie du Nord, then the métro to the Gare de Lyon, and then who knows?'

'Sounds all right. I don't know that I'd do it, though. You've got more courage than I have.'

I thought it would take more courage to stay at home, but said nothing.

'Take care of yourself. Is there anything you want me to do in the flat while you're away?'

'No, nothing. Any other news? Anything I should know about while I'm off message?'

'I can't think of anything. Oh, yes, this will amuse you. I saw that man Gibson in Selfridges Food Hall yesterday. He was with that nurse, you know, the one with the teeth.'

'Sue.'

'I must say he's made a remarkably quick recovery. He looked positively cheerful. So did she. I was surprised that he remembered me. Us, I should say. "Give our love to Claire," she said. They even reminded me of the telephone number, although he added that they might be leaving the flat, were thinking of moving out a little way. "Not that we're in any hurry," he said. Claire? Are you there?'

'Must go,' I said. 'Things to do. I'll ring when I get back.'

The burning blush that crept all over me was for my own stupidity, not emotional this time so much as intellectual. This was one connection I had failed to make. It was the greatest failure of my life and no future success could ever obliterate it. When the heat in my face and throat subsided and I could bear to get up from my chair, I walked to the window and looked out. I must have stood there for some time, because when I turned round the room was in darkness. I had no conscious thoughts. All I knew was that now, as never before, I should find it easy to leave.